# Tirumalai Jain

## E.R. Mason

**Editors**

**Frank MacDonald**
**Contact:**
**SciFiProofreadingDoneRight@gmail.com**
**https://sites.google.com/site/scifiproofrea
ding**

**Sam Thornton, PE PhD**
**www.facebook.com/SamThorntonPE**
**SamThorntonPE@outlook.com**

**ISBN: 978-1-7328697-8-3**

# Chapter 1

"R.J., how can we be going to Earth? Look at you, you'd stand out like a sore thumb. You've got no beard and no hair. You look like a walking phallic symbol."

"I have immersed myself in the cleansing pool of Ramu, the fountain of creation, the purification from all materiality. One must be free of all imperfection to do so."

"Wait, all? Are you saying you removed all the hair on your body just to go in that thing? Do you have any hair on your body at all?"

"Not a one."

"Oh my God, you're a human noodle!"

"I am free of all unnecessary physicality."

"And yet you're wearing farmer's coveralls, a T-shirt and sneakers."

"I am purity existing within materiality."

"Does the word normality fit in there anywhere?"

"Consider yourself, oh unenlightened one. You are Lord of the Manor here on the garden planet Enuro. You should be dressed in knee-high riding boots with a vest and cravat. Instead, consider those worn Earth jeans you're wearing with a New York Jets T-shirt, your day old beard, uncut brown hair reaching down to your shoulders, your six-foot-two frame marching around like every woman's dream. Compare the two of us. What do you see?"

"I see me walking beside a human popsicle."

"Yes, while I am forced to accompany a Neanderthal who has forgotten where he left his cave and his woman."

"Hey, I'm not lost. Both suns are on our left. We just go straight ahead through those trees and we'll hit the horse trail."

"By the way, Elachia said I *could* go, provided Fantasia came along."

"R.J., what are we, kids needing our mothers' permission to go somewhere?"

"Close. Did you ask Fantasia for permission?"

"I do not ask for permission to do something, R.J."

"So what did she say?"

"It just so happens she wants to come along."

"So she doesn't trust you."

"It's been a while since we all visited Earth. She just wants to go."

"I'll bet it was the Acrua Maru incident. You really got us in deep on that one."

"I was stuck on that moon, R.J. It wasn't *my* fault!"

"You realize that until you showed up the planet Lemoria was a peaceful self-governing world, its people enjoying luxurious android servant lifestyles."

"God, don't remind me. I think my left hip is still sore."

"I'll disguise myself on Earth. I'll wear a false beard and wig."

"R.J. if you wear a false beard and wig you'll look just like yourself."

"You're just never satisfied. Anyway it's a two-week trip to Earth, by then I'll have erupted back into Cro-Magnon man."

"You know, that could be your superhero name."

"Faster than a speeding bullet, able to leap tall buildings in a single bound?"

"Who, disguised as a mild-mannered noodle...."

"Hey! I don't believe it!"

"What?"

"I do believe you've found the trail, sir."

"Not saying nothing."

"Go ahead, gloat. Modesty does not become you."

We looked up and down the narrow well worn trail. Dense overhanging tree limbs made it look almost like nature's tunnel. Streaks of golden light broke through in some places. I did not know which way to go but was unwilling to admit that, besides I had a 50-50 chance.

"She may have already passed by here."

I shook my head. "No. She would have been running him. We would have heard the horse hooves from a long way off."

"We go to the left, correct?"

"Of course."

"I wonder how far away Fantasia is?"

"Not far. Maybe a minute or two."

R.J. stopped. "Are you getting that from the link?"

"Yep."

"Tell me something, how is it for you with the link, after this much time I mean?"

"To be honest, I love it. She's always there in my heart. Always feels good there."

R.J. resumed walking. "To be accurate it's in your solar plexus you feel that. Even more accurately, your anahata chakra."

"What about you and Elachia? Are you still comfortable with that connection?"

"I love the link also. I'm glad to hear you do. I was a little bit afraid I might be losing myself in it."

I nodded. "I have no idea how that mad scientist doctor managed to give them the power of the link with their chosen mate but I'm thinking he did us a huge favor."

"Yeah, that trip we took on the Star Seven was one of the worst nightmares I've ever lived through but I'm grateful I was there. It was the worst of times and the best of times as Dickens put it."

"I think that's backwards."

"You know, that creature on the Star Seven really was a Jabberwocky."

"Oh boy. Here we go again."

"And has thou slain the Jabberwock? Come to my arms, my beamish boy. O frabjous day! Callooh! Callay!"

"Yeah, I'm over the moment."

"Let us go galumphing back then."

I stopped. "Do you hear something?"

"This sand is full of glints of real silver."

"Hold up a second."

The sound of a horse at full gallop faintly filled the air. It was coming from up ahead. They came around a turn in the distance; Fantasia's silver veiled dress billowing in the air behind her. She was barefoot. Her horse's nostrils flared from the run. No saddle. No bridle. The two of them working as one, both equally enjoying the moment. She looked like an angel riding out of heaven. I became hypnotized by her as I always do. The scene became slow motion. She slowed and trotted up to us. I stood with a doofus half grin.

R.J. said, "You always ride so beautifully, Fantasia."

"When I bestride him, I soar. I am a hawk. He trots the air. The earth sings when he touches it. The basest horn of his hoof is more musical than the pipe of Hermes. I've been studying Shakespeare for our trip to Earth."

R.J. added, "I think Shakespeare would have been inspired."

"Shouldn't you two be headed back to the manor? It's the other way."

R.J. gave me a terse look. I rolled my eyes.

Fantasia laughed, gave me a daring look and galloped on. To me, it looked like slow motion again.

"It's the other way," said R.J. dryly.

"Well okay, if you'd rather take the short route."

We turned around and started walking.

"So Elachia is sending us the false paperwork for the trip, complete with our false names," said R.J.

"Oh, that should be a riot. Please tell me you didn't have any say in what name I got."

"Fantasia is supposed to be securing commercial passage for us."

"Remind me again, are we wanted criminals on Earth or legendary heroes?"

"It just goes to show how much damage you can do in only six seconds."

"There you go, blaming me again."

"Hey, if they knew you were coming some people would probably show up with signs saying *all is lost*."

"Why isn't Elachia coming? I know you told me but I forgot."

"She has an important seminar with the Enuro High Council. She's a speaker for interplanetary relations."

"So all four of us will be away."

"Yes, but our little blue people will take care of both estates with loving care."

"You were kind of blue yourself there a while back, weren't you?"

"How dare you bring that up."

"My bad."

"I should remind you that you were the one who fell for the story that Fantasia could get pregnant just by being near someone for too long?"

"Like I'd have any chance at resisting her anyway."

"Yeah, you know how our women are in bed."

"Though she be but small, she is fierce."

"That's my line."

In the distance a small cloud of silver sand told us someone was coming. A moment later a small open speeder came into view driven by a petite blue woman with long blue-gray hair wearing white cargo-styled clothes. It was Geni, one of our manor house managers.

"Alas, we are saved from you!" exclaimed R.J.

She pulled up smiling and let the tiny hovercraft settle.

"Geni, can you give us a ride?" I asked.

"Certainly, my lord. I was just on my way to tell Lady Fantasia the soup is almost ready."

"What kind of soup?" asked R.J.

"Many kinds, sir."

We jittered the vehicle getting into it. Geni rotated it back in the direction from where she had come and took off at a pace that seemed unsafe but male vanity prevented either of us from mentioning it. We sped through the section of woods I had nicknamed Sherwood Forest. It reminded me of the irony that Fantasia's castle was adorned here and there with fancy examples of real suits of armor. Enuro had never endured a period similar to the Dark Ages, but they had watched Earth survive that age and had been enamored by the courage shown during the Crusades.

We broke out of the forest. Lake Menoir was on our left and ahead, far across green fields, were the towers of the manor-castle. On a crest of rolling fields on our right horses grazed. The lead stallion Emperor raised his head at our passing. There was a psychic greeting between the two of us. We had come to know each other well.

Geni dropped us at the main entrance steps then zoomed off into the woods.

Inside the castle's receiving area near the base of the grand staircase we were greeted by four-foot-tall central wing manager Lua, silver hair down to her butt, short cream-colored skirt over pink leggings. With a big blue smile she said, "Sir, the soup is ready."

R.J. persisted, "What kind of soup did they make, Lua?"

"A soup of many flavors, sir."

I nodded appreciatively, "Lua, could we have our soup in the east sitting room?"

"Right away, my Lord."

"And would you tell Fantasia that's where we are when she gets here?"

"Of course, my Lord."

She dashed off, seemingly happy to have important information for the kitchen staff. R.J. and I headed off to our favorite den of reclusion. Within the heavily decorated, high ceiling chamber we took our favorite seats by the huge unlit stone fireplace. R.J. fiddled with an end table and pulled out his pipe and tobacco.

"A purified man smoking a pipe?"

He ignored me and packed the pipe. A long stem lighter put fire to it.

"This pipe is hand carved from a single piece of rosewood. The tobacco is natural, gathered wild from the forest, dried and seasoned locally. It has natural ingredients that sooth the sinus tracks. It is not carcinogenic."

"Touché."

Lua appeared carrying two heavily carved deep brown steaming wooden bowls on a silver tray. The smell triggered my stomach. She carefully placed a bowl on each of our side tables, paused to see if there was anything else, then said, "Chef has asked that you please not eat the bowls. They are intended to preserve the flavoring."

I considered the difficulty that would be involved in trying to eat my bowl but Lua dashed off before I could ask.

"Wooden spoons," commented R.J.

"To keep the soup hot, I think."

"Oh my God this is good!"

"If it was any thicker it wouldn't be soup," I replied.

"Oh my God this is good!" repeated R.J.

"Oh my God, it is!"

"Every spoonful tastes completely different but better!"

"Maybe there' s drugs in it?"

"Either way I'll have seconds."

"Now I understand why she said not to eat the bowl."

Fantasia came cruising in the door still wearing her sheer riding veil and still barefoot. She carried a bowl of the soup in one hand and a paper-thin tablet in the other. She smiled at us and eased slowly down into her red, high-back chair.

She put down the tablet and smelled her soup. "Oh my God, this soup is so good!"

I gave her a narrow stare. "You've had it before?"

"He only makes it when the second moon is full. I can never tell if that really has anything to do with it or he's just pulling my leg, as you earthlings say."

"Who cares?" said R.J. as he shoveled soup into his mouth.

Fantasia asked, "Did he tell you guys not to eat the bowl?"

We nodded.

"I can never tell if he's serious about that either."

As we neared the bottom of our bowls, Lua appeared with three more. We continued in silence.

As I neared the second soup halfway point, a flash of light in the center of us suddenly gave way to a translucent image of Fantasia's sister Elachia. The image spoke, "The passports and other paperwork are complete and will be delivered to you shortly on special tablets. Do not lose them, children."

"She must be referring to you," said R.J.

I couldn't stop eating long enough for a comeback.

Elachia disappeared. R.J. began slowly eating his soup again.

"What the heck just happened?" I asked between spoonfuls.

Fantasia answered in a matter-of-fact tone without looking up. "Four-way link."

I paused with a spoonful halfway to my mouth. "You and Elachia can create psychic holographic group links?"

"Elachia is much better at it than I am but yes, when three of the four are in close proximity a group link can sometimes be created."

"You never told me that."

"It never came up until now."

"But there was even an image of her?"

"Yes, the close proximity of the three provides a much greater degree of astral energy which can be used in that manner. Of course no one else could see that image of Elachia except we three."

I ate my spoonful and wondered what else I did not know. We quietly finished our soup. R.J. relit his pipe.

Fantasia said, "I've booked us on the Serenity Nova. It is a holomatter deck-based ship. You will both enjoy it."

"Care to elaborate?" I asked.

"Yes. All of the suites are furnished by holomattergrams. So are most of the communal areas. Many of the staff are also holomatter. You do not feel the same confinement you experience on most ships. All chambers can be of any size and design the hospitality managers choose. They typically alter the environment of various rooms on a daily basis."

"I could go to sleep in one place and wake up in another?" I asked.

"No. You control the environment of your own suite."

"The entertainment is holomattergraphic?" asked R.J.

"Yes. Performances by almost any artist you can think of. The facilities are equally diverse. They have a twenty-minute water slide that takes you through canyons and waterfalls."

"What's the travel time?" I asked.

"It's been shortened to ten days. They have a jump-stop system. Halfway through the trip they are able to compress the warp field and jump five days off of the Enuro-Earth leg."

"Why would a cruise ship like that have an Enuro-Earth connection?" I asked.

"They are willing to adjust their travel route in some cases."

"Sounding pretty luxurious to me," commented R.J.

"Fan, you didn't *buy* that ship, did you?" I asked.

"Certainly not. That would be decadent."

R.J. laughed. "I could create a holomattergram of myself."

Fantasia smiled. "Spacesuits are available for guests who would like to visit the star deck."

I asked, "What happens when we get to Earth?"

Fantasia nodded. "The Serenity Nova is not designed for orbital insertion. We will be met by a contracted shuttle outside of Earth orbit. The shuttle will take us directly to Chennai Spaceport. We'll pass through customs and immigration there. Our paperwork will be quite good. Our true identities should not be detected by any government agencies. I've obtained clothing for both of you. We will need to blend in during passage through several different social settings. An air taxi will take us to Arani. We will meet with Parth Sharma there. He's made arrangements for us."

"You bought clothes for me? It's not like robes, is it?" I asked.

"No, silly. The Tirumalai Village is a major tourist site. You can wear almost anything as long as it's respectful. I didn't want you walking around in a flight suit or something else that might make you more recognizable. You'll have casual tourist clothing with dark sunglasses. You don't want to end up signing autographs and alerting the wrong people to who you really are, do you?"

"No."

"You'll also have appropriate clothes for the caves."

"Okay."

R.J. bit down on his pipe and snickered.

## Chapter 2

The Serenity Nova was spectacular. It almost seemed as though the ship was made entirely of contoured windows. From space the forward bridge section looked like the nose of a Klingon battle cruiser. The bareness of the receiving hanger did not prepare you for the living areas. The instant the elevator doors closed we were ascending a kind of space elevator overlooking a well-populated star system. There was a sombrero galaxy on our right and a distant pulsar on our left. It was like spacewalking without a suit.

What I assume was a standard hallway leading to our suite looked like the Sistine Chapel, and though I knew the real walls must be within nine or ten feet of us for the life of me I could not detect them. Our suite was an arched open door that slid open for us. I barely got off a wave to R.J. as he entered his.

The suite was heavily decorated and furnished. Fantasia tossed her satchel onto the nearest chair. I expected it to fall through the hologram to the floor but it did not which left me wondering how to tell which things were real and which were not. It was a large suite. At least it looked large. The kitchen area was sectioned off by a bar. As I stared at it, a man in a black and white tuxedo appeared behind the bar. He called to me, "would you like anything Mr. Arnt?"

"Me? Oh, no thank you."

The bartender disappeared.

14

Fantasia laughed without looking up from her satchel.

"What's so funny?"

"You, Mr. Arnt. What a perfect alias."

"Yeah, how'd I get that?"

"It's just the T in Tarn, moved to the end. The paperwork forger always makes everyone's names as close as possible to their real names so they react to people speaking to them better."

"So what's my first name?"

"Adrie."

"How about R.J.?"

"He is Arjay Miths. I am Fanaise Arnt. Do you like the room? I selected conventional to start with."

"It's fine. Are those waiters going to be popping up all the time without warning?"

"He appeared because you were staring at the bar-kitchen area. It's not random."

"Geez. If I stare at the bed will a naked woman appear?"

She laughed again. "You could have relations with a holomattergraphic character but it would be like making love to a statue."

"Really?"

"Although I understand there are add-on options that can be purchased on the ship's net to make them more sentient."

"Oh brother."

"You're not thinking of...."

I gently took her arm to interrupt her. I shook my head. I kissed her lightly on the lips and smiled.

"What a wonderful trip this is going to be," she said and she went about putting her things away.

I asked her to show me the bedroom. She gave a quizzical stare and led me there.

Later, I awoke on the bed wearing nothing at all, wondering if it was a holographic bed. Fantasia was faintly snoring beside me. Clothes had been left on a chair for me. Light-colored tourist slacks and loafers, both of which I winced at. The robin's egg-colored short sleeve golf shirt was okay. I realized I'd not even taken the time to inspect the suite. In the main living room there were two sitting areas with reading chairs and tables here and there. In one corner near curtained windows was a heavily carved oak desk and high back chair. There were heavily engraved ivory images on the ceiling and off-white carpet on the floor. I looked at the kitchen and wondered what real food might be stocked there.

The butler appeared.

"Yes, Mr. Arnt?"

"Can I get a nice fat multi-layer sandwich and a beer?"

My butler went to an odd-looking food dispenser, pressed a button to make a silvery screen disappear and behind it were both items. He brought them to the counter and looked at me to see if that was the right spot.

"Anything else, sir?"

I came to the counter and watched him disappear.

Was the sandwich holographic? This place was taking some getting used to. It tasted like turkey and ham, lettuce, and tomato. I could feel it in my stomach so that meant it had to be real, right?

A voice came from overhead. "Mr. Arnt, you have a call from Mr. Miths. Will you accept?"

"Yes."

"Mr. Arnt, this is Mr. Miths, shall we conduct recon?"

"I'll meet you out there in the Sistine Chapel."

"Roger."

Fantasia was awake when I looked in. She smiled and stretched.

"Want to come exploring?" I asked.

"You go ahead. I need to visit the shops. It's a moral imperative as you so often say."

"We'll be hanging out in one of the lounges on the promenade wherever that is."

"I'll find you."

R.J. and I followed the huge, glamorous false hallway to the nearest elevator. We stepped in. The doors closed and we were suddenly in a glass elevator in the deep sea ascending to the surface. Ocean life swam around us. Through the glass floor the ocean bottom fell away.

"Promenade deck," I said.

Lights on the tiny control panel blinked acknowledgement. A large tiger shark followed us up.

The doors opened to a giant, four story gallery of shops, theaters, restaurants, game rooms and lounges. We choose a drinkery with a name I could not pronounce. Inside we sat at a luxurious bar and looked at menus illuminated in the surface of the counter. It stepped through many languages apparently trying to identify ours which it never did.

"How are your translators working?" I asked R.J.

"Just fine. Those Euronians know their translators," he replied.

"Let's hope the bartender are just as good."

"Oh, they've gotta be. I'm guessing she's a hologramian."

"Good one."

We were approached by a sizzling red head with hair down to her waist. Her eyes and nose were unusually small, but her red lips a bit too wide. "Yes, Mr. Arnt, Mr. Miths? It's my pleasure to serve you. What would you like?"

"Do you have bourbon?" I asked.

Her eyes went blank as a computer somewhere searched the records.

"Yes. We have that."

"With ice, please."

"And you, sir?"

R.J. answered, "Do you know what a martini is?"

Blank eyes again. "Yes. We have several versions."

"Let me have your most popular version then."

"Very good, sir."

I only had time to glance at R.J. and say, "Things are looking up," and the drinks were in front of us.

We sipped and scanned the lounge. It only took a few seconds to realize we were the only humans in the place. People were sitting at tables in front of a stage with a piano which looked like it had melted in a fire even though the colorful keyboard was fully intact. There were other brass instruments along with items I did not recognize.

The assortment of guests was diverse. A few looked very nearly human but ears and eyebrows set them apart. Other non-human guests needed child seats to raise them up to table level. A few species were completely unknown to me.

The band appeared on stage. They were a collection of equally varied players. I wondered if I'd be able to stand the sounds they were about to make.

With a few discordant notes they checked their tuning. I braced my ears. They all hit on the first note without a count. To my amazement, it was jazz! The closest I could relate it to was jazz fusion and it was good. The multi-armed drummer stood behind his strange set, but the kick drum beat was strong and he was getting a well-metered snare sound from somewhere. R.J. and I sat back and watched the strange crowd and took in the solid tunes. Partway through the night a fight broke out between two frail looking bald humanoids in gray silk body suits who seemed unable to hurt each other. Hologram security appeared out of nowhere and led them aside.

Later in the evening we began to get tipsy. We were laughing at each other's comments whether they were funny or not. Fantasia failed to show leaving me to guess at the new wardrobe that probably existed in our suite.

R.J. began to get uppity. "You know that twenty-minute water slide ride is probably getting very little use right now."

"The one where you slide down through a canyon with waterfalls?"

"That's what it said."

"We don't have suits."

"Don't need one. You get a holographic body suit to help with the slide."

"Hey, at this point I'm game for anything."

"Let's do it."

"Maybe there will be a sign that says to use this ride you must be less than fifty-percent inebriated."

We both spit-laughed.

Under the watchful eyes of holographic security we groped our way out of the bar. The music was still so good I gave a shifting wave to the band.

In the elevator R.J. commanded, "Canyon water slide please."

The elevator remained an elevator.

The entrance was on the uppermost deck. For a moment it crossed my mind that we would probably be sliding down quite a few deck levels. Even under the influence that gave me a moment of pause. I looked over at R.J. to see if he was still determined. We both spit out another laugh.

You couldn't miss the entrance. There were no less than four slide attractions with big Disney World type signs. We had to ask an attendant in a booth which one was the Canyon ride. She pointed us on. We studied her for a moment to see if she looked worried for us. She was a hologram.

I pushed R.J.'s shoulder and we laughed some more.

Inside the canyon slide greeting area we were directed to a changing room. We were told to strip down to our underwear and stand in the suit booth. There, colorful body suits were woven out of thin air on us. They felt light and flexible and had a wet feel to them. Though our movements were still staggered and awkward from alcohol, the staff didn't seem to care. They were holograms.

The launch points were clear tubes with floor panels that opened to drop you. There was no safety briefing. They closed us in our tubes. I looked over at R.J. in his tube. There was a moment of sobriety between us that said, "Do we really know what we're doing?" We both spit out laughs again.

The floor dropped out.

Those first couple of seconds falling through wet darkness made me have second thoughts about the whole thing. Then bright light flashed on. I was in a rushing river flowing alongside a stone plateau with trees in the distance. I could just see over the edge of the plateau but a moment later I was falling along a cliff side, bumping against stone ground occasionally as the river forced me downward. I managed to focus ahead only to spot what looked like a waterfall's edge a short distance away and before screaming was even possible I was thrown from the river out into the air, falling backward into the thundering flow, then swept away even faster. I turned a three hundred and sixty degree turn against my will before regaining some control with my hands and arms. The cliff wall was racing along on my right, wide open space of the canyon on my left. I managed to look down in time to see a long steep drop to the next waterfall. Once again over I went, cast out into canyon space then splashing down into the rapids. It went on and on, twisting turns, passage through phosphorescent caverns, drop offs when you least expected them. After fifteen minutes of it I just gave up and went limp with the ride, the canyons walls rising far above me.

Ride's end flushed us into a still pool of warm shallow water. R.J, popped out a second after I did. We coasted aground on the shallow end and did not bother to sit up. We were two drunken bodies washed ashore.

R.J. finally said, "Let's go again."

"Are you insane?"

"I didn't get to see everything."

"No shit."

"The signs said we were never in any danger."

"Except maybe for cardiac arrest."

"Were you injured?"

"I'm sober. All that drinking wasted."

We managed to climb out of the pool.

I held up one hand. "Hold on. I think my soul is still trying to catch up with my body."

R.J. said, "Our lockers were supposedly transferred down here somewhere. It's got to be one of these doors."

I chose the nearest one and pushed out it. It snapped closed behind me.

I was standing in a busy thoroughfare. Dozens of guests were passing by in both directions. I looked down and found my hologram suit had disappeared and I was standing wet and dressed only in men's bikini underwear. People were staring.

The door popped open behind me. R.J. stuck his head out. "It's this other door."

We dressed and headed back to the bar. Fantasia was seated at a table when we arrived.

"The Serenity computer said you two were at the Canyon water slide. How was it?"

A waiter appeared. She was identical to the bartender. We ordered restorative drinks.

Fantasia persisted. "The water slide ride. How was it?"

I nodded. "Personally I think I should have gotten a discount. I barely touched the slide all the way down."

R.J. snickered. "At least the slide didn't break down, you being on it and all."

Fantasia smirked.

R.J. added, "Adrian posed in the concourse in his bikini underwear."

"No!?" responded Fantasia. "Did you get any tips?"

"Very funny. It was the wrong door."

The waiter brought our drinks. I escaped to mine.

"You want to try the canyon water slide, Fantasia?" asked R.J.

"Not today. Next I want to visit the stargazer deck. They have deck chairs out there made to fit the custom spacesuits."

"Wow! Sitting outside a ship at faster than light speed. That must be something."

"Been there, done that," I suggested.

"Oh, not like this dear," added Fantasia. "The suits are not made for work. They're made for comfort. There is no helmet. It is a clear plastic fabric bubble. You have three-hundred-and-sixty-degree views, plus up and down. They say you can barely feel the suit at all. It's just like being outside."

R.J. said, "I'm game. Let's finish these drinks and head up there."

So we did.

This time the suits were put on us by attendants. We stepped out of the most luxurious, automated airlock I had ever seen to find we were on the very top pinnacle of the Serenity Nova. We had wide open three hundred and sixty degree views. That first look on any EVA is never routine. It's always like unexpectedly embracing God. The effect might be brought on by how apparent the depth of space becomes, or the number of stars multiplied to a power of ten. Whatever it is, you never get over the totality of it. So many stars there's almost no room for the black. And the Serenity Nova people had done their best to maximize the experience. The suits felt like suit liners, not suits. They were slightly warmer than body temperature. And, as promised, white adjustable deck chairs with suit plug ins were available. After turning in circles for good half hour we sat together, plugged in, and stared out at infinity. We all fell asleep within God's embrace and ended up there for the entire night.

## Chapter 3

Aside from being at Fantasia's castle, the Serenity Nova was the most fun I'd had in a long time. There was too much to do to experience everything. There was a sensuality ride that I refused to go on for fear of catching a glimpse of some alien custom I just didn't want to see. It made Fantasia laugh and laugh. We played and ate the entire trip. I did not even care about not seeing the Klingon-looking bridge or Engineering.

They brought us in above the Terran ecliptic. Dropped out of light just before the moon's orbit, then used sub light engines to get as close as they could without entering Earth's orbital control area. The contracted shuttle that met us was much more than a shuttle. It even had artificial gravity, so we were in gravity for the entire trip. We dropped in to Chennai International Spaceport and suddenly we were back in stark reality.

The first suspense was at check in. They made us take off our sunglasses. Fantasia had applied some type of lotion to our faces claiming it would mess up anybody's face recognition software. I sat in front of the stern man in uniform checking my registration, expecting that any second he would point accusingly at me, declaring me to be the infamous Adrian Tarn, disruptor of world events everywhere.

When they finally waved us on I had to conceal my arrogance at having fooled them. It was also then R.J. and I discovered Fantasia had brought follow-along luggage. It was dropped off by the shuttle crew and as Fantasia began to walk to our next pick up point I stepped over to pick it up but the luggage took off and followed along behind her. R.J. smirked. We hurried and caught up and followed along with the rest of the luggage. The walk to the air taxi area was refreshing. Nearly everyone was human.

Our air taxi looked beat up on the outside but almost luxurious on the inside. We sat on couches along the windows. The flight deck was open. The pilots spent more time getting clearance than it usually took for an airliner. We rose up and dashed away.

Our pilot seemed to be holding at about five hundred feet. We sped over city blocks of colorful roofing, past villages and street markets, and agricultural areas. Civilization soon disappeared as we passed over a river followed by green forests and fields. Eventually the landscape became patches of housing and industry separated by large sections of forest and field. A very large, dry river came into view, sand colored and winding. I heard the pilot call out, "Palar." A few minutes later we came to an area of lakes and heavy population. The pilot called out, "Arani." We were swung around and maneuvered into place before lowering down into the parking area for the GVS Residency Hotel. With the air taxi engines still idling, the pilot hopped out his door, pulled out our luggage and opened the cabin for us to exit.

We paraded toward the hotel. Nice building. Big glass windows. In the middle of a residential area. The A.I. luggage became stuck in a few places along the way and had to be helped. There were steps at the entrance. The baggage bumped repeatedly at the bottom step as though impatient for more help.

Quite a beautiful though small lobby. Walls of black and white swirling marble. Snow white flooring with the same back marble borders. A woman in casual dress shorts with her sandals kicked off was seated on a bench, waiting. The Indian lady behind the small gray desk was very beautiful. Long black hair past her shoulders. Red lipstick smile. Tiny nose, narrow stare, comfortable and friendly.

She spoke with a musical Indian accent, "We have been expecting you, Mrs. Arnt. We have two rooms on the top floor, both luxury suites. Someone will be down shortly to catch your luggage." She smiled at her own joke. "Do you know how long you will be staying?"

"Not just yet. Will that be a problem?" asked Fantasia.

"I do not believe so. You have reserved them for one week but we will gladly extend that until you check out. There is one message for you." She turned and pulled an unsealed envelope from the counter behind her and handed it over along with three key cards.

R.J. and I read over Fantasia's shoulder. It was a handwritten note;

*Thank you so much for coming so far. I will meet you at the hotel tonight or tomorrow.*

*Many thanks,*
*Parth*

A very clean but very worn elevator took us to the top. Our suites were surprisingly modern and well-kept. Everything was a tan color. Tan carpet, tan curtains, tan bed covering, headboard, couch, and chair. Our picture windows overlooked blocks of colorful residences and businesses. Most of the streets were not paved. Frequent hovercraft sped by above them. It was the perfect contrast of future and past.

The three of us got comfortable, ordered room service, and waited for Parth. We had chicken tikka masala with chana masala. There was no entertainment center but thanks to Starlink our cell phones worked.

Parth showed up around 8:00P.M. IST. He brought a bottle of something. We rounded up glasses and ice. We shuffled furniture around and sat around the couch drinking and sharing greeting stories.

"Can you still play the piano, Parth?" asked R.J.

"Earth music is written slightly differently but I am able to read it. Yes, I do still possess that ability."

There was a long pause as we exchanged glances. Finally I could wait no longer. "Parth, we had a wonderful time on our trip but it's time you told us why we're here."

Sharma balked for a moment, took another drink for fortitude, and nodded. "It is my wife."

R.J. straightened up. "I did not know you were married, Parth."

"It was an arranged marriage. We seldom saw each other. But we grew up as friends so it was an easy thing. Diya Singh is an archeologist, another reason we do not often see each other. Two years ago she wrote me to say work had begun at the Tirumalai Jain Complex but I was not to tell anyone. I did not think much about it at the time. She had helped in so many excavations. I was scheduled as Science Officer on a six-month cruise to the Kuiper belt. When I returned, her family met me at the spaceport. They were very frightened. They insisted something had happened to her. Her letters had stopped coming. Her cell phone was not answering. They searched for her in Tirumalai. She had been there working but no one knew where she was. They asked me for help."

Parth paused for a drink of water, then continued. "I came here and searched. I learned that she had not been working under university authority. There had been no dig team. She had been working with another archeologist, an American by the name of John Bischard. I began to ask around, all the people who supply and support archaeologists. At first no one would talk. Finally it took money. At one place that rents horses and guides I found one man who had been taking them to the mountain. He would not admit anything but he said he thought they were searching the mountain for something. It took more money but I finally got him to show me where he would drop them off each time. I searched. Not far from the drop off I found a small hidden entrance into the mountain. It was locked with a steel gate. It took a week but I made a key. I went in there. There was a trail of burned-out chemical light sticks. Deep down a secret side entrance to a tunnel had been covered with stones. It took me two weeks to find it. Within the secret tunnel there was a kind of antechamber. They had left tools behind there. I found some of her belongings there. They had set up a table and were collecting strange samples of machinery and metals. This smaller chamber opened to huge cavern and in the middle of that cavern rested an intact virmana. Many ancient documents found in India describe virmanas as flying vehicles. I know that sounds crazy. It is shaped like a huge saucer. It sits on a large center pedestal. There is an entrance in the pedestal but it is sealed. In looking for a way in I realized this virmana was alive and active."

"How?" interrupted R.J.

"When you place your hand on the virmana it is vibrating and humming."

We all sat quietly and tried not to look skeptical.

"I know Diya went into that cave and did not come out."

Once again R.J. asked, "How?"

"Stones were stacked to hide the path to this secret cavern. When I broke through them I could see they had been stacked from inside."

Fantasia asked, "You think we might be able to help with this?"

"It is illegal. That gated entrance was sealed by the government for some reason. I cannot ask the police for help. I cannot ask the universities. It is likely I would be prevented from searching for Diya if I reported any of this. I do not think the government ever discovered this virmana or the place would be overrun by officials and probably sealed off forever. That is why Diya and her associate were working on this in secret."

"What do you think happened to them?" asked Fantasia.

"I only know they went in that chamber but did not come out. They are still in there somewhere."

I asked, "Parth, how long did you say they've been missing?"

"Months."

"So is this a rescue mission or a recovery mission?"

Fear flashed through Parth's eyes. "There can always be hope."

I asked, "Do you have any idea how to get into this virmana craft?"

"Yes. There are control consoles for it also in the main chamber. Power is available to them but I do not know from where. I did not want to make any attempt to operate them without someone backing me up. That is why I contacted you."

Fantasia asked, "Isn't there anyone here who would be more qualified about these machines than we are?"

"I cannot risk telling anyone about this. There is too much chance word would leak out. I do not think anyone is more qualified than you, my friends. You have experience with exploration and the unknown. I trust you."

R.J. asked, "What about this guy who rents you the horses?"

Parth nodded. "I was fortunate. He drops me off about a mile from the hidden entrance. He does not know about it. He believes I have been searching the mountain for signs of Diya. We must stay in the caverns while we work. We cannot make daily trips back and forth. That would be too suspicious. We must take enough supplies to set up in the virmana chamber and remain there until we find her."

R.J. said, "So if we disappear also, no one will come looking for us either."

Parth nodded. "There is danger, I agree. But it is the only way."

R.J. looked at me with concern. "What do you think about this, Adrian?"

"I don't really see a problem. Cells won't work in the caves but all we'd need to do is climb outside to call for help. To begin with, we'll be looking for some other way out of that chamber. If there isn't one, we'll need to get into that machine, whatever it is."

R.J. looked at Parth and nodded. "I'm game."

We all looked at Fantasia. She laughed. "Of course I'll go. I can't wait."

R.J. looked at Parth and me.

I said, "Well, if the doctor is in, I'm in."

Parth continued, "I will come in the morning and we will drive to the villages. We must walk from there through the marketplace to meet the man with the horses. We must pack a lot but make it look like a little. I am sorry for asking this, Fantasia, but can you ride a horse?"

R.J. and I laughed loudly.

The next morning we were up early. We had room service Nihari for breakfast. It was just okay. We dressed in Jungle Jim styled clothing with lace up boots; R.J. and me in brown, Fantasia in gray. Fantasia had a round brim hat with optional fold down veil, I wore a NY Jets cap, and R.J. became the farmer in the dell with a sagging round straw hat. Parth Sharma parked out front and came up. He was in purple-colored jeans with a long sleeved gray work shirt. He wore hiking boots. He had backpacks for each of us, heavy with stores. We had to cram the few extra things we needed into them. I tried to take Fantasia's away from her but she pushed her med kit on me instead.

In the car we gave Fantasia the shotgun seat. The white sand narrow roadways were lined with frequent foot traffic. Colorful, tightly fit businesses and residents bordered them. Frequent hovercraft sped by overhead. No one paid them any attention. Pedestrian dress was the most diverse I'd ever seen. Men in dusty business suits. Others in wrap around lungi skirts mixed with standard short sleeve works shirts. Women in wonderful, colorful shawls and long skirts.

We came into a section of city. Narrow hardened streets separating stone and brick buildings. The mass of pedestrians slowed us greatly. Everyone seemed very busy and in a hurry. There were colorful shops with their wares displayed out front. High power lines ran along the street, nearly touching the buildings. No one paid us much attention.

We tightened up emotionally as Parth parked the car in a lot just beyond the end of an alley barely wide enough for the car. Had we broken down in it none of us would have been able to get out. Parth opened the doors for us and gathered his bags. We helped each other into our backpack straps and looked to him to lead.

A different, single file alleyway brought us to a busy outdoor market, a place so packed with color it was like a huge painting. Parth gathered us together.

"Here is money for you in case you want to buy something. It will make us look more like tourists. When you buy, look to me. My fingers will show you how many coins to give. If I shake my head, you do not want that. You must all be very respectful. There are some older merchants who still keep to the old ways. If you stare at their goods for too long they may accuse you of contaminating them. Then you will have to buy all that they have. You must look people in the eye always or they will not trust you. Stay together please."

We remained together for about ten yards. From that point on I could barely keep R.J. and Fantasia in sight. They were all over the place. I looked at Parth and he just shrugged. The market was a such an enchanting collage to explore there was no escaping the wonder of it. It was noisy with conversations, a thousand words at once that the translators in our ears could not keep up with. The smell of delicious food was everywhere, mixed with pottery, weaving, animals, and people. There was a lot of human contact required to get from one spot to another. Men in white turbans and white robes squatted by their vegetables for sale. A barefoot woman in a colorful wrap-around selling a thousand hanging lamps, no two of the same color or design.

Somehow, we made it a good distance down the street, though we were never together. At one point Fantasia came to me wearing an expensive-looking red crystal set in gold on a chain. Apparently American money could be exchanged here. The stone was the size of an almond. She looked up at me with a wide smile and I immediately remembered why I loved her.

"How could you have bought that?" I asked. "It looks very expensive."

"Oh, believe me it was."

"But how could you have paid for it?"

"The kind old lady had a cellular phone with a card reader."

"How much did you pay?"

"Don't ask. She packed up her displays and left after I paid her."

"You may have been robbed, Fantasia."

"No. I could see into her aura. She was telling the truth. She said this crystal was found in the caves beneath the temple. She said it is rumored to be thousands of years old."

I smiled at her. "By the way, I love you."

She smiled back. "I am officially your wife here. I think I like being your wife."

R.J. rejoined us wearing a new Raiders of the Lost Ark hat. He had traded his straw hat for it. I tried not to laugh but failed. Thankfully he had no whip.

Farther down the street the crowd began to thin. Stone cliffs came into view in the distance. We finally grouped back together and left the street fare behind us. Parth led us down a dusty road to a stable. It was not a busy place but a few tourists were discussing price with the proprietor. I noticed five horses saddled and tied to a hitching post near a corral of rough-cut tree limbs. A man in bagging brown slacks, a brown work shirt and sandals emerged from the stable and noticed us. He gave Parth a big bearded smile and came briskly over to shake his hand.

"It is good to see you again, my friend. I see your friends have arrived safely. Are you ready to go then?"

"We are ready, Sai. Let us go."

Sai leaned in and spoke in a low tone, "Parth, my friend, the woman, has she ridden a horse?"

This time Parth laughed. "More than any of us, Sai."

Sai looked at Fantasia and gave a loud laugh. He motioned us to the horses.

My horse was willing to bite me if the opportunity arose. His name was Jack. Our saddles were surprisingly western. I made sure to remain facing his head as I pulled up and on. Jack seemed dejected by the lack of ass opportunity. We headed down a narrow dirt trail bordered by stone and boulders growing in size as we went. Fantasia pulled up alongside me.

"Darling, in my backpack, the very front pocket. Carrot slices. Would you bring out a few?"

"You brought carrots all the way from Enuro?"

"I have blue cookies for you."

"You are wonderful, you know that?"

"Uh-huh."

I fumbled with her backpack, found the carrots, gave her a handful, and pocketed a few in my thigh side pocket. I kept a couple in my hand and carefully leaned forward to give them to Jack. Our relationship changed immediately.

We came to cliff side, riding close enough to the wall to drag our hands on it. Boulders on the opposite side kept us in close. The path began to lead upward through stone and scrub brush and

34

more cliffside. Some passageways were so steep we had to lean forward to the saddle horn for the climb. Eventually we broke out to wooded plateau on the left and mountain stones rising on the right. After an hour more we came to a fork in the trail. Sai brought the parade to a halt.

"Would you like to go beyond this time?" he asked Parth.

"No, Sai. There are some pictures we would like to take along this north trial. We will hike."

"Will you camp, or should I bring them back later?"

"We are not sure, Sai. We will call you if we wish to come back today."

"Very good."

We dismounted and pulled off our packs to get water and rearrange them. Fantasia gathered up the rest of her carrot slices and passed them out to the grateful equines. I fed mine to Jack. We were now established friends.

We watched Sai link up the horses and lead them back down the trail. Everyone looked to Parth.

"It's not the north trail," he said. "That was to throw him off. It's this one that follows the mountain." He pointed to a rocky, narrow uphill trail.

We wiggled back into our packs and followed him.

It was another forty-five minutes of carefully stepping along a path that really could not be called a trail. On our right, the mountain still rose steeply. Parth got ahead of us and finally stopped and removed his backpack. We caught up to find a four-foot-high cave entrance hidden by bushes and guarded by a steel grate with a padlock. Parth nodded to us that this was the place. He fished his key out of his backpack, unlocked and let the grate fall out of place. It looked like a deep, dark hole.

Parth said, "There are headlamps in your packs. You will need them and your jackets or sweaters. It is cool in the caves."

Fantasia added, "Parth, we should eat before we go in there."

Parth nodded. "Yes. You are correct. Let us gather our energies."

We found seats and rifled through our packs for food. We ate under blue sky and clouds, all the while eyeing this ominous hole we were going into. Dressed and with lights we grouped at the entrance and waited for Parth to lead.

At the darkness, Parth turned and gave us all a last look to be sure we were ready. He ducked down and disappeared inside.

# Chapter 4

I was second inside with Fantasia behind me holding on to a strap on my pack as though she was afraid of losing me. The small entrance had concealed a much larger passageway. We were immediately able to stand. Parth added a chemical light to his headlamp. The cavern came into view in detail. It was a much rougher rock surface than I'd ever seen, a naturally formed ragged dome cave with a hard flat walkway through it. The rock walls which surrounded us were gray and black and porous, almost like a demon's lair. The path led down.

R.J. called out. "Parth, no breadcrumbs?"

Parth's laugh echoed. "I have mapped this place from when I first searched it. We will not be lost."

The place had a musty smell to it, no airflow I could detect, and my face became chilled as I adjusted to the environment.

One hundred yards in the rock walls became less ragged and began to be decorated with stalactites that grew in length as we progressed. The walls lost their porosity and became wet in appearance. We had to slide down a few sections of floor.

An hour into the descent I began to wonder just how far Parth was taking us. To my relief he stopped at a rock fall not far ahead and turned to us.

"These stones were collected and placed here. When I first found them, they had been stacked from the other side to hide the opening. We must do the same once we are inside."

Without further discussion Parth began to pull down stones. We joined in as the echoes of moving stones bounced around the small cavern.

It was another four-foot opening. Inside we regrouped and re-stacked the wall. We were burying ourselves alive. The passageway had a five-foot ceiling and was narrow enough that I could touch both walls with my arms outstretched. It was a winding path. Gentle downward slope.

We eventually came around a sharp left-hand turn and found a bigger chamber the size of a tractor trailer. At the end of it there had once been iron bars sunk into the rock. There was no ceiling. Instead, an overhead shaft rose up and out of sight. Rusty pieces of iron were scattered around the floor. A few broken iron ends were still embedded in the rock. The passage the bars had once protected was big enough to drive a vehicle through. Parth paused and looked back at us.

"This is it," he said. "This smaller chamber once provided a ladder or elevator that led up to the temple. We are directly below it."

The cavern beyond was the size of an aircraft hangar. Jagged black walls and overhead. The object that took up most of the chamber made Fantasia gasp. It made me hold my breath for a second.

R.J. said, "I really don't believe it! This thing is ancient but it looks almost new!"

There in the center of the room was a disk-shaped vehicle. Like the old saying went, two teacup saucers, one inverted atop the other. It sat upon a chrome metallic barrel that was part of it. On the top there was a large frosty half-bubble, also a part of the craft. The main body was silver gray. There were bits of stone rubble on its surface. There was now a faint charred smell in the cold air. It took a long time before I could look away to check out the rest of the cavern.

R.J. said, "There's a static charge in the air."

Parth replied, "Yes. That is the way it always is."

There were test consoles at various points around the room. Their markings were strange, almost hieroglyphs. Parts and other equipment also were scattered against the walls. There was dirt and bits of stone on everything. Some of the consoles had dim illumination here and there.

R.J. stepped forward, raised his hand above his head and touched an outer edge of the craft. "It's vibrating!"

"Yes," responded Parth with a nod.

"I think we all need to rest," said Fantasia.

"Yes. Let us sit," agreed Parth.

We found a place off to one side with a stone shelf seat and other cut rock. We sat and removed our packs. Our water bottles quickly emerged.

"You now know all that I know," said Parth.

"You've searched this entire cavern for another way out?" I asked.

"Yes, but there are some rough areas up high which are recessed and difficult to see."

I said, "That should be our first job. We'll split up and search every inch of this place including the floor and overhead for another way out."

"I am holding out hope, but I do not think we will find such a pathway," said Parth.

"Do we all agree we are looking at a real UFO?" asked R.J.

There was a long silent pause.

"I have never seen a craft like this one," replied Fantasia. "I see no avenue for it to leave this chamber."

"So maybe it's not a vehicle at all," suggested R.J.

Parth said, "There are many carvings and drawings from old India that show this craft. There are even diagrams of the interior etched on the walls of some temples. The Sanskrit word virmana is often translated to temple or palace, and in other translations it is said to mean aircraft. I do not believe we are looking at a temple or palace here. We are seeing a machine. More than that I cannot say."

When we were sufficiently bulked up with packaged food, we spread out and began the search. Halfway around the cavern I met up with R.J.

R.J. paused and looked back at the disc. "You don't think this thing can dematerialize and then re-materialize somewhere else, do you?"

"R.J., with the things you and I have seen...."

He nodded. "Yeah, anything is possible."

There were no alternate exits. One way in. One way out. We met back at the starting point and stood staring at the monstrosity before us.

"So we are left with this," said R.J.

"Have you found any way into it, Parth?" I asked.

"Not so much as a seam anywhere, Adrian," he replied. "But the path here leads directly to that center column."

I turned and looked at the three consoles nearby. "The answer must be in these."

We gathered around the consoles. Buttons, dials, and switches. Gauges and lights. Individual symbols above each control, a cross shape, upside down U, upside down and backward P, the rest just as unidentifiable.

40

I said, "We need to find the controls that have the most wear and tear. The controls used most frequently."

"I have a scanner that will help with that," said Fantasia, and she went to her pack.

With careful dusting and wiping, we narrowed the heaviest use down to two sections of panels. Both had dim illumination in their gauges.

"It's a guess from here," said R.J.

"I'm not sure," said Fantasia. "These two symbols, a filled in circle and an open circle. That is an open-close pair if ever there was one."

"It's just push-in buttons. Do we dare?" asked R.J. "Who wants the blame?"

I stepped up. "It's this or turn back."

"Please, push the button, Adrian," said Parth.

R.J. mused, "I agree, oh frequent destroyer of things everywhere."

I rolled my eye at him, reached over and pushed in the damn button.

There was a sound.

We all jerked around to look. A vertical, oval black hole had appeared in the center column.

"Well, if *we* figured it out, they would have," said R.J.

We went to the opening and carefully looked in. It was an empty room the size of a circular elevator. There were no controls.

I stepped back. "Elevator."

R.J. added, "Or, a waste disposal port which disintegrates anything put into it."

Parth said, "There is no smell of such things and no markings in there. It is an elevator."

R.J. said, "So do we all go in and get fried together or does someone want to volunteer?"

Parth answered, "I will do it. I am the one causing us to be here. I believe it is an elevator. I will test it."

R.J. looked at me. "He may find them not alive in there. You going to let him do it?"

"I don't know but I think Parth is right. One or all of us have to go up inside."

R.J. looked at Fantasia. "What do you think?"

Fantasia said, "I am in agreement that if there is any entrance to this machine, this must be it."

Parth stepped inside. As he turned to face us, the door filled in. We were cut off. There was a faint machine noise.

We waited.

R.J. said, "We could push the console button again and see if he's a fried skeleton still standing there."

Fantasia shook her head. "Patience, R.J."

It took a good five minutes. I had just begun to worry when the oval door reappeared. Parth was standing inside. He was whole.

"It is an elevator," he said.

"What did you see?" asked Fantasia?

"Incredible things. You must all come."

R.J. spoke, "Wait a minute. The last people we know of who went in there never came back. Shouldn't at least one of us stay back in case that happens again?"

I looked at R.J. "Okay, you want to stay here while the three of us check it out?"

R.J. straightened up. "No way."

The three of us joined Parth in the elevator.

The magic door again filled itself in automatically. It was a very plain elevator interior illuminated by a golden light that seemed to be coming from everywhere.

The floor began to slowly rise up. Overhead, a hatch parted to allow us access. A few moments later we were standing in the very complex interior of what had to be a ship.

A round, softly glowing core occupied the center of the craft. Consoles and seats circumvented the outer area. The ceiling sloped down sharply. Near the core there was enough room to stand. We walked the circumference of the cabin, staring down at consoles alive with power. Fantasia pulled out her scanner and began scanning the central core.

I said, "Okay everyone, I know you know this but I have to say it anyway. Do not touch anything. Do not put your hand on any console. Do not lean on anything. This machine is powered up. Let's keep our cool and see if we can figure any of this out."

They all stopped and looked at me for a moment then continued on.

I touched Fantasia's arm. "Fan, I'm not sure you should be scanning anything."

"Yes, darling. Perhaps you're right." She tucked her scanner back in her pants leg pocket and went on.

"I think this is the pilot's position," said R.J. and he pointed to two seats positioned close together.

"And I would guess this is some kind of navigation station," said Fantasia. In front of her was a very complex looking station. A blue 3D hologram was projected above the console. It had orbs of different color within each other, moving in place, and alternating shades of color.

Parth looked at me. "This is far, far more than we can understand."

"What could Diya have done in here?" I asked.

"I do not know. But they had been studying this machine for some time. They must have thought they understood some of it."

Fantasia said, "I believe this navigation array would be safe to operate. The controls are set up in a very basic common-sense manner."

R.J. added, "Adrian, we're going to have to run some kind of test or we're at a dead end here."

I held up one hand. "Okay everybody, just hold on. Let's sit down and talk this through. Let's figure out what we can do, if anything, and where to go from here."

I brought the pilot's seat around and sat. Parth sat next to me, Fantasia took the navigation station. R.J. went to the nearest empty seat, rotated it, and sat.

And that was our first mistake.

There was a blinding flash. It was very strange. It was not of light but rather seemed to be pure intensity. It lingered for a few moments then slowly dissipated.

"Oh, my! That was amazing!" said Fantasia.

"What was amazing!? What just happened?" asked R.J.

We all refocused and looked around. The ship had changed. Few consoles were now illuminated. The hum from the central core had decreased. Cabin lighting had dimmed.

"Is everyone alright?" asked Fantasia.

"I'll let you know," replied R.J.

"Did anyone touch anything by accident when we sat down?" I asked.

Everyone shook their head.

Path said, "Perhaps it was just an automatic power reset or something of that nature."

"I believe there was some sort of physiological effect, one I am not familiar with," said Fantasia.

"It might be a good idea to leave before it happens again," suggested R.J.

"It is possible that something like this is what happened to Diya," said Parth.

I stood. "R.J.'s right. Let's regroup outside and talk about this."

We gathered at the elevator. Without any command it lowered us down. The door unsealed itself. We stepped out.

More had changed. The cavern was now well lit by daylight. The entrance we had come through was still there, but beyond it was a short tunnel section that opened to outdoors.

"Oh my!" exclaimed Fantasia. "I do not believe we are where we were."

"There are no control consoles here," said R.J. "It's a different cavern."

Parth looked at me. "I believe they are correct, Adrian. We have been transported somewhere but I do not know where."

R.J. said, "Look!" and he pointed at the ground. Leading out of the cave were two sets of footprints.

"Diya," said Parth.

R.J. said, "We are either hot on their trail, completely lost ourselves, or both."

We looked at each other.

R.J. added, "Well guys, there are only two choices; we either go after them or stay here and try to figure out how to get back."

I tried to sound sympathetic. "There really isn't a choice, R.J. We left our packs back there. We have no food or water. We can't gamble that we'll figure this thing out before we die of thirst. We've got to find food and water somewhere."

R.J. said, "And you guys all realize this ship must have left a completely enclosed cave to arrive here in this one, right?"

I answered, "Let's just hope we're near civilization wherever we are."

R.J. persisted, "I'm just saying, we all apparently passed through solid rock to get here."

We headed for the exit. The daylight beaming through was reassuring. Stepping outside we had to shield our eyes from the sun. It took a few moments to focus.

Once again Fantasia exclaimed, "Oh my!"

R.J. followed with, "What the hell?"

I had to blink a few times from the light. We were standing on a small plateau halfway up a mountain overlooking the deadest brown landscape I'd ever seen. There were scattered forests, all brown. There were fields of grass, all brown. Dry riverbeds ran through some of it. Far in the distance there were two good sized lakes also brown.

Parth came up beside me. "I do not believe this is Earth, Adrian."

I nodded to him. "I have to agree."

R.J. called out, "There are two suns, one just about behind the first. No wonder it's so bright, even with the brownish sky."

Fantasia pointed and said, "Diya and her friend left here and headed in that direction."

Two sets of tracks wound down the mountain side, a shuffling through the brown dirt.

Fantasia exclaimed, "Wait, over to our right, halfway to the next mountain, I see a town."

We all studied the terrain. Far in the distance, within a cluster of forest, there were buildings. A path passed through their center; a road covered in the same brown dust. I scanned the brown path as it led into and out of the cluster of civilization. There was no sign of life, no lights, no traffic, no movement.

"Does the air smell strange to anyone else?" asked Fantasia. She unclipped her scanner and began to take readings.

46

"It's the dust," answered R.J. "It's everywhere."

"There is radiation here," said Fantasia. "But it's strange. It appears to be passing right through us. We do not seem affected."

"I'm guessing Diya and her companion headed for that town. If we follow their tracks it will probably lead us there. Anyone have any other ideas?" I asked.

"Not a lot of choices," commented R.J. "Fan, can you measure distance with that thing?"

"Oh! Yes. I can if I just make a few adjustments. It's a medical scanner but it's smart." Fantasia held the scanner against her hip and reprogrammed it. She held it up and read the display. "It is twelve miles in a straight line."

"Probably at least fifteen for us," said R.J.

Parth said, "It is lucky we had our jackets on. The air is cool here."

Fantasia checked her scanner. "Sixty-eight degrees F to be exact."

I asked, "Anyone have a guess of how much daylight we have left?"

R.J. answered, "If this was Earth those suns would be at about eleven o'clock in the morning."

I looked lovingly at Fantasia, "Can that be set up to map us so we can find our way back?"

She took a step close to me and looked up with a smile. "Yes. I can also record the surrounding terrain."

I turned to the others. "Gentlemen, shall we try to cover some ground?"

It was a winding, broken path down between rock and brush. There were prints from Diya all along the way. The walk down was easy. It took almost an hour to reach level ground. From there it became a pathless weave through brown woods. Most leaves had remnants of brown ash. The ground was covered with it. We kept the suns to our left and followed Diya's shuffling marks as we went. Our lack of water began to be more and more relevant.

Nearly two more hours into the march the tree line opened up and surprised us with a roadway. It was completely covered with dust in both directions. Diya had followed this road and gone to the right, the general direction of the town.

We were another forty-five minutes into the hike when Fantasia took a quick scan as she walked. She stopped abruptly and called out, "Wait a minute."

"What is it Fan?" I asked.

"Metal object through those woods. A big one."

## Chapter 5

We went to the roadside and searched.

R.J. said, "The brush has been trampled down here like something went through."

R.J. and I headed into the woods, following a vague path of crushed brush. Parth and Fantasia followed.

Ten minutes in I asked, "You really have something, Fan?"

She held up her scanner. "Yes, it's right there."

A few more steps gave us another surprise. It was a vehicle, jeep-type, with a torn canvas roof. It had been there for some time.

R.J. worked his way to the driver's side. "Oh man."

I caught up and looked in. A skeleton was driving.

Parth joined us. "He must have lost control."

R.J. said, "Yeah, after the bullet went through him."

It was then we noticed the bullet hole in the driver's seat just behind the body's rib cage.

Parth said, "There are carry-alls in the back."

We opened the back and pulled out two satchels. The first contained military styled food packets, still sealed. I placed the second satchel on the ground, opened it and found two weapons, one similar to an Uzi automatic, and the second a large handgun, probably a nine-millimeter automatic.

Fantasia stood watching over us. "Well, this certainly tells a story, doesn't it?"

R.J. called out, "Canteen on the passenger seat. It's three quarters full of something."

I looked up. "R.J. don't you test that. Let Fan scan it."

"Duh, okay cause I'm stoopid."

Parth asked, "Fantasia, do you have a theory about this place?"

"We are in a world which still uses projectile weaponry and fossil fuel driven vehicles. We are also in a world where people shoot each other to death. We may have been lucky not being assaulted already along the way, that is, if there are any people left."

R.J. appeared with the canteen. Fantasia scanned it. "Water. With that same small amount of radiation. I believe we can drink this."

R.J. sneered at me and took a drink. "Gee, tastes just like water."

I waited and took the canteen from him and handed it to Fantasia. She carefully sipped from it and handed it back. We all took drinks.

Parth said, "So this man was shot on the road, lost control and crashed into these woods."

I straightened up from searching the pack. "I don't think so, Parth."

"Why not?" asked R.J.

"They didn't take the guns or the food. This doesn't seem like a place anyone would leave guns, ammunition, and food behind. I think he was shot somewhere else but lived long enough to drive here and crash. That's why his stuff is still here."

R.J. asked, "I wonder if we could get this thing running? Let me pop the hood."

We looked on as R.J. reached into the skeleton's window and found the hood latch. I followed him to check out the engine compartment.

50

"Damn," said R.J. "This engine looks like it would run but the battery terminals have corroded off from age."

"Pretty stale fuel if there is any left in the tank," I added.

"Yeah, but if it's fossil fuel I'll bet it would fire."

"No way we'll push this thing through these woods."

"Yeah, I guess skeleton man gets to keep his jeep."

"This thing is black but I couldn't even tell that until you opened the hood."

"Dusted in brown," replied R.J.

We returned to the others.

"How about I take the Uzi thing?" said R.J. "I'm the worst shot. You get the automatic."

"Okay, but sling that thing over your back out of sight. If we run into anyone, we don't want them to think we're road warriors. Parth, you want a weapon?"

"I think not, Adrian. Not until they are needed."

"There is a long knife in this pack if it comes to that."

Parth nodded.

I brought out the pistol and looked it over. It had odd markings on it but otherwise looked like a standard automatic. The safety was on. The magazine eject button was nearby. I popped it out. Standard looking bullets, definitely nine-millimeter. I slid it back in and tucked the gun into my waistline behind me.

R.J. ejected his curved magazine, confirmed it was loaded, and set the gun up. He strapped it on behind him and looked at me for approval. We brushed brown dust off ourselves and headed back to the road.

"At least walking will be much easier," said Parth.

"Diya's trail will be easier to follow also," said Fantasia.

We made the roadway and began following along the footprints.

"I have seen no aircraft in the sky since we began walking," said Fantasia.

"What do you deduce from that, Fantasia?" asked Parth.

"We have seen a vehicle, weapons, and some sort of settlement that suggest this society was comparable to twentieth century Earth. If that is correct there should be frequent air travel overhead."

"But there is not," replied Parth.

Fantasia continued, "We also see an underlying level of radiation in the air and a layer of dust covering the entire surface. All of these together suggest some type of catastrophe befell this planet, or at least a large part of it."

R.J. looked back at Fantasia as we walked. "Are you suggesting a natural catastrophe or a man-made catastrophe?"

"We cannot be sure," answered Fantasia.

Parth added, "The murdered man back there may also suggest there was a period of anarchy after the catastrophe."

I said, "You two are making me feel better about this old-fashioned handgun tucked into my belt."

"Damn right," added R.J.

"Let us not assume the worst, gentleman," said Parth.

I asked, "Fantasia, what kind of natural disaster could cause something like this?"

"There are many, darling. A super volcano could easily eject this kind of ash and lay waste to a large portion of the planet's surface."

Parth said, "There is also an hypothesis by a Professor Foester based partly on research by scientist Paul LaViollette which proposes the center of our galaxy is not a black hole but rather a pulsar that releases its energy every twelve or thirteen thousand years. The energy from that release strikes our sun causing it to emit giant blasts of plasma that scorch Earth's surface in various places. So it may be that cataclysmic destruction within a galaxy is more frequent that we realize. Such an event could also account for what we see here."

"I would have guessed the giant meteor theory," said R.J.

"There is one other major possibility none of you has mentioned," I added.

"What is it?" asked R.J.

"Global thermonuclear war."

We considered that in silence as we walked.

R.J. asked, "Fan, how far have we gone?"

Fantasia checked her scanner. "Almost seven miles. And in tracking the suns, they have moved approximately twelve degrees per hour. I have calculated that Earth's sun moves at roughly fifteen degrees per hour so that means one day on this planet is longer than that of Earth. But, we must also consider that as the orbits of those suns diverge, the length of the day will vary."

I guessed we were making better time than Diya and her companion. The farther we traveled, the more we saw signs they had stopped to rest. I began to worry we might find their bodies. If they had arrived here without supplies like we did and had lingered around the ship too long, they may have succumbed to dehydration. But so far, the tracks kept on.

We rationed skeleton man's water carefully and rested as often as Dr. Fantasia ordered us to. As the shadows began to grow long we reached the top of a small hill and found we were looking down on the town a few more miles away. We found places to sit where we could rest and watch for activity there.

I asked, "Fan, can you reprogram the cameras on the scanner for visual long distance?"

"Yes, dear. It will take a few minutes." She drew out her scanner and began punching in commands.

To the naked eye it was a ghost town. A creepy ghost town. There were vehicles scattered around the streets, covered with dust. Some were parked, others had been in accidents. The buildings were in disarray. No power apparent. No movement.

Fantasia said, "Look at this!"

We crowded around to try to see the small scanner display.

"It's difficult to hold it steady enough but look; that's a dress in a shop window."

She did her best to scan along the buildings. Some had open front doors. There were some broken windows.

Suddenly Fantasia groaned, "Oh, no." She had found an image that looked like a dust covered body in the street.

I put a hand on her shoulder. "We've been expecting that."

R.J. commented, "Have you noticed in some spots there are two sets of footprints in the dust in the street. I hope they found water."

"I hope *we* find water," I added.

R.J. leaned in over Fantasia's arm for a closer look. "Fantasia, can I hold that for a minute?"

She handed him the scanner.

R.J. braced and pointed the instrument at a certain point. "Look at this," he said.

We all squeezed in.

"It's the sign above that store. I'm trying to keep it steady, sorry. See what it says? H-A-R-D-W-A-E-R. Hardware! And right next to that place it looks like a closed-up restaurant. Here's the sign. D-I-N-A, Dina, meaning diner. English is being used here except it's skewed."

I said, "You've convinced me we have no idea where we are, R.J."

Parth said, "It will be getting dark soon, I think. We should get to that town for shelter."

Fantasia nodded. "The canteen is empty."

Down the hill we went, still shuffling through brown ash. Though it hadn't looked that far it took another two hours. We came to a farmhouse on the outskirts of town. Early evening had set in. There were no lights in the windows. The house was wood construction with a long porch. Garage in back to the right. One of two garage doors open, no vehicles inside.

R.J. stepped up on the porch and knocked. Silence answered. He tried the door. Locked. He looked back at us to ask if he should break in. We all shook our heads before he had time to ask. We turned away and continued into town.

We dared to walk down the center of the street, looking inside abandoned cars as we went.

R.J. said, "There's keys in some of these."

I replied, "You can be sure the batteries are gone."

"Yeah," he answered.

Parth said, "That looks like a hotel up ahead. The doors are open."

It was one of the few buildings that did not have a broken window. It was a modern building with a glass front. Three stories, steel construction, open vestibule with twin arched entrances. The glass doors were blocked open by rubble and a wave of dust on the floor. Long main desk counter on the left. Two dark computers on a shelf behind it. Old fashioned CRT monitors. Made me guess we were looking at an early Windows era. Couches and chairs in the adjacent waiting area. Their fabric was giving way from age. We stood for a moment at the reception desk. As ominous as the place was, it felt good just to be inside.

R.J. exclaimed, "My God, they look just like us!" He was staring at a picture on the wall hanging by one corner. We gathered there and appraised the long-haired young man in sport clothes holding a shiny silver trophy, his benefactor in an open corduroy style jacket smiling alongside him. As R.J. had said, they looked perfectly human.

Fantasia said, "I don't think we should stay here tonight. The temperature is dropping. We don't know how cold it will get. We need a heater or a fire."

I said, "Lets head farther down the street and look for chimneys."

We returned to the street and resumed our walk. The light had become dim. Past another dust-covered body form Fantasia looked ahead, pointed, and said, "Perfect."

It was a two-story doctor's office. Stone chimney ran up the side. Metal steps led up the side to the second floor. Split wood was stacked beneath the steps. The glass in the ground floor front door window had been smashed. The door was slightly ajar. We choose the steps on the side instead. I insisted on going first.

At the top of the stairs the door was unlocked. I pushed into a hallway that had escaped the dust bowl. Living room on the right. Office with messy desk beyond it. Two bedrooms on the left. No one home. Back at the top of the stairs I waved them up.

R.J. and Parth arrived with bundles of wood. We went to the living room fireplace and built our fire. None of us had anything to light it with. A search began. R.J. returned with pipes in a revolving pipe holder, pipe tobacco, and a lighter. I motioned Fantasia to a nearby chair less deteriorated than the others we'd seen, and we set our fireplace ablaze.

I headed for the office and did a more thorough search. To my delight there was a flashlight and in one closet a box of dry cell batteries. Back by the fire I loaded up my treasure and found that it worked.

"It's going to be a long night without water," said R.J.

Parth said, "There has to be a water tower in this town somewhere. Tomorrow in the light our chances of getting water from it are good."

"I will also probably be able to put a med kit together from what I can find downstairs. The doctor couldn't have taken everything."

"Is there any chance there might be water downstairs somewhere?" I asked.

"Others have probably beat us to it a long time ago," said R.J.

Fantasia looked up. "Wait! There's a chance. Let's go down and take a look."

We never doubt Fantasia. We left Parth to guard the fire and the three of us went down.

The doctor had left nearly everything. The locked medicine cabinets had been broken into and rifled through. In a back room there were several large tanks and to our surprise Fantasia cheered. She held up a large, sealed plastic container. It was labeled: AQUA ADD INJECTIONEM.

We looked at her inquisitively.

"It's water, silly. Purified water," she said, trying not to laugh at us.

We headed back upstairs.

"I'll put together a really good med kit tomorrow. Those poor people. They stole the drugs that make you feel good but left all the most important ones. Antiseptics, anti-inflammatory, blood pressure, sutures, scalpels, all the really important items."

"I doubt they were thinking ahead," said R.J.

Upstairs we rounded up cups, took seats around the fire and quenched our thirst. We rifled through the food packs, checked to be sure they were good and ate as much as we wanted. Despite our situation we were able to relax and rest. R.J. packed and lit one of the pipes and sat back contemplating the nature of the universe as all pipe smokers do.

Path asked, "Fantasia, any new insights to this world?"

"Yes. This town is fairly large. It would have supported thousands but we have only seen the remains of a few residents left behind. These people had time to leave. Many of their vehicles were left behind on the street."

I added, "Most of the parking lots we've seen are almost empty."

"Many left in their own vehicles and others in mass transit," suggested R.J.

"There is one other ominous observation," said Fantasia. "There has been no wildlife, not even birds in the sky, but also no signs of deceased animals."

Parth responded, "The wildlife must have also gone into hiding and the domestic animals were taken with their owners."

"It must have been a crazy exodus," added R.J. "And where did they all go?"

"You know what this place reminds *me* of, R.J.?" I asked.

"Yep. Mars."

Fantasia asked, "Oh, I have not studied Mars. Why do you say that?"

R.J. answered, "Mars was given the name Planet of War a very long time ago. Many centuries ago there was a war between advanced cultures there. It destroyed the planet's atmosphere and almost everything on it. There are still remnants of destroyed cities on the planet. That's part of the reason life on Mars is based mostly underground now."

"There is no evidence of that kind of battle destruction in this town," suggested Parth.

R.J. answered, "True. But it is still eerily similar."

I said, "Fan, you were right. It's gotten very cold outside."

"We'll need to take turns keeping the fire going," said R.J.

So we slept in shifts and waited for the two suns to rise.

# Chapter 6

Parth had the last fire watch and let us sleep past Browntown sunrise. There was coffee in the Doctor's kitchen which we brewed over the fire. The morning was cold. We sat around the fire sipping our coffee and planning.

"I need to assemble a med kit downstairs and something to carry it in," said Fantasia.

I added, "We have to find water that is drinkable or can be made drinkable and canteens or some kind of containers to carry it in."

R.J. said, "You know, if there was any way to get one of these vehicles running…."

"I would bet there's not a functioning battery to be found anywhere," I said.

"Maybe we could push start something."

I said, "That's a long shot. It would have to be a manual transmission and after all this time it might not fire. We'd have to find something parked at the top of a hill."

R.J. persisted. "There has to be an auto parts store in this town. If I could find a new battery in a box which hasn't been activated, that would work."

"Who knows, you might get lucky," I said. "One thing, though, no one should go wandering around alone."

"Maybe we can find some walkie-talkies in a store somewhere," added R.J. "The dry cell batteries still work."

Fantasia said, "Watch for water in outdoor barrels or anywhere else. We can purify it as needed."

Parth said, "I am wondering, should we really continue the search or should we return to the craft and try to get back if we can?"

Fantasia said, "Parth, it's possible Diya knows more about that ship than we do. We may need her to get back."

R.J. added, "Yeah, we wouldn't want to go back and fail and then have to come all this way again. Let's keep going."

No one objected.

Parth said, "I am very grateful to you all. I would have asked that I go on alone had you decided to return."

We spread out and began our snipe hunt. Daylight showed just how ransacked the doctor's office was. But, as Fantasia had said, the really important stuff had been disregarded. We cleared junk off the exam table and used it to lay out the tools and supplies she wanted. A hardshell briefcase fitted with cut out foam made a perfect kit case.

We walked to one end of the town and found a small food market. Most of the shelves were bare, not a single can of food. A drug store farther down was just as bad. There was a set of kid's walkie-talkies but not a battery of any kind in the place. We took them anyway. There was also a set of plastic binoculars. On the way out a display rack caught my eye. Yellowed plastic maps were sticking out of it. We took them all.

On the way back we spotted R.J. and Parth coming back. As they neared I realized R.J. was pushing a handcart with something on it. It was a box about the size of a standard car battery. He had a big smile on his face.

"Always check the hazmat dumpsters," he said. He proudly opened the flaps on the box to reveal a new unused car battery. "The case is badly cracked," he added. "But we can patch it up long enough to start a car."

"Did you find any electrolyte?"

"All the electrolyte containers had dissolved on the shelves. We'll have to make our own electrolyte. But when we add electrolyte to this baby it will automatically be eighty percent charged. At the top of the hill back there we spotted a military jeep vehicle parked at a garage. It's worth looking at."

Fantasia said, "You will need sulfuric acid to mix with water for that battery."

Parth said, "There is other good news, also. Fantasia, your idea was correct. At the end of the street behind a business there is a gutter down spout that channeled water into a closed barrel. It is full."

I said, "Let's go check out R.J.'s jeep. If there's any chance of getting it running that would give us the best chance of catching them. R.J., bring your battery. We'll patch it up there. Maybe we'll get lucky again and find some electrolyte."

We marched up the deserted street. A gentle breeze had picked up. It caused wisps of brown dust to come off the nearby buildings and vehicles. The place was spooky. I kept thinking I'd seen someone looking out a window but there was no one there. The garage was up a small hill at the end of main street, surrounded by trees and brush. It could have been a set for Mayberry. A dust covered red and white office gave the place its best visibility: glass front, checkered bay doors. R.J.'s jeep was parked facing them. Ancient gas pump. No overhead. The place was locked up tight. We broke in the back door.

They had left everything. In the office the scheduling book and last day's receipts were stacked up. The front counter and cash register were clean and waiting for customers. In the bays, tools were still hanging in place. In the storeroom R.J. found a can of powder marked, Battery Activator. We opened the bay door and stood looking at our ride while Parth and Fantasia set our battery up on a counter to patch it.

"The engine may be frozen solid, R.J." I said.

"Let's change the oil, then we can push it and pop it into gear and see if it turns over," he replied.

We did and to our glee, it did.

"We're only going to get a few chances before our battery dies. We better make the best of it," I said.

R.J. popped the hook and braced it open. "I'm thinking pull the plugs, clean and set them, and clean out the distributor."

"You have a commendable knowledge of the gas combustion engine, sir."

"My collectors' 1960 Corvair. Still the best car ever made. You didn't have points in your Vette, did you?"

"Nope. It's an optispark distributor. Don't ask me to explain it. I think we've gotta pull that carburetor and clean it. No gas, no go."

"Yeah, you're right. You take the carb, I'll get the plugs. The plug wires are pretty brittle. We'd better keep our fingers crossed."

We went to work. We had everything we needed. Tools, ancient gas in gas cans for cleaning, rags, and workbenches. I tore down and cleaned my carburetor alongside Parth and Fantasia. She and I continually exchanged provocative glances. Love never gets old with her. They made acid resistant glue for the cracks in the battery, found a roll of tape that still worked, and bandaged the thing up. The electrolyte powder mixed properly but we held off adding it to the battery until we were ready.

When it was all back together a quick check of the jeep's gas tank showed it nearly full of old, old gas, but it still smelled like gas. We stood over the engine and stared down at it with doubt.

"It was worth a try even if it doesn't light," said R.J.

"We'll definitely need to spray a wisp of gas into the carb when we try to start it."

"If by some miracle it runs we'll need to put the air cleaner back on or the thing will ingest all this dust in the air."

I looked at R.J. and smiled. "Now or never?"

"By your command, sir."

We set the activated battery in place and connected it. There was a clicking of relays. I set up a spray bottle with gas and stood ready at the carb.

R.J. stood at the open driver's door and said, "Ready?"

"Go for it."

I sprayed. R.J. twisted the key. The engine turned over which made us both jump. There was a bang and a rumble and R.J. switched off the key.

"Oh my God! It almost started!" he cried.

"One more time, sir."

R.J. twisted the key and the little four-cylinder engine rumbled to life, ran rough for a few seconds but smoothed out.

R.J. called out, "I don't believe it!"

He came up beside me admiring the rocking, noisy engine.

I held up one hand, "You are a mechanic of great merit, sir."

"As are you, my friend."

We high-fived.

We looked at Parth and Fantasia standing behind us. They were smirking.

"I do believe we have wheels." I said.

"It was the battery that did it," joked Parth.

R.J. looked at me and nodded. "It *was* the battery."

After a furious cleaning of our jeep we used it to collect large empty plastic containers from the pharmacy then spent the rest of the day developing a filtration system to purify the water from the rain barrel. Fantasia's scanner showed some particulates remained but the water safe to drink. With our supplies collected and stored we returned to the doctor's upstairs apartment to spend the night. A grand fire going in the fireplace, we spread out our maps on the floor and began to study the world where we had ended up.

"It really is mostly English," said Fantasia.

"There is no way to know where we are on any of these maps," said R.J.

Fantasia said, "If we call sunrise the east and sunset the west, that may not be correct but if it is, the road we followed that runs through town is a north-south road."

"So a small town somewhere on one of these maps, with mountains to the north or south and a north-south road running through it," I added.

"There are quite a few major cities on these maps," said Parth.

"And we know Diya came though this town and left heading in the direction we call south," said Fantasia.

I added, "This map over here is a street map. That has to be us, right?"

"The town of Jeffson," said R.J.

"Here on this one," said Parth and he pointed to a spot on the main map. "A north-south road along mountains leading to Jeffson."

"Got to be," said R.J.

"This is very helpful," said Parth. "The main road heading south leads to a major city, Britonia."

"If this map legend is using anything close to miles, Britonia is about eighty miles away. That would be maybe a two-hour trip by jeep," I added.

Parth said, "I am growing more concerned as we go. How could they possibly get that far on foot, yet we know they left here on that road?"

Fantasia looked at Parth. "Parth, you said Diya is an archeologist."

"Yes, an assistant Professor."

"She must be very smart."

"She has always been."

"And they've gotten this far."

"That is true. Perhaps there is still a chance."

We all bundled up near the fire and held on to hope.

In the morning we gathered up our treasures, climbed into the jeep and cheered when it cranked and started. We began a slow follow of the footprints left by Diya and her companion.

About a mile out of town in an area bordered by trees and thick growth, the footprints suddenly turned into the driveway of a farmhouse. They did not come back out. In their place were two narrow lines in the dust that came out and continued along the south road.

"They found bicycles," said R.J.

"Good for them," commented Fantasia.

"We may not be as close as we thought we were," said Parth.

We picked up our speed and made good time.

The legend on the map turned out to be very close to Earth miles. Just about two hours into the trip, we climbed a steep hill that crested overlooking the city of Britonia.

66

It was shocking.

As untouched as Jeffson had been, Britonia was equally destroyed. The place looked like a modern city which had been photoshopped into a World War Two bombed out area. Lots of roofs missing. Lots of windows out. Piles of brick alongside damaged walls. Holes in the streets. Burned out cars everywhere. A few lumps on the ground that looked like former people. But the worst of it was at the north and south side of the city. Two giant melted rings probably two miles in diameter. The remnants of nuclear bombs. Along the side of one of these melted rings a long section of six lane thoroughfare had been broken off and pushed a mile away from the rest of the highway. Cars were still lined up on that piece. The second blast ring had created a huge crater and underpass of the same highway. We stood gawking and speechless. The silence was deafening.

"Oh, my heavens," said Fantasia finally.

"Now we know," added R.J.

"I had hoped it was at least natural phenomena," said Parth.

"Another point for the inevitable end of man everywhere," said R.J.

"The radiation here is higher, but still for some reason it does not appear to be affecting us," said Fantasia as she fidgeted with her scanner.

I looked down at the bike path. "They went down there." I drew out the plastic binoculars and began a slow scan of the streets. "It looks like there are too many tracks in the streets. They couldn't all be from our guys. There may be other people still living here."

R.J. said, "We must be cautious."

"Okay, Obi-Wan."

Parth asked, "Do you see anyone moving down there?"

"Not yet. I see two separate airports. One looks international, the other regional. Both have control towers intact but nobody's flying."

"That could be useful," said R.J.

"We can't just go driving though the city, guys. It's too dangerous. We have a very valuable jeep, water, and food. We can't go waltzing in there," I warned.

"You are right, of course," said Fantasia.

R.J. shook his head. "If there are survivors down there this place will be ruled by gangs. We've seen it happen a dozen times. Once back in the nineties on Earth after Louisiana got hit by a bad hurricane gangs took over a big part of New Orleans. Police and firefighters were shot at. They couldn't even get into some areas. Down there it will probably be worse."

Parth added, "If, as you say, there are survivors."

I continued to scan. "There is a subway system here. I see two entrances to the underground."

Parth said, "That is where the people would have gone."

I handed the glasses to Fantasia. She began her own scan.

I turned and looked at the others. "We need to stay out of sight, camp out here and watch the city for a while. We need to get an idea of who is down there and where."

R.J. said, "When we're ready we can drive down as close as we dare, hide the jeep, then go in on foot."

Parth asked, "What will we accomplish?"

I answered, "We'll keep an eye out for signs of Diya, but I think R.J. is talking about supplies.

We're okay on water for now, but we'll have to find food somewhere before we run out."

There was a spot nearby where we could pull off the road and conceal the jeep behind brush. We took turns sitting on the jeep hood and watching the city with our plastic binoculars.

Fantasia said, "We need to get inside before nightfall, Adrian. The cold will be dangerous."

R.J. added, "Most of the places we've passed have chimneys. We just need to find one between here and the city and park the jeep out of sight."

Parth called out, "There is smoke rising from a chimney near the center of the city."

R.J. said, "Wow! For all we know that could be them."

I came up beside Parth. "See anything else?"

"It is too far. I am not able to see the streets that far away."

"Do you think you could find the building the smoke is coming from?"

"I think it is a two-story residential building next to a four-story office building. Yes, we could locate them." Parth continued to search with the binoculars.

"Parth, can you see any farmhouses or businesses down in the valley we might use for shelter?"

"Yes. I have been looking. There is a farm or ranch house about halfway to the city. It might suit our needs."

We climbed aboard and continued south toward the city. The farmhouse Parth had found was big and deserted. It had a double garage in back with doors. We shut in the jeep and checked the home's back doors. Rather than break in, I climbed through a window and let everyone in. Parth went for wood while the rest of us searched the place.

We met in the main living area where the blackened fireplace waited for fire. R.J. came in carrying a cardboard box.

"It was their stash. Hidden in the back of a closet," he explained.

He pulled out a dozen cans of what looked like franks and beans. He left again and came back with a can opener from the kitchen just as Parth arrived with firewood.

Fantasia stood looking at pictures on the wall. "It was a big family," she said. "I count six children, two parents, and two grandparents."

"They left stale food in the fridge and clothes in the closets," added R.J.

I said, "We know this city was bombed. They must have had warning and headed for the underground."

R.J. made another kitchen trip and returned with a cooking pan, smaller bowls, and silverware. He and Parth dished out what I hoped was franks and beans and set the pan on the growing fire.

Parth stirred the food. "It is much easier to understand the cost of war when one sees it in this fashion."

"It is a stark hell," said R.J.

Fantasia said, "It is not the fault of everyone involved. It is the fault of the immature ones who respond only to their basic instincts for wealth and power."

Parth asked, "But do not the mature ones eventually join in?"

Fantasia said, "When too many immatures group together and gain too much power, they can impose their will on the people. They can force them to comply. That is how world wars are started."

R.J. said, "Actually, that is historically true. All through history when one dictator or warlord

70

obtains technology ahead of everyone else's, that advantage has been used to make war on neighbors to commandeer their wealth and property. Those who disagree with the warlord are killed or imprisoned. The warlords and their supporters take control of the news media and use it to manipulate people. On Earth that was precisely the formula for World War Two."

Parth stirred and added, "Yes, it is fortunate Earth was not a nuclear society at that time. Because when one side begins to lose a war many times they would prefer to die than to be taken over, so the doomsday weapons are used."

"Which brings us to the planet outside this farmhouse," said R.J.

Fantasia asked, "You have been awfully quiet, dear. Don't you have an opinion about this?"

I looked up. "You've all left out religion. The people who tell you to believe what they tell you or they'll kill you, but I think in the end it adds up to the same thing."

The flames licked at the side of Parth's pan. He began spooning out franks and beans and handing out bowls. The hot food made us all silent. We ate and stared into the fire. The food seemed more delicious than it should have. I dared to read the label on one can; Horg's Beans and Tubes. On the ingredients list all it said was, meat tubes one hundred percent meat. Apparently, these people didn't care what kind of meat it was. I was left to hope it wasn't Soylent Green.

We pushed furniture closer to the fire. There were good sheets in the bedroom to use as covers. Fantasia and I were given the couch although it was an exercise in narrowness. We took turns keeping the fire and listening for unwanted guests. We slept in doomsday land and waited for its two suns to rise.

## Chapter 7

R.J. insisted on driving. He claimed the best marksman needed to have his hands free. Holding on for dear life due to wild driving made marksmanship a questionable benefit.

As we neared the city we turned off on a side brown dust road that circumvented most of the buildings. There were occasional tracks in the road which were disconcerting. The road became a single lane dirt path between trees and brush. We found a concealed spot that would allow for a quick escape, parked, and covered the jeep completely in brown branches. We filled our water holders and took the two packs with ammo and some supplies. We were near the back end of a tall hotel with many broken windows.

"Think you can get us to the smoking chimney, Parth?" I asked.

"Yes, Fantasia took images from the hilltop with the scanner. With those we should be able to find our way."

"I think our best bet is to follow along behind these buildings. That should keep us out of sight."

We pushed brush aside and headed toward the hotel. A wall of giant gray dumpsters in the back of the hotel hid our approach.

R.J. said, "You know, there may not be any danger at all. It's possible we could waltz right down main street without any problem."

As we crossed the clearing to the hotel, R.J.'s hypothesis was immediately disproven. A figure

72

appeared out of nowhere and stepped into our path.

I had been leading. The others caught up and gathered around me.

The man was wearing a dirty leather vest with no shirt underneath which surprised me because we were borderline cold in our jackets. His trousers were so overdue for washing it made the dark color indefinable. He wore brown boots which ran up under the ragged hem of the trousers. His black hair was swept back behind his head, hairline receding. Darkness around a narrow stare. Pretty much a standard human. Big smile that wasn't friendly. He did not see the weapons tucked in behind us.

He smiled rotten teeth. "What you got there? You got anything?" He spoke in a tone that suggested bad things would happen to us if we did not. "You got a fixer on you?"

Parth looked at me in surprise. "Adrian, in India the term *fixer* is slang for handgun."

Immediately I felt that a solid punch to the nose would have been an appropriate response to the question but R.J. jumped in before the idea reached my right hand.

"Sir, we do not want any trouble but I should advise you we are quite good at mitigating it when it does happen."

He cocked his head back in disapproval and asked again. "What you got there. You must got somethin'. What you got?"

R.J. persisted, "My friend, right now you're in good health. If you just step aside we'll be on our way. It will not cost you a thing. If you continue to interfere with us however you may end up losing some of the meager affluence you now possess."

I looked at R.J. "Meager affluence? Really?"

Fantasia had her scanner out and was reading him. "This man is suffering from radiation poisoning."

Our friend reached behind and drew out a rusty but formidable hunting knife. He widened his revolting smile. "You just lay out the ground and we see what you got."

The sight of the rusty blade caused me to take pause and consider how long it had been since I'd participated in mortal combat. Were my reflexes slowing up? My technique getting sloppy? Nah. It was time to conclude show and tell by displaying the automatic weapon tucked into my belt, but R.J. interrupted again.

"Friend, please, you're going to get messed up and lose your nice knife too. Please, just walk away."

Indignation set in. The guy grimaced and came at me apparently because I was the largest and most threatening. I did not have time to bring out the automatic. He lunged forward and took a knife swipe at my throat. He was dead serious.

He was quick but was a single technique kind of guy. No follow up. I leaned back from his advance and let the knife swish by at a safe margin. Then it was my right hand grabbing the back of his arm as it passed by and holding it away, my left hand clamping over his face, my left foot kicking into the back of his weight bearing knee, and down he went. I stepped back to let him try to get up. He spread out both arms to push up allowing me to step on his right wrist and take the knife. I slowly back peddled a couple of steps and let him be.

He sprung up as though he was going to try something else, realized he was no longer the owner of the knife, and looked at me like a dejected cat that just had fallen in a pond.

R.J. was beside himself. "You couldn't listen, could you? You had go and mess yourself all up. I tried to tell you but did you listen? No. Now look at you. You got nothing and lost your nice knife. Why don't people ever listen?"

Without taking his eyes off us the disheveled man brushed the dust and leaves off his bare arms. He was really pissed about the whole affair. He started to back away. He turned and took a few steps and stopped again to look back.

I held the knife by the blade and threw it so that it stuck in the ground halfway between us. He looked at me questioningly and with the greatest of care stepped forward and drew it from the ground. For a split second he seemed to be contemplating a second attack. I drew out the automatic and held it up for him to see. He scoffed and hurried away into the woods.

R.J. said, "Well, welcome to doomsday world."

I replied, "It was a good lesson in what to expect."

R.J. answered, "Yeah, you probably shouldn't have given that back to him."

"I had a feeling he might not survive too long without it."

We waited to be sure he wasn't doubling back, then headed for the back of the apartment complex. We were mostly in the open and had to stay low and use what cover there was. The line of dumpsters had achieved a very mature ripeness. We dared not look inside fearing it might be bodies. I kept glancing back to check on Fantasia and each time was surprised by how well she moved with us.

It was a messy advance. Garbage and broken furniture had been tossed out the hotel windows. We moved with stealth past building after building. There was no one around. An hour into our foray, we came to two dilapidated office buildings that had a two-foot alley between them.

I turned to the others and kept my voice low. "This might be a good place for a position check. These buildings are both four stories. They're so close together we could jump from one roof to the other if we got cornered. Let's see if we can get roof access and look for our target chimney."

Through a missing back door and up four flights of stairs strewn with litter. Still no people. The lock on the hatch to the roof had been broken off. I pushed up very slowly and scanned the flat stone roof surface. We were alone. We all climbed up and scanned around fearfully. There was no one. As we walked toward the far corner of the roof, Parth pointed and said, "There it is over there. It is the chimney with the black cap."

At the side of the roof we searched the cityscape. Buildings of various heights were above and below us, all tinted in brown. Glass, brick, stone, and wood. The construction designs were similar to twentieth century Earth. In the dust on the street below there were signs of foot traffic, too many to have been created by two people. I pulled the plastic binoculars out of Parth's bag and began studying the target building. It sat on the far side of a four-way intersection. I could see into some of the windows.

Parth tapped me on the shoulder. "I see people. Let me borrow the glasses."

I handed them off. He stared down at the street in front of the suspect building. Two people in dark clothing were crossing the street. Weapons were slung over their shoulders.

Parth followed them intently with the glasses. He looked up at me and said, "It is not Diya."

R.J. said, "Glad we didn't go knocking on their door."

Parth said, "This is interesting. I can see an airport control tower between those two far buildings." He handed me the glasses.

He was right. I'd seen it before. I studied it as best I could. It looked like a control tower you'd see at an international airport. "Fantasia, can you find this on the map?"

She drew out one of the maps from our pack and spread it open.

"What are you thinking?" asked R.J. "You're not thinking...."

"Yes, my love. It is right here. It is a large facility."

I kneeled beside her and studied the map. Two, long, X-shaped runways. Five miles or so beyond it was smaller municipal airport, one runway. I looked up at the others. "Guys, I suggest we go take a look at these airports."

R.J. asked in a drawn out comical tone, "Whhyy?"

"I measure six miles to the large airport and another five to the smaller one," said Fantasia.

"Again, why?" asked R.J.

"What are you thinking, Adrian?" asked Parth.

I stood. "Where do we go from here? Anyone have any ideas?"

There was a somewhat tense pause where the three of them were trying to come up with any answer at all.

"Did Diya and her companion leave this city? If so, what direction did they take? Should we try to walk the entire perimeter of this huge city in search of two sets of tracks leading away? Do we try to search the whole city on foot? Or, do we give up here and take the jeep back to cave and try to get home? You guys choose. I'll do whatever you decide."

Again there was the long pause.

R.J. begrudgingly asked, "You want to try to find a working plane and fly it?"

"Gee, what a great idea, R.J. Why didn't I think of that?"

"You want to use a jet if there are any, to search the outskirts of the city," said R.J.

"It wouldn't be a jet. We'd need a propeller job, something that could fly slow."

Parth asked, "Are you familiar with propeller aircraft, Adrian?"

R.J. answered, "He has done scary things in almost all types of aircraft, Parth. That won't get us out of this."

I added, "If there is anything airworthy I could go up alone."

"Not on your life," said Fantasia.

R.J. looked at me with a raised eyebrow. "She has really picked up on Earth idioms."

"So do we head back for the jeep or what?" I asked.

Two hours later we were back in the jeep on a narrow paved and dusted road lined with good tree cover headed south. Fantasia insisted on driving. Though again fearing for our lives none of us had the courage to object, so as inconspicuously as possible we held on tightly as she tested the jeep's limits at forty miles per hour on an unmarked dust covered narrow roadway.

R.J. called to me from the back seat. "Flying doesn't seem so bad
now."

Parth said, "We will be fortunate to not be seen."

I answered, "There have been no tracks in the ash. I don't think anyone's been out here."

R.J. added, "Besides, how could they ever catch us."

It was the perfect airport road circumventing the city. The control tower came into view above the trees in the distance. There began to be turn off roads that headed that way.

"This airport or the next?" yelled Fantasia.

"We'll have a better chance of finding smaller aircraft at the municipal so keep going."

Thirty minutes later we came to a long drainage ditch bordering the road. Brown ash floated on water, slowly moving along it.

"Wow! Open water," said R.J.

Parth said, "So water is not such a scarce resource."

A few miles more brought us alongside a good size brown ash lake. The bows of several boats poked through it in some places. We next came to a bent over metal sign that read; **Terbro Airstrip**. To R.J.'s relief, Fantasia slowed.

The second control tower came into view. Fantasia turned onto the next road to head in that direction.

Parth asked, "Fantasia, back there you said that our robber was suffering from radiation poisoning."

Fantasia looked partly back at Parth making R.J. nervous again. "He was. It was killing him."

"How long did he have?"

"I would guess less than a year."

"But this radiation, it is not affecting us?"

"I've been scanning everyone regularly. It has not affected us at all."

"How do you explain that?"

"I can't but it's a fact."

The airport fence came into view. It had been run down. The area beyond was wide open as all airports are. We found a place to pull off the road and hide the jeep. We took the duffel bags. Fantasia insisted on bringing her med kit claiming she knew us too well.

Inside the airport perimeter we kept low and to the wood line. It was a north-south runway probably five thousand feet. I was able to make out three flight service stations, one to the west, two others to the east. The control tower was located between the two east-side stations. There were quite a few planes parked askew around them. Some were upside down, others in pieces. But several looked intact. Most were propeller, a few looked like Lear Jet era private jets.

The perimeter was too far to follow. We took a chance and crouched across the runway and made it to the first flight service station. There still had been no sign of anyone.

"There's nobody here, Adrian," said R.J.

"Let's not bet our lives on that," I replied.

Fantasia pointed to a nearby blue and white high wing airplane. "That one has four seats."

I squeezed her hand affectionately. "Four is not enough, Fan. Many four-seaters won't get up with four full grown people in them, depending on density altitude and other stuff."

"Oh, I understand."

R.J. said, "We're going to have to cross over by the tower. I don't see anything else in this airplane graveyard that looks promising."

We stayed close to buildings, darted across to the base of the control tower, then on to the second flight service station where more airplanes in various states of disarray were spread out on the tarmac.

R.J. said, "I see two that would fit the bill except one has a crumpled wing and the other no prop. What do you want to do?"

"Past the tarmac, those are hangars. I'll bet we'll get lucky there."

We wove through airplanes and made it to a long row of hangars. There was roof damage to one corner of the place, a few bay doors were open, and several others still intact and locked up. The first hangar with an open door had no airplane but was loaded with tools. We grabbed a long arm crowbar.

The first three bays we broke into had either disassembled airplanes or the wrong kind of airplane but the fourth hangar had treasure. The marking on the nose of the high wing aircraft said 'Air 210.' All six seats were already installed.

"Okay, this thing looks good enough that I'm worried again," said R.J.

Fantasia came to me. "Are these the keys? They were hanging on that board over there."

"Good job, doll. We won't have to hot wire it."

R.J. opened a cowling door and looked at the engine. "Better shape than the jeep was," he said. "It does look like magnetos."

Fantasia asked, "How will you start it? Surely this battery is just as discharged as all the others."

"With magnetos I can spin the prop and start it, Fan. We just need to do a little preflight work first."

Parth appeared with a service ladder, climbed up and looked into both wing tanks. "About half full, Adrian."

R.J. closed up the cowling and came to us. "There was a fuel truck back by that building but you can bet that it's empty. I'll bet there's fuel in the underground tanks though."

I nodded. "They always keep a fuel hand pump around somewhere for emergencies. We just need to find it."

R.J. asked, "Think we should test start this thing before we bust our butts lugging fuel?"

"I don't think so, R.J. A start up might attract too much attention. Let's gamble on getting it all ready then open up and if she starts we'll roll right out and get the runway. Be gone before anyone can get here to disagree with us."

R.J. nodded. "I'll get Parth and we'll start pumping fuel into cans, I hope."

I climbed into the pilot's seat while Fantasia loaded our bags. The instrument panel was odd but readable. The airspeed indicator was labeled *airflow*. The gauges all had the standard speed and operational limits marked. The landing gear was retractable but I wasn't sure I'd have the nerve to trust putting it up. It was a dual controls cabin. I checked the rudder pedals. Toe brakes. The throttle was a shaft coming out of the instrument panel with a golf ball on the end of it.

It took almost two hours of sneaking around bringing fuel cans in and hoisting them up on the wings, along with spraying cleaner up into the carburetor, draining sumps, and checking cable linkages. The tires were flat. A long stint of hand pumping brought them back up though they looked questionable and had slight flat spots.

R.J. asked, "What do you think about those tires?"

"I'd say a very gentle landing will be called for."

He laughed but looked concerned.

We gathered around the prepped plane for a preflight meeting of the minds.

R.J. asked, "So exactly what is our flight plan should we actually get into the sky?"

I nodded. "We circle the outskirts of the city and look for a trail leading out left by two people or more. If others left here, Diya and her friend may have gone the way they went. We can also make some passes and get a better idea of what's going on in the city and where all the people have gone."

Parth said, "I fear that when the engine starts it could attract unwanted attention."

82

R.J. said, "He's right, Adrian. We've managed to avoid being discovered so far, but when that prop starts turning it can be heard over this entire airfield."

I nodded agreement. "You're right. The instant that prop starts we need to haul ass out to the runway. I'll do the run up on the way. We'll need all of the runway in case there's a problem so we'll have to taxi all the way to the end. The ignition looks like it's dual magneto and if we get a dead one we're going to have to go anyway on the one."

"Seating?" asked R.J.

"I'll set the hand brake but whoever is in the front passenger seat will need to be ready on those toe brakes just in case."

Fantasia interrupted, "Gentlemen, what is the term you all use? Is it dibbies, I think? I am formally calling dibbies on the front passenger seat."

There was a moment of silence but no one dared challenge.

"You may need to work the throttle fan if it runs too rough," I said.

"I'm certain I can manage that," she replied.

I said, "So I will spin that prop until it starts, then I'll make a beeline for the pilot's seat and we'll taxi out as fast as possible. Don't be alarmed if a wing dips down in a sharp turn. The idea will be to get to the end of that runway fast. The wind is from the north so we'll be on the three-six end. Does anybody have any questions or suggestions?"

R.J. said, "I think it's time to reopen the hangar door."

We all stood there as though none of us believed we were actually going to try this. Finally, R.J. went to the door and warily pushed it open. We did not see a soul anywhere.

I went to the pilot's door, leaned in and set the parking brake and the throttle, then switched the key to; BOTH. The others climbed in. Fantasia squeezed into the copilot seat. I gave her a quick rundown of the controls.

It was a three-blade prop. You reach as high as you can on the top blade, extend your left leg for added power and yank down and away as hard as you can, following up with steps back so you don't get sucked into the air stream if it starts.

The first crank did not even make a sputter but I felt a pang of joy at how well the engine had turned over.

Two more crank attempts and nothing but on the third, it coughed. I heard R.J. call out an apprehensive, "Oh, boy!"

The next one brought a loud bang and the prop sputtered a moment and whirred to life. Like an idiot I stood there waiting to see if it would quit. My brain kicked in and I practically vaulted around and into the pilot's seat. A test of the throttle gave us more, smooth power. We coasted out of the hangar. A quick kick to the right rudder pedal turned us toward the runway. A second push put us alongside it. Racing toward runway's end, I flipped the key and found we had two good magnetos. A quick flip of the master switch and power flowed into the instrument panel.

At the end of the runway we did a tailspin to face north and without waiting I shoved the throttle all the way in. Engine noise filled the cabin.

R.J. yelled, "Did you hear that?"

I had to concentrate on the airplane but I had heard a sound like a loud crack. As we picked up speed there were several more.

Parth yelled, "Right side of the runway, several men with rifles shooting. Three more are running toward the plane."

There was a smattering more of gunfire loud enough to be heard over the revving airplane engine. Suddenly there was a smacking sound on the side of the plane. Parth lurched forward in his seat.

"Parth's hit!" cried R.J.

We were now faced with the realization that if this airplane did not get up we would be in serious crap.

"Parth, how bad is it?" called out R.J.

The airspeed indicator crept up to what I thought felt right. I eased back on the control yoke and held my breath. The nose came up. Another hundred feet and I felt the rear wheels spin as they left the ground. Climb-out felt routine. Good air pressure over the wings, good airspeed indication.

We climbed away from the rifle fire.

## Chapter 8

As the altimeter turned upward I tried to steal a glance back at Parth.

Fantasia had unbuckled and was on her knees backward in her seat working on him. We had no headsets so yelling over the engine noise was required.

R.J. said, "That's quite a bit of blood."

Parth answered, "I don't think it's too bad."

Fantasia ordered, "R.J. get my med kit."

"Where is he hit?" I asked.

"Right upper leg," answered Fantasia.

"Those fucking assholes," yelled R.J.

Fantasia said, "Parth, I don't want to cut up your pants. You've got to pull them down."

At what I thought was two thousand feet I nosed the airplane over and backed out the throttle. A quick trim of the yoke gave me a stable level flight. I looked back at the chaos going on behind me.

Parth was up in his seat trying to pull down his bloody pants. R.J. was hunched over facing him trying to help. Fantasia was straddled over her seat back holding pressure against a bullet wound in Parth's bare thigh.

Somehow, they got Parth's shoes and pants off. The med kit was brought forward and set up in R.J.'s lap.

Fantasia said, "Parth, the bullet is not very deep. It needs to come out. You should be under anesthesia for this."

Parth yelled back, "Fantasia, I do not believe I want to miss a moment of any of this."

Fantasia persisted, "Parth, the bullet was very hot. It has bonded with your skin. The removal will be very painful."

"I will use the Vedic sciences to transcend the pain. You may proceed, Fantasia."

Fantasia looked at R.J. "Give me a syringe and open the medication flap. Use your meditation all you want, Parth. I'm at least using a anesthetic for this."

I could not see but I knew she was injecting something around Parth's injury.

"Can you keep it straight and level, Adrian?" asked Fantasia.

"No problem."

"That scalpel and the forceps, R.J. You keep dabbing with the cotton. No, the narrow scalpel. Thanks."

I did not hear a peep from Parth though she spent a good ten minutes on what I guessed was carving the bullet out of his leg.

"Okay, the sutures, R.J. You're doing good, Parth. More antiseptic."

Still not a sound from Parth.

I had to keep glancing at the directional indicator and holding the three hundred and sixty degree heading so we could retrace our path back. The sewing went on for about fifteen minutes.

"Okay, help me clean it up, R.J. Gauze and tape."

I finally felt a release of tension in the cabin. Fantasia kept bumping me as she tried to clean up.

"The alcohol, R.J. Would you try to clean up his pants while I do the rest? We need to put them back on him. It is too cold up here."

There was a bunch more bumping around with twisting and turning. Finally, Fantasia turned in her seat and sat back with a long exhale.

"So what's the verdict?" I asked.

"He will be fine. No major arteries."

Parth called out, "My most devoted thank you, Fantasia. You too, R.J."

I asked, "Permission to turn this plane around, dear?"

For the first time we all began to look out our windows at Doomsday World. I made a slow turn back in the direction from where we had come. The city was far in the distance. The blanket of brown ash was everywhere as far as the eye could see. Large patches of forest bore bare branches and fallen trunks. The roadways were clearly visible but undefined. There were clusters of residential homes which had not been maintained for years, ponds with swirl designs in brown ash and businesses with abandoned trucks at their loading docks.

As we neared the city, a root cause to all the destruction again became apparent. Ahead of us a major elevated highway ran the length of the city. On the near side we were approaching a great circle of molten earth. I guessed it to be fifty miles in diameter. It was not really a crater since it was not very deep, but it had liquefied everything within it. It had fractured the multilane thoroughfare, broken off a ten-mile section of it, and somehow pushed it away and to the north. There was a massive tangle of vehicles still on it and for the first time we began to see the shapes of bodies, lots of them. Beyond the cityscape was a collection of mono-colored high rises and business all supporting ash-covered roofs. There were brown-coated roads and parking lots strewn with debris. Far in the distance it looked like two broken towers had once supported power plants. I leaned the plane over to begin circling the city limits.

"How are you feeling, Parth?" I asked.

"Quite well. The injections have not worn off yet so there is no pain but I must say the scene outside is not uplifting."

R.J. asked, "How is she running, Adrian?"

"There's an ever so slight roughness but otherwise fine," I answered.

"Yeah, there had to be at least some water in the fuel. We couldn't drain all of it from the sumps."

"I believe you are correct, inspector."

"Wow, you're really bringing back old memories now."

"Who has the binoculars?"

"Parth, you want to start the ground spotting? Might take your mind off your leg."

"Thank you, R.J. I'll take them."

Our air-cooled engine kept a steady, reassuring drone. I backed off on the throttle and dropped down to one thousand feet and began our first loop around the outskirt of the city.

R.J. called out, "This may actually work. There's so few signs of movement down there."

As we came around the west end, Parth yelled, "There is a main highway down there that leads out of the city. There are many signs of foot traffic. There was an exodus to the west from here after the ash had fallen."

As we came around the south side, R.J. yelled, "Weapons flash down there. Someone is shooting at us."

I yelled back, "We're at a thousand feet at about ninety knots. It would take a heat-seeking missile to hit us."

R.J. answered, "Maybe we'd better not push our luck."

Fantasia added, "I do see a few people occasionally in various areas."

We came around for a second loop. I widened the circle. There were more call outs of weapons flash.

On the west side R.J. said, "I see what Parth means about the exodus to the west. It's a wide trail in the ash. We should follow that for a ways, Adrian."

So I dropped the right wing and turned to the west. Parth held the binoculars against the window to steady them. R.J. and Fantasia both stared intently down looking for signs of life in the tracks. I held to the right of the road and did my own share of scanning in between keeping an eye on altitude. I had secretly scared myself with the mention of heat-seeking missiles.

We followed the tracks for forty-five minutes. Somehow it reminded me of the Trail of Tears.

Suddenly Fantasia called out, "Oh, my! Look at that!"

We all stopped searching below and looked forward in the direction Fantasia was pointing.

Far ahead there was an enormous opaque bubble structure rising up from the land. It was dome-shaped and almost luminous. It was so large that estimating the size of it was difficult. We were at one thousand feet. This dome was at least as high as we were. The breadth and width of it had to be measured in miles. I adjusted our course to head for it.

"I have seen these before," said Fantasia. "On the planet Icronia the surface is uninhabitable. These are used to make the surface accessible for food production and scientific studies."

"What kind of structure is it?" asked R.J.

Fantasia replied, "On Icronia it is an electronic curtain radiated from shield generators placed at strategic points around the designated area. It is

90

very similar to the protective domes Earth uses against severe storms but it is more substantial than those. Solid matter cannot pass through it."

Parth said, "I believe we may be finding where all the people went."

Fantasia said, "I do not believe so, Parth. I would estimate that this structure is perhaps thirty miles in diameter. It would accommodate only a limited population and I do not see any additional domes anywhere."

Parth added, "I believe I see the remnants of another city just before the Dome, but the buildings seem to have been torn down or destroyed."

I added, "We'll be there in another ten minutes. I'll circle the thing for a look around it."

As we approached the next destroyed city, Parth still had the binoculars. He said, "Yes, most of the buildings have been torn down to nearly ground level. There are many footprints everywhere. There are heavily used trails that lead to underground transportation, subways perhaps. Many, many people have gone there."

When I was as close as I dared to the dome structure, I banked over and began a flight path around it. Nearby there were more sections which had once been housing developments but those were gone also. Single family homes were scattered far and near to the dome, most in complete disarray. Farther from the dome a few farmhouses had remained intact.

Parth said, "One very odd thing, I have not seen a single entrance to the dome anywhere."

We continued the rest of the way around.

R.J. said, "Parth is right. There is no way into that dome. It must be done from underground."

I banked away to put a little more distance between us and the structure.

"We need a plan," I said.

"We've got to go down," said R.J.

Parth added, "This aircraft is vital for a return trip to the cave."

I asked, "Do we really think Diya and her companion made it this far and are down there?"

Fantasia said, "We know they made it to the previous city. There were no signs of them returning to the cave. Therefore they are either still at the last city, or they are down there."

Parth added, "If they are still alive. We have been shot at numerous times."

R.J. asked, "Adrian, can we land and find somewhere to rest up and talk about this?"

"Any suggestions?"

Fantasia said, "I saw a farmhouse with a large barn on the north side."

I banked around and we searched the land of brown ash until Fantasia spotted the place again. A long straight road ran in front of it. It looked wide enough.

I said, "I can land on that road but we can't be sure there aren't potholes in the ash. We would be in a bad way if we hit one."

R.J. replied, "Do a really low pass, maybe you can blow the ash away enough."

So we did. We dropped down over the road below the tree line, applied full power, and dusted the dust. I pulled out into a crosswind leg and the road looked okay. We came around and there was enough road for me to carefully ease it onto the wheels, none of which blew.

"Nine-point-eight," said R.J.

Fantasia did not understand the scoring reference. Parth laughed then grimaced and held his leg.

We taxied into the driveway and up to the big barn doors where I shut it down. Weapons drawn, we spread out to clear the place.

No one was home. No footprints anywhere. We backed the aircraft into the barn and shut the doors. At the farmhouse back door a good bump with the hip popped it open. They had left split wood by the fireplace. We dropped our packs on the floor and settled in.

Fantasia said, "Parth, I need to unwrap the wound and take a look at it now that we're not being rocked around. I'll see if I can find you some other pants around here somewhere."

Parth answered, "Thank you but I think I would prefer my own trousers. There is a well out there. I'll wash these and stitch up the bullet hole."

Fantasia didn't argue. "Okay. I'll need to rewrap that if the stitching looks okay."

"I am in your debt, Fantasia."

We made as smokeless a fire as possible. Out came the cans of all-meat franks and beans. There was something that may have been actual coffee stored in the kitchen and a pot to make it in. Hot food and coffee were a dream come true. Once we were fed and relaxing, R.J. drew out the pipe stolen from our last home invasion and lit up.

R.J. asked, "So do we find one of those underground entrances and chance going in, or do we scout out the dome?"

Fantasia said, "I would like to scan the exterior of the dome to determine the nature of its construction. We should know how absolute the structure is and how difficult escape from it might be."

"Makes sense to me. How far will we have to hike?" I asked.

"I scanned the area between this farm and the nearest portion of dome. If we travel directly through the woodlands it will be a five-mile journey," replied Fantasia. "The nearest underground entrance is two miles beyond that."

Parth said, "Because we are in search of my consort, perhaps I should first venture into the underground alone to see if it is safe. There is nothing to be gained by all of us walking into danger."

R.J. said, "Parth, I don't think those toy walkie-talkies have much range."

Parth replied, "Nevertheless, my proposal is sound."

R.J. said, "At least if we find Diya we have a fast safe way to get back to the cave. Of course we have no way of knowing if that virmana is even still there."

Fantasia said, "I believe that craft will be there. It was active and waiting to go when we found it, but when we arrived here it shut down completely. That indicates to me that it was not set up to travel, as it was when we found it."

We slumped back and took naps in shifts though not quite as deeply as before. There had been too much shooting.

The Doomsday World morning arrived marked by the hazy brown sky. We added hot water to our MRE meals and had coffee. We suited up and let Fantasia lead us to the dome with her scanner.

It was an easy woods to walk. The trees and brush were dead. Except for a slight limp, Parth's leg did not seem to bother him too much. We made good time.

We came to a short clearing just before the massive dome wall. We watched and waited for any patrols which might be acting as security. There were none. We approached cautiously for a close look. The dome surface looked like silver glitter. It was almost transparent. We could make out fixed rectangular shapes within but no fine detail.

Fantasia scanned. "This is definitely an electronically generated wall, but my scanner is unable to identify the frequencies or subatomic structure. It is puzzling."

I cautiously tapped lightly at the surface with the fingers of one hand. It felt like it was vibrating, almost like an ultrasonic cleaner.

I stepped back. "So do we go around a ways and see if there are any changes to it?"

R.J. said, "Wait a minute." He stood sideways to the wall and lightly tapped at it as I had.

He began to worry me. "R.J. don't...."

He pushed his hand into the barrier up to the palm and pulled it back out. He wiggled his fingers to test them. "It's all right. It's not harmful."

"R.J., just wait a minute, will you?"

R.J. ignored me and leaned his upper body through the barrier. I started to step over to pull him out but he passed completely through to the other side. He was so intent on doing so his weapon slipped off his shoulder and fell to the ground on our side.

I turned to Fantasia and rolled my eyes. "I hate it when he does this. He's done it before, you know."

Before Fantasia could respond, R.J. stepped back through.

"Wow! I dropped my gun. Luckily there was nobody on the other side shooting at us."

Fantasia asked, "What did you see?"

"It's a controlled atmosphere. Warmer, cleaner air. There are two buildings near here. One looks like a big laboratory of some kind, the other looks like a small manufacturing plant. I did not see people anywhere, but I'd bet there are some in those buildings."

Path said, "Once again this sounds like a situation I should investigate alone. I am responsible for all of you being here. I will go through to see if it is safe."

I interrupted, "Parth, that's not a good plan. We have been shot at everywhere we've gone. You need R.J. and I to back you up in case a rapid retreat becomes necessary and we can't leave Fantasia here alone. So the most logical thing to do is we all go though and check the place out as carefully as we can. I'll go through and set up cover. You guys give me two minutes, then join me. Is everyone okay with that?"

No one objected.

"Okay, stay ready." I stepped through the curtain of glitter. Something momentarily held me back but an extra lean got me through. There were green trees and manicured bushes at various points around the buildings. I kept low, reached for my automatic and found it was not there. I searched the ground and could not find it. I stepped back through the curtain. The others were staring. My automatic was on the ground near where I'd stepped through.

"How the hell did I drop that?" I picked it up and tucked it back in.

R.J. said, "It looked like the curtain knocked it off your belt."

I redrew the gun and tried to push it through the curtain. It would not go. Try as I may the gun could not be made to pass through the dome wall. As far as the gun was concerned, the wall was as solid as concrete. There was even a clacking sound against the curtain.

Fantasia stooped down and picked up one of our satchels. She tried to push it through the wall. The satchel simply flattened out and would not go. She looked at us as though enlightened.

She unclipped her scanner and passed it through the wall and back out with no resistance.

"Okay, doll; you know something. What is it?"

She held up one finger for pause, grabbed the other satchel, and found the results were the same.

We stood waiting for an explanation.

Fantasia smiled. "Nothing from this world can pass through this dome wall. Anything from our world can."

"Wow!" said R.J.

I said, "Well, that bullet was from this world and it sure didn't pass through Parth too easily."

Fantasia replied, "Lower grade of matter. This dome is made from this world's high frequency subatomic particles. They don't have any effect on us, just like the radiation here isn't making us sick. But you are correct. The denser lower forms of matter affect us just fine. We eat it and we feel it."

R.J. asked, "So you're saying if they shot a particle beam weapon at us it wouldn't affect us?"

Fantasia nodded, "Probably not, but don't bet on that. Heat is a transient component."

Parth said, "Perhaps your safety hypothesis is not so relevant now, Adrian."

"No, it is Parth. We can still cover your back in there. Splitting up would just leave some of us in the dark."

Parth replied, "As Fantasia has suggested, if Diya is alive I believe she is here somewhere. I must continue on."

Fantasia said, "We must all go. We can't lose track of each other. And, Parth, those stitches are from this world. They are going to try to pull out as you pass through. I should remove them and replace them with pressure bandages made from whatever Earth materials we have on hand."

So we hid our weapons and packs within the brush, waited for Fantasia to redo Parth's leg, then took a position just outside the dome. I went first followed by Fantasia, Parth, and R.J. We grouped together on the inside and found ourselves in yet another different world.

## Chapter 9

We could see the twin suns and we could stare at them with the naked eye. There was no glare or burn. Fantasia immediately began scanning.

"Most of these green trees and other landscaping objects are imitations. They are not alive. There are life signs in the buildings, many of them."

We began a cautious walk behind the two buildings nearest us. A fake green forest blocked our view to the right. The buildings were metal and oddly constructed. The walls and windows seemed to be piecemealed together. There were just the two buildings R.J had described. Ahead of the larger, second building we could see what looked like a transportation depot with a long, large open awning which covered the rails and narrow roadways leading into the fake forest.

A voice behind us took us by surprise. "Yes. It is a wonder, isn't it? But really, you must come back inside. You won't want to delay the others."

The gentleman who had spoken so kindly was a slender, mature man with thinning gray-brown hair. He wore a red drake vest and a white long sleeved collared shirt underneath it, dark slacks, and black leather boots beneath the pants legs. He had age lines. His face was pale from indoor lighting. Brown eyes that had a hidden sadness to them. He projected himself as caring.

He smiled and continued, "I certainly understand your desire to explore. None of you have probably ever seen green trees and forest except in photos, I'm sure. But if you'll bear with us. We apologize for the delays. The effects of that baffling transient pulse has really set us back. We had so hoped the first one was just a one-time phenomenon, but this second event was even more insidious than the first. Even the core memory was affected in some areas. I see the four of you have already dressed for the part. That is a very smart way to prepare."

He held one hand out for us to follow. We communicated with eye contact and followed along silently.

He continued, "Paper is too much of a precious commodity of course to be used for backing up memory. So we are having to reconstitute our visitor information since much of it was lost in the pulse."

He led us around to a side door to the office building. We climbed iron steps as he held the door. We entered an auditorium. Big, slightly elevated stage; many rows of red seats. Projection windows high against the back wall. Tall red curtains bordering the front. Our guide motioned us to take seats. The front row was dramatically curved, allowing all of us to see each other. Several other people were already seated.

As we scanned around, a man in coveralls appeared in the back pushing a cart with a computer terminal on it. Unlike those in the outer world, this one had a large flat screen monitor.

R.J. leaned in front of Fantasia and spoke in a half whisper. "Adrian, what are we doing?"

I leaned in. "We need to know about them. We don't want them to know about us."

R.J. straightened up with a perplexed look.

Our guide looked up at the stage. "Oh, they've neglected to put up the images. Please excuse me for just a moment." He raced off toward the back.

Fantasia said, "Adrian, look over there by the stage steps. That's a large globe of this planet. I'll be right back."

"Fan...."

She went to the stand-mounted globe and with one had adjusted it slightly. She looked around and as inconspicuously as possible scanned the thing. A few more moments of studying it and she scooted back and sat.

She looked at me, "As you Earthers like to say, wow!"

"Wow what?" I asked.

"This place is marked on that globe. It shows the latitude and longitude. We are at the same exact latitude and longitude here as we were on Earth."

"Okay wow, but what does that mean?"

"I don't think that ship ever moved at all. I believe it shifted dimensions. Or, it exists in two dimensions at once."

"You're saying we are in a different dimension? A different universe entirely?"

"Yes, that's what I'm saying," replied Fantasia.

R.J. said, "Wow!"

An image appeared on the center stage screen. It could have been the main street of Dodge City on Earth. Horses were tied to hitching posts. A stage was stopped at a hotel.

R.J. leaned over again, "Adrian, at what point to we take our leave of this place?"

"And go where?" I asked.

Parth leaned in also. "We must stay long enough to talk to these people. Someone may have seen Diya."

Our commentator returned and took a position front and center. He leaned back against the stage. "To refresh your memory, I am Chancellor Doun, your guide through the insertion process. It is always such a pleasure to meet and introduce the next visitors to Oldtown. Of course this time is a bit different because of the computer memory corruption we experienced. So after I quickly recap your coming visit, Mr. Jenkins there with the computer will attempt to recreate each of your files. Behind me on the screen, you see Main Street, Oldtown. How many generations has it been since we have been able to live on the surface? I've lost count again. Life in Underworld has become reasonably comfortable but don't we all wonder what it was like once on the surface? We've all seen the photos and movie files. But what did it feel like to live like that? Well, now the science of dome shielding has been perfected enough to allow us to experience life as it was on the surface. We could have chosen any period, modern or ancient, but we would all like to forget about the war so going back to a time before it seemed logical. At the same time we have all grown accustomed to modern conveniences, so a time period was chosen where we could incorporate the more basic luxuries into our surface life setting. That time period was the age when new territory was being settled. Mining and agriculture were the mainstays of society. The dome now allows us to recreate that period. Some aspects are artificial, others are real, but the effect is quite believable. The dome gives us three months on the surface without harm from the residual war radiation. Three months to live in Oldtown as it was so long ago. Of course you are all already very familiar with the Oldtown vacation. It's why you're here so I won't ramble on. Mr. Jenkins will now visit with each of you to reconstitute our participant records."

There were eight other individuals seated with us. The others were a mixed bunch. Mr. Jenkins wearing a white lab coat pushed his cart over to the first two people on the opposite side as us.

"Names please?"

The gentleman had a small crop of black hair sticking up about two inches. He had a drinker's red button nose and beady black eyes. He reminded me so much of Bert from Bert and Ernie that I had to resist smiling about it and when he answered Jenkins' question by saying, "Bert Shrack," I nearly lost it.

"And this is your wife, Mr Shrack?"

The lady next to Bert could have been Marilyn Monroe in white shorts and an overflowing white blouse. Her shapely legs were crossed and she kept kicking one out in time to music that wasn't there. She kept curling one of her long blond locks with one finger.

"Candy Shrack," replied Bert. Candy popped bubble gum as he said it.

R.J. leaned over. "People are the same everywhere."

I nodded.

R.J. continued, "I fear we are going down the rabbit hole, Adrian."

"R.J. we're *in* the rabbit hole."

Jenkins asked, "And what is your occupation in Underworld, Mr. Shrack?"

"Resource manager," replied Bert.

"And you, Mrs Shrack?"

"Home Engineer."

"And what positions in Oldworld did you originally request?"

"I would like to be a successful gambler," answered Bert.

"And you Mrs. Shrack?"

"Saloon owner," replied Candy.

"And you both understand you will still be a married couple in Oldworld. We find it very necessary to preserve relationships in there to prevent harming them."

They both nodded. Neither looked concerned in the least.

Jenkins pushed on to the next three grouped together. "Names please?"

"Jack James, this is my brother Luke and my wife Mae."

With a giant picture of Oldtown projected in the background, the name James immediately brought to mind the James brothers of the old west. The two brothers fit the bill perfectly. Both had dark hair slightly long. Deep set dark eyes, too many lines in the face from too many celebrations. The brother Luke looked like he was still getting over one from the night before. Mae James seemed too delicate for the James family. She had innocent blue eyes, ivory soft skin, tiny nose, thin lips, and sandy-colored hair wrapped behind her head. It made me wonder what Jack had used to win her over. In Earth world, Jack and Luke were the kind of people I might have had trouble with. Of course I'd always been famous for wrong first impressions.

"And what occupations did the three of you select for Oldtown?" asked Jenkins.

Jack answered, "Me and Luke want a horse ranch. Mae wants to be the town schoolteacher."

Mae did not look like she agreed.

Jenkins typed in his data. "That will all be just fine, sir."

Jenkins moved on. The next client was a surprisingly young man dressed in jeans and a western styled shirt. He also had on stovepipe boots. Short sandy hair and too serious an expression for a kid his age. I put him at about fifteen Earth years old.

Jenkins smiled. "Riley, it is nice to see you again. The winner of the Radio Six Oldworld contest. You must be excited."

"Yes sir, I am."

"You're kind of famous now. You'll be a sort of celebrity when you come out of Oldworld."

"Yes sir."

"Okay, Riley Kit. And if I recall you said you wanted to be a drover, is that still correct?"

"Yes."

Jenkins pushed on to the last two people before us. They seemed like a subdued couple not sure of what they were getting into. The man was overweight in a way that his button-down shirt was spreading near the naval. He had brown hair receding evenly on both sides. Big dark eyebrows, slightly sunken dark eyes, and an almost bulldog expression. His wife was competing with him for girth. She had brown hair, razor cut to suit the egg-shaped head. Her expression was pudgy. She wore an off-white flowered long dress.

Jenkins pushed up to them, typed something and asked, "May I have your names?"

"I am Roy Nick, this is my wife Melda."

"Thank you, sir. Occupations?"

"I am a manager in population control. Melda was an accountant."

"And what positions have you requested?"

"I would like to be a Judge," said Roy

"I would like to own the bank," added Melda.

"Positions very well suited I would say," replied Jenkins. "I do not see a problem at all. Thank you."

Jenkins pushed his cart toward us. "Names please."

I jumped in to take the lead. "I'm Adrian Tarn. This is my wife Fantasia. My friends here are R.J. Smith and Parth Sharma."

"Thank you, Mr. Tarn. Occupation?"

"I'm a pilot."

"A pilot? Oh, you mean an engineer on the underground railroad. Wonderful. And you Mrs. Tarn?"

"I'm a doctor," answered Fantasia.

"Oh, how wonderful. Oldtown will have a physician who is actually a real doctor. And you, Mr. Smith?"

"Inspector."

"Oh, for the underground railroad also?"

"Yes."

"And you, Mr. Sharma?"

"I am a science officer."

"Oh, you mean at the university. Wonderful. You will make a strong support group in Oldtown."

"Mr. Smith and Mr. Sharma are either of you married?"

Parth answered, "We both are. My wife had too many obligations to join us. Perhaps you've met my wife. This is her." Parth drew out the photo of Diya.

"No, I'm sorry to say I have not had the pleasure, Mr. Sharma. In any case you both will be registered as married individuals in Oldtown to help prevent any indiscretions you did not intend. And tell me, have you all decided on chosen positions?"

I jumped in again. "We have been finding it difficult to decide. We thought you might make some recommendations."

"Indeed I can, Mr. Tarn. Since you command on the underground railroad you would make an excellent town sheriff. And Mr. Smith since you both work together already I would see you as a deputy. Obviously, Mrs. Tarn would remain a doctor, and Mr. Sharma we could place you in the assayer's office. Do those posts sound acceptable to you all?"

We nodded reluctantly.

Jenkins waved to his boss and pushed his computer cart off to the side.

I sat back in my seat and for the first time since we had come to Doomsday World I felt we had a handle on things. We could infiltrate this society without being discovered, show Diya's photo around and eventually pick up a lead. We had gained control of a wild situation and I was certain we would track down Diya and make our way back.

Speaker Doun checked some notes on a paper and took the floor again. "My friends I believe we are in a position to proceed. There are one or two items I need to review with you since they tend to raise the most questions. First, weapons in Oldtown. They cannot kill or even harm you. The bullets used in Oldtown are smart bullets. When fired toward a warm object they turn red and liquefy just before impact, leaving the appearance of a serious wound but causing no injury. When fired at a cold object they remain solid. Because of the implants you will believe all bullets are real and you may think someone has been serious hurt or even killed though they have not been. Oldtown is a busy place. Most of the criminals are animatrons as are the horses and animals. I know you are familiar with these facts from your earlier interviews but it is necessary to touch upon them due to the frequency of violence which was a way of life back in the days of Oldtown. There are frequent bank robberies, saloon fights, and shootouts in the street. Whether you choose to involve yourselves in them is of course completely up to you. Either way no real harm can come to you."

Doun's use of the word, *implant*, began to bother me.

He continued. "The other item we need to reassure you about is the implant procedure. We have promised you that you will not be frightened by the procedure at all and you will not feel any pain whatsoever. You may have noticed a feeling of well-being coming over you in the past few minutes. That is the gas sedative that has been released into the air here to prepare you for the implantation. You may also notice you are unable to move in those very comfortable seats we have provided. That too is to aid in an exact implantation process. The injector is inserted into the left nostril and the implant is injected into a shallow part of the brain from that point. The implant allows us to block your long-term memory and replace it with a new Oldtown computer memory chronology. The implant will also inhibit you from wanting to go beyond the Oldtown outer borders. This process is entirely safe. The implants are powered by radiated energy in the air. The moment you leave the Oldtown limits the implant loses power and dissolves completely in a matter of minutes. You should be feeling tranquil enough now that our medical staff will bring in the service cart."

I sat in my chair like a zombie. The world looked pretty damned good from where I was sitting. People were so damned nice. Nothing was better than friendship. Every breath I took was a miracle. If I could have moved my hand and arm I could have made swirls in the room light. I could only look straight ahead but what could be better than straight ahead? There so much to see.

The only strange thing at all was the screaming voice way, way in the back of my mind. What the hell was that about?

Two immaculately clean men in white coats pushed their silver cart up in front of me. They were both smiling so I was sure they liked me. One of them put a silver gun in my nose to help me. There was a pop. They smiled some more and went on their way.

## Chapter 10

It had been a long train ride. All four of us had fallen asleep in the compartment. Fantasia had her head on my shoulder, still faintly snoring. R.J. had fit himself into a corner and Sharma had his sample case in his lap. For R.J. and me it was supposed to have been a simple prisoner extradition. We were supposed to have had rooms reserved at the Pamona City hotel. Instead they put us upstairs in the busiest saloon where the bed in the next room kept banging against the wall. Fantasia managed to sleep though it all. Just wait until the next time, they ask.

The conductor walked by calling out, "Oldtown." It woke everyone up. R.J. opened his eyes but his body remained in the shape of the corner. The train began to slow. I looked down and found my badge was clipped to my belt but I wasn't wearing my gun. It's hard to sleep with a holster on your hip.

Fantasia moaned and opened her eyes. She blinked and smiled at me. Sharma lurched up and grabbed his bag.

R.J. asked with a hoarse voice, "Are we there yet?"

Fantasia laughed but none of us seemed to understand why.

R.J. said, "I've got to get out of these clothes. I feel like I've been wearing them for a week. Just as soon as I can move...."

Fantasia straightened up and adjusted herself. Sharma stretched. The train jerked to a

110

stop. There was a rush of riders passing by our compartment.

The conductor passed by again calling out, "Five minutes, five minutes."

We stood and pulled down our luggage. I grabbed mine and Fantasia's.

R.J. stopped and pointed at my waist. "You're not going out there naked are you?"

We both put our luggage down, unsnapped them, and drew out gun belts. We strapped them on, repacked the suitcases, and slid open the compartment door. At the end of the narrow corridor, we stepped down and onto the depot platform. A sign on the nearest post said "Welcome to Oldtown, population 1158." The shortest route was past the telegraph office and through the depot so there we went, nodding to the man behind the window at the ticket booth, then out onto dusty Oldtown Main Street.

Main street looked busy but reasonably peaceful, but it was early yet. We passed by the livestock pens on the right and the tax register's office on the left. It was a good thing Main Street was wide because there was enough wagon and carriage traffic on it to cause accidents. The growing boardwalk and awning business had kept Motly and Sons Lumber in good shape this year. I dared a glance down the length of Main Street at the colorful businesses packed in tight along it. As I looked, there was the faint sound of arguing voices about halfway down. A moment later a man came flying out of a saloon's swinging door, backpedaling, and falling to the street. He got up, brushed himself off, and walked away.

"Welcome back, Sheriff," said R.J.

"I believe that was Obi."

"Yeah, trying to get his complimentary morning drink."

Fantasia moved in and held onto my arm. "Adrian, we need to go look at the Bennet place before the real estate people get it."

"Yes, Fan."

"We can't go on staying in the back room of my upstairs office. It's crazy having to get patients up those side stairs. If we had the Bennet's place I could set up an office in the drover's barracks. It would be a real medical clinic."

"Your office served Dr. Harding pretty well right up until he got too old."

"Oh don't get me started on that."

"You know I love you, Fan?"

"Well that's a nice thing to say."

"Can we afford the Bennet place?"

"Easy. The ranch would be collateral, and we both have monthly income from our inheritances."

"I'll leave the finances up to you."

"It's the only ranch right on the outskirts of town. It's perfect. I could finally have horses again."

R.J. said, "Adrian, I'll go see if anybody got thrown in jail."

"Okay, I'll meet you there."

Fantasia and I climbed the stairs to her office. Inside we found an IOU from a farmer for stomach pills. In our back-room apartment we tossed the suitcases on the bed and flopped down alongside them.

Fantasia gathered up a pillow and looked at me with her special cute face. "So let's go out there as soon as you're ready."

"I'll check in with R.J. at the jail then we'll walk out to her place."

A quick change into jeans and my long-sleeved sheriff's shirt and I headed for my office. R.J. was seated behind my desk with his feet up.

"Anybody?"

"Cells are empty. All we got is these new wanted posters. There's also a telegram from the district marshal's office saying these three are headed our way." R.J. tossed a wanted posted over to me.

"You'd better round up a couple more deputies."

"I already checked the bank book. We can afford it."

"Post one at each end of the town."

"Yeah."

"I'm going out to the Bennet's place with Fan. I'll be back shortly."

"Going to buy it then?"

"Yeah. You want to move out there when we do?"

"Nah. The back room of the hotel has the best hearth in town. I got a great view of the plain out my east window and I hear every damn thing going on in Oldtown. I'd better stay where I'm at."

"I salute you, sir."

"Don't salute me. I'm trying to forget the cavalry."

We both laughed. I reached for the door, gave him a last nod and headed back to Fantasia's office.

Fantasia was ready to go when I arrived. She was seated at her desk playing with something.

She waved me over to look. "What is this, do you think?"

I tried to make heads or tails of the thing. It was a colorful, strange looking little box with buttons and dials. "It looks kind of like those oriental puzzle boxes. Where'd you get it?"

"It was in my pants leg pockets. I don't know how it got there."

"Does it do anything?"

"Not yet that I can see. But it's strange, very strange."

"You could have Parth Sharma look at it."

"Not yet. I want to fiddle with it myself for a while."

"You ready to go?"

"I've been ready."

Mrs. Bennet wanted to sell really bad but not to the real estate people. There were too many buildings and corrals on her ranch for her to maintain, especially at her age. She wanted to move back to Pamona to live with her sister.

"The railroaders want it," she said despairingly. "They want to put in a spur and unload freight here. This place would disappear."

I pulled out my wallet, took out a silver dollar and handed it to her. "That will be our down payment to make it official, Bet. If the bank approves your asking price, it's a done deal."

"Praise the Lord. Here I come, Pamona! Let me get some paper and the pen and we'll put this in writing. I can come and visit the old place whenever I want. Deal?"

Fantasia smiled. "Anytime you want, Bet. No reservations necessary."

Fantasia kept studying the one sentence receipt as we walked back. Every now and then she let out a small laugh.

"I'm guessing you're heading straight to the bank?"

"You should come along."

We stepped up onto the boardwalk, passed by my office, the town hall, the North Hotel, trading post, leather shop and Sharma's assayer office.

In the bank, Vice President Peal came out to greet us. I never warmed up to the slicked back hair parted down the middle. The chain for his pocket watch was hanging out of his vest too far to give a sophisticated look, but his broad smile was genuine. "We're going through some big changes, Sheriff. You know there's a new judge in town and his wife has bought the bank. So until Mrs. Nick formally comes in and sets up her office, I guess I'm in charge of contracts."

"Ours should be easy, Mr. Peal," said Fantasia.

Peal nodded, "Yes, yes, the town's Sheriff and Doctor wishing to purchase a property which will be more convenient for everyone. I should say so."

"You already know why we're here?" I asked.

Peal smiled, "Gossip in Oldtown is faster than any telegraph, Sheriff."

"We just came from the Bennet place!"

"If you two will follow me into my office."

He led us past the teller's area to his office. He took a seat behind his desk and pulled out paperwork. "Do you have a written agreement with Mrs. Bennet?"

Fantasia placed it on the desk.

"Okay, just a couple signatures from each of you and this can be hand carried to the committee members today and I expect you can pick up the mortgage paperwork tomorrow and the place will be officially yours."

"Thank you, Mr. Peal," said Fantasia.

We exited the bank and stood outside looking at the foggy Oldtown sky.

"I could move the horses out of livery to the Bennet's today," said Fantasia.

"You sure?"

"I could turn them out into the pasture. They'd be jubilant."

"I've got to get to work."

"I'll see you later upstairs." She blew me a kiss and hurried off. I headed for the jail.

R.J. was seated in front of my desk with his feet up. I sat down and skimmed through the paperwork on it.

R.J. said, "I know I'm the suspicious type and all, but I don't get something."

"What is it this time?"

"I just took a shower in the jail wash down. When did Oldtown get hot and cold water in pretty much all the buildings in town?"

"When they put in the water tower and central boiler outside of town. Somebody invented that new copper pipe stuff. The National Trust people came out and put it in the same time the electricity cables were put in. They also put in the central generator up at the Tawnee river damn."

"Yeah, but do you remember that being done? People digging ditches to all the building and running pipes and cable?"

"We may not have been here. We may have been doing another extradition or supporting an operation out of town."

"So you're saying we went out of town for a week and when we got back all that stuff was just here?"

"I can prove that, R.J."

"How?"

"Because it's here!"

"You want to go make the rounds?"

"We better before you think of something else you don't believe in."

"You want the west side or the east?"

"Don't matter to me."

"I'll cross over, then."

We followed the boardwalks on opposite sides of the street, passing folks on horseback and in carriages. Business owners were sweeping dust off the boardwalk. Feed was being loaded onto a wagon in front of the feed store. We reached the general store on my side. R.J. crossed over and joined me.

"I need to stop in here a minute," he said.

Inside the store, two kids were eyeing the candy jars. I checked my pocket and found a quarter silver. I flipped it to the store owner. He opened his jars so the kids could grab a hand full. They charged out yelling, "Thanks, Sheriff!"

R.J. asked, "How much for this one, San?"

"That's our best hand carved pipe. Two coin for you, R.J."

"I will take that and I need good pipe tobacco and matches."

"Comes to three coin even, Deputy."

R.J. paid and gathered up his stuff.

Outside he asked, "How come I don't own a pipe? How is that possible?"

"Here we go again."

"So are we stopping in gossip central?"

"Of course."

We pushed our way through the swinging doors of the Main Street Saloon, wove through the mostly empty tables and leaned on the bar. The never-ending poker game was going on in a far corner. Two cattlemen were eating steaks on the opposite side of the room. The stage was closed off for repairs.

Bartender Hugh wiped his way over to us. "Bout time you two were back."

"We think so too," said R.J.

"Coffee, Sheriff?"

"Yes, sir."

"R.J.?"

"Beer. What did we miss, Hugh?"

"Well, for one thing believe it or not, they sold this place to a gambler's wife name of Candy Shrack. They'll be changing the front sign tomorrow."

"You met the new boss?" I asked.

"Not yet. There's also a new judge in town name of Nick. I hear his wife took over the bank. Lot of things changing in Oldtown."

"Any trouble while we were away, Hugh?" I asked.

"Couple things might be comin' up. Rumor is there's three no-goods headed for Oldtown. Don't know when, though."

"Yeah, we know about them," replied R.J. "Anything else?"

"Just one thing brewing. I hear the James brothers are bringing in a new drover but it's just a kid. Only thing is he ain't really just a kid. Old Mabel down at the diner got a letter from her sister saying this kid was in a shootout with somebody and got the better of them. He was asked to leave town so I guess he's coming here for the job."

"Got a name?" I asked.

"Riley Kit. Supposed to be all of fifteen. They say he wears a six-shooter custom made to fit his hand. One of the men out at the James' place has been talking bad about this kid comin' in, like he won't pull his weight or somethin'. You may have a problem coming there, Sheriff."

I sipped my coffee and looked out over the barroom. It had been cleaned and polished, ready for the evening's chaos. As I looked, a girl came in from the kitchen with pan full of clean glasses.

"I need those over here, Diya. Just put them down right there. Thanks."

Diya did what she was told and hurried out.

A gray-haired old man pushed his way through the swinging doors and approached the bar.

Hugh leaned in and said, "Oh brother, here comes Alien Andy. Keeps insisting he's seen people from outer space out in the desert."

Hugh left us to serve Andy.

R.J. took note. I shook my head as he slid over to Alien Andy.

"How you doing, Andy?"

Andy looked up and wiped his gray beard with one hand. "Fine, Deputy. You wanting something?"

"Yeah, I want to hear your story about out in the desert."

"Cost you a drink, deputy. If you're gonna laugh at me you're gonna have to make it worth my while."

R.J. motioned for a drink.

Andy waited for it to arrive, then tested it for quality. He leaned sideways against the bar, took a few more samples for courage and eyed R.J. suspiciously. "I'm way out on the flats. Thinking about doin' some prospecting in the hills. I ride around to the far side of the first hill looking for the right signs. I dismount, climb halfway up the hill and suddenly there's this sound like mill grinding. I scramble up the hill to the top to see what's goin' on. I get there just in time to see this machine set down hard on the desert. I could not tell what it was. Then a door opens in the thing and two creatures get out. They're all back with shiny black heads and sunk in faces. They open some other doors on the machine and are fiddling with it. They work on it for a while, close the thing up and get back in. The machine floats up off the ground, turns and flies off out of sight. People say I'm crazy, but I saw it."

"I don't think you're crazy, Andy," said R.J.

"Well, you'll be one then."

R.J. motioned for Hugh to give him another drink and came back. "See? I'm not the only one who thinks there's something strange about Oldtown."

"You done with that beer?"

"Yeah."

"Let's go finish rounds."

We walked the rest of Main Street and watched the Waylay brothers moving their stage to the blacksmith shop to repair a spring arm. They kept that cherry wood stage in pristine condition complete with gold lettering and trim, even though the railroad was putting them out of business. At the far end of Main Street, Sally Risen came out of her dress shop with a plate of fritters and made us each take one.

"You want to do Second Street?" asked R.J.

"Let's skip it. The train ride kind of wore me out."

Back in the office we sat around the desk and drank coffee.

"So what's the plan for the three coming our way? You know they're coming here to hit the bank, right?"

"We're going set up four temporary deputies in separate rooms upstairs across the street from the bank. We'll put them on two shifts to watch over the bank with rifles day and night. We'll pay all the kids to watch for those guys. As soon as they're spotted, you'll set up inside the bank where you can't be seen but where you have a clear shot. We have to let them rob the place or there's nothing to arrest them for. When they enter the bank I'll be waiting out in the street. If any of them raises a weapon to shoot a teller or the manager, you open fire, but I don't think they'll kill anybody. Bank robbery is a lot of time in jail. Murder is the hangman's noose. They'll rob the place and as soon as they step outside I'll be there and tell them to drop their guns. They won't. The first one raise a gun will be the signal for the deputies to open fire. It will be three against three and when you move forward into position behind them it will be four to three. We will be shooting to kill. You don't give someone pointing a gun at you a chance to use it. How does that sound?"

R.J. fidgeted with his new pipe. "It sounds like a Sheriff Tarn plan to me. The undertaker would approve. What if one of them waits outside with the horses?"

"Then I'll take care of him quietly if I can. If not the sound of shots fired will be your cue to open up on the two inside. I'll be inside with you a second later or I'll meet anybody trying to come out."

"We'd better put in some range time out back, don't you think?" said R.J.

"Wouldn't hurt."

We collected up ammunition and went out back to the area where grain sacks were set up as targets. We dampened paper with water and plugged our ears. We took turns drawing and firing at the grain bag outlaws. As usual I was okay with my speed but not happy with my spread.

"Damn it," I said as I picked up my spent shells and reloaded.

"Don't worry," replied R.J. "That's the way you always are. You're a little scattered on the range but every time you're facing down a real gunman you are fast as lightning and you never miss. It's part of the Tarn legacy. Your mother was the same way. She couldn't hit the broadside of a barn with that old peep-sight hex barrel twenty-two she had, but any woodchuck tearing up her garden a hundred yards off didn't stand a chance."

"You're looking pretty tight today. That's nice grouping."

"It was the beer. It relaxes me."

When we were finally shot-out I asked, "You want to take the office the rest of the day? I need to pay off some kids and I'll drop off our shells at the gunsmith for reloads. I'll see who he's got for temporary deputies. Then I need to check on Fantasia. I think she already moved our horses out to the Bennet place."

"No problem. I'll be here testing out that new pipe. Looking forward to sitting around your new fireplace someday soon, by the way."

"Yeah, that oil heater in Fantasia's is getting really old."

I made the rounds, paid off the town's kids and set up a deputy rotation using one room above the jewelers and a second in Mrs. Maglies apartment. The old woman loved company and having a deputy at her disposal around the clock was a dream come true.

Fantasia was fussing with her new toy in her office.

"Figure that thing out yet?"

She looked at me with raised eyebrows. "Look at this. If I press my finger against this little slot, it lights up! It must have a battery of some sort."

"I think I get it. It's one of those kid's music boxes where they push a button and there's gears and a tracker bar inside that plays a different tune."

"No, no. Look, if I point this at you and push this first button, numbers appear at the top. These last letters look like blood type, and next to them looks like blood pressure, and next to that might be temperature. This thing is amazing. I've never seen anything like it."

"Maybe you should show it to Parth Sharma."

"No, no. We've got to keep this secret until I figure it all out. Someone might try to take this away from us."

"Okay, doll. It's your toy."

"I don't think it's a toy at all."

"Did you move the horses?"

"Yes. You never saw two happier horses in your life. They are grazing as we speak. The only one happier is Mrs. Bennet. She's packing."

We retired to the back bedroom, cooked fresh fish on the oil burner, then sat around while I read and she played with her toy.

"Look at this," she held up the device. "It's a map of something I don't know what."

"Interesting."

"So when were you going to tell me about the outlaws heading for town?"

"You heard about that?"

"The whole town knows, silly."

"We're ready for them."

"What are they going to do?"

"They'll try to rob the bank."

"How do you know?"

"Telegram from the district marshal's office."

"What are you going to do about it?"

"Deputies upstairs across the street. R.J. inside."

"There's going to be shooting then, isn't there?"

"It's possible."

"You want me to...."

"No!"

"Where will you be?"

"I'll be outside where I can duck."

"I don't like this one bit."

"We're ready for them."

We did not speak much the rest of the evening. We crawled into our roped feather bed and took turns waking up to find the other one already awake. Each time I tried not to appear worried.

## Chapter 11

Things always look better in the morning. The sun was up in the hazy Oldtown sky. The street was busy. R.J. and I sat in the office drinking coffee as usual.

"How many times have you cleaned that gun?" I asked.

"This is my spare. Only twice."

"You pick your spot in the bank?"

"Yep, leave the VP office door open. I can see the whole area in front of the tellers from there."

"You know they may not show for days, even a week, or they may just pass us by and move on to the next town."

"I got a feeling."

And R.J. was right. I pushed back to get another cup of coffee and the front door burst open. A kid so out of breath he could barely speak yelled, "They're at the Bennet place! They're watering their horses!"

A streak of fear shot through me. I had not included Fantasia in my readiness plan. "What are they doing there?" I asked.

"They're just watering the horses and looking over the town."

I flipped the kid a silver dollar from my desk drawer. "Go spread the word, everybody off the street."

The kid waited for a moment as if there would be more. He ducked out the door and ran like hell.

R.J. nodded, "I'm on it." He headed out the back door.

"Don't forget to signal the deputies."

R.J. cast me a sarcastic look.

I tucked my spare gun into my belt behind me, checked my holstered gun and followed him out the back door. Across the street from the bank, two stores down, was an alley where a delivery wagon was parked. It was the perfect place to check up and down the street without being seen and at the same time I could keep the bank in full view. The town's exodus was quick. Main Street had never been so deserted. There was still dust in the air from people leaving.

It was a long twenty-minute wait, worrying they might mess with Fantasia. But all three rode in slowly, big bandanas hanging down on trail-dusted clothes. Their hands and faces were clean. They had splashed their faces in the water trough. Their shirt fronts were damp. Their hats had a wet ring.

They were vain types, which pleased me. Overconfidence is usually a big mistake. They were not afraid. They didn't think anyone in this town could stop them. I kept down behind the wagon as they passed my alley. They pulled up to a hitching post at the lawyer's office next to the bank, dismounted and tied off loosely. Like R.J. had said, had they been more concerned one of them would have held the horses outside the front door of the bank for a quick getaway. These guys were belligerent.

They walked casually up to the bank's front door, two entered, one stayed outside checking the street in both directions. I held my position, hoping not to start gun play while the two were inside.

Ten minutes of holding my breath, praying R.J. wouldn't have to set it off. The bank door opened and the two came out. Their guns were still holstered. They were carrying stuffed bank bags.

I drew my gun, cocked it, and kept it pointed to the ground. I stepped out into the street and took measured steps toward them. From the corner of my eye I caught the flash of my badge glinting in the daylight.

The three spotted me immediately. They stopped to appraise the lone lawman headed their way. The outside man started to reach for his weapon. The gang leader caught his arm and stopped him.

I picked a spot twenty feet away from them in the center of the street. They had the high ground on the boardwalk. They looked almost amused.

"Gentlemen, you can start by dropping your money bags and weapons right where you are."

The leader replied, "Sheriff, you really gonna take on the three of us alone?"

"One way or another your weapons are going to end up on the ground."

"Sheriff, you might get a shot off and wing one of us, but you'll be dead. You really want to die there in the street for nothing?"

"Gentleman, I am not alone."

They all searched the street and buildings.

"You look mighty alone to us right now, Sheriff."

"I'll give you every chance to drop your guns. There are two deputies with rifles upstairs across the street, and one behind you in the bank."

The leader gave an insolent grin. "You don't really think I'm going to look behind me do you Sheriff? That's the oldest trick in the book. And all I see across this street are curtains. You wouldn't be tryin' to bluff us would you now, Sheriff?"

"If any of you so much as touches the grip on any of those guns you will find out I am not bluffing."

"But Sheriff, you'll still be the first one to drop."

"Like I said, I'm giving you every chance not to die where you stand."

"You got guts. I'll give you that, Sheriff."

The bank door was open. I could see R.J. in position with a gun in each hand leveled at them.

Someone in the bank trying to see out a front window knocked something off a table. It hit the floor and shattered.

All hell broke loose.

All three went for their guns.

It was one of those moments when time slows down and almost stops. I knew exactly what to do. It was all automatic. I brought my gun up to the one who was quickest at trying to put a bullet in me. Before I could even fire, gunfire and bullets from upstairs across the street filled the air on my left. The three of them were experienced. They all tried to dive one way or another but the barrage of bullets peppered them. The leader was the fastest and did his best to keep his word. My shot caught him squarely in the chest and caused his arms to jerk together. A shot in the back from R.J. drove his body forward and down. Shots from the other two went wild, one into the bank awning, the other into the street. All three fell. All three had multiple bullet holes in them. With the three of them lying on the boardwalk not moving, that strange ghostly silence fell over the street. The bank bags had holes in them and had spilled out money. A light wind was carrying some of it off. There is always that momentary wait to see if it is really over.

I turned and waved to the upstairs deputies. They waved back and withdrew. R.J. emerged still holding his guns ready, still pointed at the freshly dead. He poked at them with one boot to be sure.

"R.J., anybody get hurt in there?"

"Nope."

"Ask the bank manager to come out and collect this money before it disappears."

R.J. nodded and went back inside. A moment later two tellers emerged ever so slowly, avoiding the dead men as much as possible as they started collecting the cash.

Next on the scene was the undertaker, measuring tape in hand, yelling to the kids that worked for him to, "get the wagon."

R.J. returned and we watched the proceedings.

"It was a good crossfire from upstairs," he said.

"Yeah, I felt it going by."

"I need a real drink."

"That makes two of us."

"We can't go in either saloon after this."

"I got a bottle in my bottom desk drawer."

"Where's Fantasia?"

"She *was* in her old office packing up medical equipment. I hope she stayed there through all this."

"You better stop by there first."

"Yeah, but that scares me more than this did."

"I'll meet you in the office, but I'm going to start without you."

I took a quick look around at the crowds forming outside the shops and saloons. Some were heading our way. The undertaker's wagon had been hitched up and the horse was being led toward us. It seemed like a nice time to leave.

I walked away and climbed the stairs to the doctor's office. Fantasia was still inside packing

128

medical supplies. She did not look up when I entered. I could have cut the tension in the air with knife. I leaned against her examination table and tried to look casual.

"Is it over?" she asked irately.

"What? Oh, yes. It's all over."

"Was anyone hurt?"

"Only the bad guys."

"Are they dead or do I need to work on them?"

"They are dead." I stepped over and stood close behind her.

"You smell like gunpowder."

"I did everything I could to avoid most of it."

She turned and faced me. We were touching. "As you Earth people like to say, this really pisses me off."

"What?"

"No one should have to wonder if the person they love is going to be killed. It was like I could feel everything that was happening."

"What was that you said about what people like to say?"

"I love you but it's going to take some time for me to put this behind me."

"You called me an earth person or something? What was that? Did you mean like a farmer or something?"

"I don't know. I'm not thinking straight."

"I'm sorry, Fan. You're all that matters to me. I'd quit this job but I don't know what else I'd do."

"No. You go on. But I'll be thinking about this insanity, you can be sure of that. Don't you have paperwork to be taking care of?"

I embraced her hard and kissed her. "What I really need to be taking care of is a stiff drink."

"Go on. I think I'll fix myself one at that."

In the office R.J. was refilling his glass. He seemed to be priding himself on adding seltzer water to it.

"Told you I was going to start without you." He pushed a ready-made drink over to my side of the desk.

I sat and tasted it.

"The deputies stopped in and dropped off those guy's identification in case there's a reward for any of them. They want to know if they're still going to get a full day's pay even though it's over."

"Damn right they are."

"There was three of them upstairs when it happened. We had real good cover. Last mistake those guys will ever make."

I sat and downed my drink. R.J. refilled. We sat in silence for a few minutes, drinking.

Finally R.J. said, "The truth is this really sucks."

"Sucks what?"

"Stinks. This really stinks. I don't even remember accepting this job."

"Oh boy, here we go again."

Before he could reply, the front door rattled opened. A man in an expensive dark suit with a vest and string tie walked in. He removed his derby to reveal a receding hairline. Big dark eyebrows and shifty eyes. He was too big for his shirt and vest.

"Gentleman. We have not been introduced yet. I'm Judge Nick. Just arrived in town. Just in time I see. You're Sheriff Tarn, glad to meet you, sir."

He reached out and shook my hand then turned to R.J.

"Deputy Smith, a pleasure to meet you."

They shook hands.

The judge closed the front door and stood near us. "I'm here to thank you for the good work you did over at the bank. I've interviewed the witnesses and it's clear no inquest is necessary. I'll have those three interred in the back of the cemetery. If anyone wants to claim the bodies they can dig them back up. I just wanted you two to know that no hearing is necessary in this matter. No citizens were harmed. No money stolen. You've both done a great service for the town. You have my thanks. If I can do anything for either of you come see me in my office. I know you don't need me looming over you at a time like this so I'll go. You two have a good rest of the day."

He opened the door, gave a quick nod, and left.

"God, I hadn't even thought about that," I said as R.J. refilled us both again.

"Oh yeah, that's all we would've needed. To sit in a council chamber and explain to the city council members why we had to shoot the three new visitors to Oldtown."

I stifled a laugh. The whiskey was getting to me. I held my drink up and we clinked glasses.

The front door rattled open. A heavy-set woman came in and stood appraising us. She wore a flowered dress that went to her ankles. Fine lace-up black leather boots. Brown hair carefully cut around her oversized face. We stared at her with looks of wonder.

"Sheriff Tarn, you don't know me. I'm Melda Nick. I've taken over the bank here at Oldtown."

"Yes, ma'am. Was it your husband we just met?" I asked.

"Yes, but that's not important. I want to ask, was there any way those bank robbers could have been taken into custody without all the shooting there right in front of the bank?"

"Believe me, ma'am, I tried my best."

R.J. tried to nod support but his voice slurred. "He did, ma'am. They weren't listening too good."

She cast an impatient glance at R.J. as though he were an unnecessary interruption. "Really, Sheriff. There was no way to avoid the bloodshed right in front of the bank?"

"The bank happened to be where they were headed, Mrs Shrack." I squinted and wondered if that was the right thing to say.

"Well, at least no money was taken. Perhaps we can discuss this again when your mind is a little clearer, Sheriff."

"Yes, ma'am."

She hurried back out the door.

R.J. looked at me with an unsteady stare. I held out my glass. He barely was able to point the bottle correctly. We drank.

"And here we were thinking it went just fine," slurred R.J.

The door rattled open. It was Fantasia. She looked slightly glassy eyed.

"Come on, Adrian. I need your help with something upstairs."

I stood but it took a moment to regain my bearings. I guided myself around the desk and patted R.J. on the shoulder. "Nice work today, sir."

He held up his empty glass. "And you as well, sir."

"I must go. I am needed elsewhere."

Fantasia hooked a hand under my arm to steady me. I caught a whiff of alcohol on her breath. She gave R.J. a big smile and shut the door behind her.

# Chapter 12

It was a peaceful hazy Oldtown morning. R.J. met me in the office looking as hung over as I did. He handed me hot coffee and started to say something cute but waved it off and sipped his cup.

I nodded. "Yeah, right there with you."

"We're going to have to make the rounds or it will be suspicious but every step I take is like a rock fall in my head."

"Yeah, right there with you."

I sat and drank. "Maybe Hugh's got some secret remedy for this."

"If anybody has one, he'd be the one."

"Let's go before we die."

We took opposite sides of the street, bent over more than would be normal, waving to each passerby like it was a normal day. We were lucky no bank robbers were visiting today. I kept looking over at R.J. hoping I didn't look that bad.

Made it to the saloon faster than usual. At the bar, Hugh stood appraising our sorry expressions. He nodded, went in the back room and came out with two cold beers from the root cellar. He opened both and used a funnel to add a touch of clear liquid, stirred them and placed them in front of us.

"Cold backwoods beer, with a touch of red oak white lightning."

We looked at him carefully to see if he was joking. He wasn't. We drank a good amount.

"Oh," said R.J. and he straightened up a bit.

"Hugh, you are a gentleman and a patriot," I said.

He smiled. "My life savings are in that bank. Two of those and you'll forget the hangover, but you'll be a little loose."

"There is a God," said R.J.

"I hear you met the new judge and his wife."

R.J. said, "He was happy. She was not."

"Figures," replied Hugh. "But you ought to hear what the townspeople are saying about you two. You're both legends so to speak."

We drank our second beers, decided we were going to live after all, and headed back to the office. The walk back was strange. People peering out their windows, some standing outside their doors talking, all of them waving excitedly and smiling.

In the office someone had left two copies of the local newspaper.

### *Oldtown Crier Special Edition*

### *SHERIFF THWARTS BANK ROBBERY*

### *Sheriff's team in place and ready.*

*Oldtown, An early morning robbery of the Central Bank was thwarted yesterday by Sheriff Tarn, Deputy Smith, and four sworn in temporaries. The Sheriff and Deputy were unavailable for comment but this reporter was able to interview several eyewitnesses who described the Sheriff as standing alone in the street facing down three armed bank robbers. The three men refused to surrender and went for their guns. A hail of gunfire filled Main Street. It is not known how many assailants Sheriff Tarn and Deputy Smith shot but all three bank robbers were taken down without anyone else being harmed. Residents will be relieved to hear that no cash from the bank was lost. According to Judge Roy Nick a telegram had warned the three robbers might be heading for Oldtown. "I had absolute faith in our Marshall to handle this situation if and when it arose and I approved of his plan completely. This is a good example of the town management and law enforcement working to protect our citizens. I applaud the Sheriff and his team for this good work."*

*Reactions from town business leaders were swift and forthcoming.*

*Story continued inside*

I sat staring at the issue. "Oh for cripes' sakes."

"So the judge preapproved your plan, did he? I don't recall that."

"His wife sure didn't approve it."

"As a matter of fact I don't recall seeing the judge anywhere near that particular negotiation," added R.J.

"You know, I do believe that's the first time I've ever *thwarted* anything."

"No, no. You've thwarted before. I've seen you."

The front door rattled open. In walked a kid dressed like a man. I guessed him to be maybe sixteen years old. Short sandy-colored hair, big blue eyes, trail dust lines in his young face. He wore a range shirt and bandanna hanging down, jeans and boots and a full set of chaps which had been cut away to allow for the six-gun hanging from his hip. His boots were covered with trail dust. I did not know him but somehow he looked familiar.

He stopped in front of my desk next to R.J. and looked down at me with his thumbs tucked into his belt. He removed his trail dust hat and held it down. "I'm Riley Kit, Sheriff. I thought I'd better stop by."

I sat up. "Riley Kit. You're working as a drover for the James brothers."

"Yep. Stayin' in the bunk house out there."

"Well, welcome to Oldtown."

"I thought I should let you know that one of the other drovers out there doesn't seem to like me too much. I don't want no trouble but sometimes trouble wants you, if you know what I'm sayin'."

"You got a name for this ranch hand, Riley?" asked R.J.

"Bard Coverton. I need this job but I don't need him."

"You're thinking this could come down to gun play, Riley?" I asked.

"He keeps pushin' and I don't believe he's gonna stop until there's no room to walk away. Thing is, if he forces my hand he's sure to lose. So where's that goin' to leave me, Sheriff?"

"I guess you must know how to use that gun then, Riley?" I asked.

"Custom made by a gunsmith for me. Got my own reloader. I know exactly how many grains are each of these bullets."

R.J. asked, "Riley, aren't you kind of old for your age?"

"Been on my own for some time, Deputy. Before that I was taking care of my old aunt. She's gone. It's just me now."

"You did the right thing coming in, Riley," I said. "If anything does happen I'll know you were doing everything you could to avoid it. I will go and have a little talk with Mr. Bard Coverton. We'll see if that helps."

"All I can ask, Sheriff."

Riley pulled on his hat, tipped it to us and left.

R.J. said, "Awfully sure of himself. You believe him? About his gun I mean?"

"I think he's got too many years on his own to doubt him."

"I know Coverton. He's a blowhard."

"Guess I'll have to ride out there and try to save his life."

"What else you got going on?"

"Supposed to join the crew to move Fantasia's medical gear out to the Bennet's place. She's got a bunch of kids helping her. The livery lent her their work horse and wagon."

"It's not the Bennet place anymore."

"Yeah, she's worried about having a medical emergency before her new medical office is set up." I pushed up from my seat, went to the front door and looked out. Two kids were seated on the boardwalk whittling a piece of wood.

"Hey, boys! You want to earn a five piece each?"

They sprung up. "Yeah, Sheriff. How?"

"Run out to the Bennet place and saddle up my horse, then bring him here and tie him off. Make sure he's watered." I dug in my pocket and came up with two five pieces and gave one to each of them. They took off running.

As I sat back down the front door rattled open. It was another kid.

"Sheriff, Hugh is asking that you come up to the saloon right away."

I dug in my pocket for another five piece, handed it to him, and out he went.

R.J. looked at me. "Oh boy."

We grabbed our hats, checked our guns, and headed for the saloon.

The new saloon sign had just been installed by the town's two natural born comedians. The fact that it was straight and true was hilarious in itself in that the two of them had done it. Of course since they were continuing to work on it, there was still a chance the entire job might end in disaster. We watched as Jeb Colton turned with the ladder and banged his brother Teed in the head after which they struggled to load the ladder from the front of their wagon. That undertaking radically completed, and having no horse, they grabbed the hitching rail and pulled the wagon away with great effort, accentuated by sounds of strain and continuous arguing. But the big new sign, "Candy's," was a marvel to behold. We watched them inch away pondering why they had not just carried the ladder.

We pushed through the saloon doors with our practiced casual attitude. The never-ending poker game was in full swing on the right. There were no other patrons except one big man leaning against the bar with a drink. He conspicuously ignored our entrance. Hugh was behind the bar wiping it though it did not appear to need it. He gave us a warning stare.

R.J. said, "By the way, I'm never drinking again."

We went to the bar and leaned against it. Hugh wiped his way to us, set up a coffee and put it in front of me. R.J. pointed to the coffee and was served one.

Hugh resumed nervously wiping.

R.J. sipped and said, "You're going to wear that countertop off, aren't you, Hugh?"

Hugh leaned in and spoke in a low tone. "That's Arny Pots. This happens every time there's some kind of shootout. Some guys get all liquored up about it. Arny's not too fast but with enough drink in him he thinks he is. He's looking for a gunfight to make himself famous. He's been on an all-nighter but I had to give him a bottle or he might have shot me. I been giving people the don't-come-in signal but sooner or later somebody's not going to pay attention."

Hugh looked at me with a wrinkled brow.

"You're a damn good man, you know that, Hugh?" I said.

"I say my prayers, I'll tell you that."

"R.J., go say hello to the marathon poker players, then take a spot at the bar on the other side of him. Real easy like."

"I know the routine, Adrian."

R.J. took his coffee, went to the poker table and began a friendly conversation. I slid down the bar closer to Arny. When I got too close he looked over at me. I nodded hello.

Arny downed his glass and turned to face me, still leaning on the bar. "I hear you faced down three, Sheriff."

I held up my coffee cup in a toast and sipped.

"You think you could face me down?"

"We're friends, Arny."

"A man's got to have respect, Sheriff."

"Well, hell; I respect you, Arny"

R.J. took his place at the bar behind him.

"You always come out on top when you're staring down another gun, Sheriff. If a man was to put you down his name would be known from east to west."

R.J. began inching closer.

"We could prove you're faster on my shooting range behind the jail, Arny. Then nobody gets hurt."

"It ain't the same, Sheriff. It ain't the same when real lead is coming at you. I'm faster and better when I think there's real bullets coming."

R.J. managed to get right behind him. He reached slowly around and ever so easy eased Arny's gun out of the holster. Army twisted toward the bar and poured another drink for nerve. He downed it in one gulp, stood away from the bar, and faced me with his hand by his holster, spreading fingers in anticipation.

"I'm sorry, Sheriff, but this is the way it has to be. All or nothin'" Arny teetered a bit.

I started toward him. He slapped at his holster and became panicky that no gun was there. R.J. bear hugged him from behind just as I popped him with a checked punch in the left side of the mouth.

Arny went to sleep.

Arny's dead weight was not easy to hoist up. I got one of his arms over my shoulder and dragged him toward the door. "R.J., bring his bottle."

The two of us managed to get him to the jail bed and lock him in. We set his bottle next to him on the floor.

"Why the bottle?" asked R.J.

"Tomorrow he'll be so hung over he won't want to hear any gun fire from anyone."

"Oh, right. I can attest to that."

I said, "I guess I'll head out to the James brother's place."

"Maybe I should come along."

"Stay here and keep an eye on things. I'll have a better chance out there if it's a one-on-one little chat, if you know what I mean. If Fan shows up, tell her I'll be right back for the moving."

"Good luck with Coverton." R.J. poured himself another coffee.

Runner was already tied off to the office hitching post. He pushed his nose into my side as I walked by. I checked over his black body, white socks, and white nose. His hooves had been well trimmed. Reins in hand, I mounted up and had to pull him in. He was more than ready to go. We did a slow canter down Main Street, ignoring

140

waves from pedestrians. The last business was Art's Cherry Wood Beef Drying. The place was smoking and smelled like steak as usual.

The James place was a short couple miles southwest of the town. It was a dry desert ride there. The word was that the James brothers kept one hundred head, but the most I'd ever seen were twenty or thirty. Supposedly they had to shift cattle groups to new grazing grounds frequently to keep from killing off the grass.

I passed under the JJ sign leading to the ranch house. Long, single story home with a porch spanning the front of it. Their chimney was smoking. I passed by the hired hand barracks and stopped at the open doors to the big barn. I happened to arrive at an awkward moment.

Luke James was inside standing too close to Mae James and Mae didn't seem to mind at all. They saw me and backed apart.

"Sheriff, what brings you out?" asked Luke.

I tipped my hat. "I wanted to stop by and see Bard. Is he around?"

"He's out on the west end fixing fence. That-a-way." Luke pointed as though he was hoping to be rid of me.

"Thanks, I can find him."

There was not a cow in sight. I rode west until I found the fence, then followed it until I saw a man and a horse in the distance.

Bard was lacing up a break in the fence. He stopped and looked inquisitively as I approached. I climbed down and tied off.

"Now what the hell are you doin' way out here, Sheriff?"

I leaned against a fence post. "I'm a little worried about you, Bard."

"*You* are worried about *me*? You just stared down three bad men with guns and you're worried about *me*?"

I laughed. "You have a point, Bard."

"What you worried about, Sheriff?"

"I'm worried about you and Kid Riley."

"Oh. Somebody say somethin' to you, Sheriff?"

"I think I know something you may not know, Bard."

"What's that?" Bard began wrapping fence wire again.

"I think that kid is fast as lightning."

Bard kept wrapping and did not look over.

"How long have we known each other, Bard?"

He stopped and looked over. "So long as I can't say."

"Oldtown would not be the same without you around, Bard. I wouldn't want to see that."

"What makes you think that kid is so fast?"

"He's got youth, Bard. He isn't old enough to have learned to be scared of anything and he's got the quick reactions of a kid. Add to that he was trained by a gunsmith and what do you get?"

Bard kept winding fence.

"You know, Bard, someday you and the kid may end up fighting side by side against rustlers or something."

Bard nodded. "True enough."

"What that kid needs is your experience, otherwise he's liable to get himself killed biting off more than he can chew."

Bard laughed. "Does sound like me, don't he?"

I untied Runner, hoisted a foot in a stirrup and remounted. "Came all the way out here, Bard. It was a nice ride."

He stopped winding and leaned against the fence post. "I'll buy you a drink next time I'm in town, Sheriff."

I nodded. "My wife's moving us into the Bennet place. I'll be needing one."

142

I pointed Runner away and cantered off.

At the end of James Road, I paused before turning onto the main trail to town. Off to the west the hills marked the distance. It would be nice to see what landscape existed beyond them, but the truth was I had no interest in riding out there.

I gave Runner a loose rein. He chose to live up to his name and opened up into a flat gallop. He kept it for a good mile and then backed off to a rocking horse canter. In town someone had set up a vegetable stand along the street. I stopped, dismounted, and left Runner at the nearest water trough. I bought a good bundle of carrots and fed all of them to Runner. He seemed to feel it was an adequate reward.

At the Bennet's-turned-Tarn's place I caught an empty-handed kid coming out of the main house and offered him a five to cool Runner down, untack him, and put him out to graze.

Fantasia was inside unpacking. "You're managing to get out of all the moving, dear."

"I'm sorry, Fan. Something important came up."

"I bet."

"What you want me to do now?"

She looked at me with a thoughtful stare. "Hey, I was thinking. Everyone has electricity in their homes. Why don't we all have telegraphs so we can talk to each other?"

"That's a great idea. There would have to be wires everywhere."

"Yes, but that wouldn't be hard, and instead of telegraph keys why not a typewriter that does the same thing? It's just dots and dashes. I type on my typewriter at home and a typewriter in your house prints it out."

"Could that really be done?"

"I could do it right now. Each typewriter key clicks out certain dots and dashes, and at the other end the typewriter sees those and depresses the correct key. It would be easy."

"Don't you think you need to get your hospital set up first?"

"Yes, of course, dear."

There was a knock on the door.

"Oh, good; the kids with another load," said Fantasia.

I opened the door. It was Parth Sharma.

"Parth, come in. How were those silver core samples you took in? Come in and sit."

Fantasia looked up. "Parth, how are you? It's crazy here."

Parth removed his business hat and scanned the room full of boxes and worn furniture. "I'm here to help if you would like."

Fantasia said, "Parth, I'm afraid the kids would rebel if you tried to cut in on their newfound income."

"Fantasia, please keep me in mind for anything you need."

"Thank you, Parth."

"I wanted to ask the two of you, have you met the woman who is working in the saloon? Her name is Diya Singh."

I replied, "I've seen her a few times. We haven't been introduced. I haven't ever spoken to her."

Fantasia added, "I rarely go in there, Parth. What makes you ask about her?"

Parth took a deep breath before answering. "I feel I should know her but I do not recall why or where."

Fantasia said, "Perhaps she was someone you and your wife knew back in the coastal cities."

Parth answered, "Yes, that is a possibility but it seems like more than that to me. I seem

144

unable to stop thinking about it. It is like a memory which is just slightly out of reach. It is quite annoying."

"Have you spoken to her, Parth?" asked Fantasia.

"Just briefly. I introduced myself. She seemed to look at me as if she had the same familiarity. She was working. I could not speak with her at any length."

Fantasia said, "Perhaps I should go and meet her. Sometimes women are more forthcoming with each other than with men."

"That would be most appreciated, Fantasia. In the meantime I will continue to soul search about it." Parth turned and reached for the door.

I said, "Fantasia, what do I need to bring from your old office? I need to go check in with R.J."

"There is a trunk of operating room clothes and a wagon at the bottom of the stairs to bring it."

I nodded. "Parth, I'll walk back with you."

We stepped outside, wound our way through the next line of kids carrying office supplies, and headed back.

"So there's a mystery woman in your life, Parth?"

"It is most unsettling."

"Could she have been a girlfriend from before you were married?"

"That is unlikely. My time at university was one of study not socializing."

"By the way, how were those silver core samples you took in?"

"It was my intent to speak with you about those. I have concerns."

"Really?"

"The metallurgic analysis showed the sample to be ninety-nine-point-nine per cent pure."

"That's good, isn't it?"

"More than that. It's exceptional."

"So what's the concern?"

"The sample was taken illegally. I checked that. There's a line of hills just southwest of the James brothers' ranch. That's where the sample came from and the James' family owns the rights to those hills. I believe they don't know anything about this."

"Okay, they don't know they're probably rich. What's the problem?"

"The prospector who brought in the core samples gave a false name. However, he did give the true location where the samples were taken. He must have thought it was open range. He believed he could stake a claim there."

"So you're not allowed to make public where the samples were found and he gave a false name so people wouldn't be bothering him about it."

"Range wars have broken out over less than this, Adrian."

"I see your point, Parth. But, by law I have to tell the brothers someone has been illegally prospecting on their land."

"And so it begins."

"And what is the law? Do I tell them what was found on their land or is that the private information of the trespasser?"

"The law is unclear about that. You will need to consult a lawyer or a judge."

"That would have to be Judge Nick and it doesn't give me a warm feeling."

"You have reservations about Judge Nick?"

"Just a feeling, Parth. I don't trust him yet. Can you let me know the next time this prospector comes in?"

"Yes. I presently have no contact information for him."

"How are things going in your office otherwise?"

"Very slow. There does not seem to be much prospecting going on around Oldtown. Fortunately Oldtown has an extensive library. I spend a good deal of time upstairs reading. But now I have this saloon woman mystery."

"Yes, we'll see if we can help with that."

"You have my thanks and the next time you will be facing criminals please let me know. I do not have a handgun, but do own a short-barreled shotgun."

"I'll keep that in mind, Parth."

We split up. I stepped up onto the boardwalk and went in the office. R.J was locking someone in a cell.

I sat at the desk and picked up the Oldtown Morning Crier.

R.J. plopped down in his chair. "It's Alien Andy. He tried to leave the saloon without paying."

Andy yelled from the back, "I told him ta put it on my account, Sheriff. I always been good for it."

"What's the plan?"

R.J. answered, "No plan. I paid it off. The cell is just to let it sink in a while. Then I'll turn him loose. How'd it go with Coverton?"

"He was patching fence. I think he's mellowing with age."

Andy yelled, "You all think I'm crazy but I'm not the only one."

"Are you moved in?"

"Fan has a dozen kids working on it."

"Yeah, don't you ever wonder about that? They only have school on Wednesdays? The rest of the days are supposed to be homework. You ever hear of a school that only teaches one day a week?"

"Those kids have to work the farms and ranches. It's always been that way."

"Seems like they're always in town to me."

"Yeah, lucky for you and me or we'd be lugging furniture right now."

"I'm just sayin'."

"You'd better be careful or you'll pick up a nickname like Alien Andy."

"I'm not the only one, Sheriff," yelled Andy. "You remember Jeck Higgs from last year? He was out late one night checking his herd. One of his cows was down on the ground. He said a door opened up in the ground and beings in strange suits came out and took the cow down under with them. Next day there was no sign of that cow. Locals tried to say coyotes dragged it off but Jeck knew better."

I looked at R.J. "See what I mean?"

Andy yelled, "Don't take my word for it. You ride out to them far hills and see what you see."

R.J. said, "I'd like to see what's beyond those hills. I just can't muster up the energy to ride out there."

"Well, if you'll stay here and guard our dangerous prisoner, I need to go move trunks."

"Remember, lift with the legs, not with the back."

"Thanks so much."

## Chapter 13

It was a busy week and except for one large bar fight in the Bucking Horse Saloon, during which no one was arrested, the town ran smoothly. With her new hospital setup, Fantasia had already treated a sprained ankle and cut on the blacksmith's head that required stitches.

When I finally got the stomach for a meeting with Judge Nick he was in his courthouse chambers. I walked in too dusty for the elegant, dark oak furniture-filled room and took a kindly offered seat at his desk. His coat was draped over a nearby chair. Red suspenders held up his trousers. The buttons on his shirt were straining to hold on.

"So this is a matter of confidential information given at the assayer's office by someone you suspect of illegal prospecting?"

"Those are the facts, Judge."

"And this particular transaction has resulted in discovery of what may be a rich yield of silver on the James Brothers' land?"

"Yes."

"Well the answer is easy, Sheriff. This prospector cannot be considered a criminal without a trial or guilty plea and until that happens his personal information is protected."

"He gave a false name, Judge."

"Yes, but until you have proof of his true identity he cannot be charged with anything."

"I will proceed on your ruling, Judge."

"Very good, Sheriff. Have a good day, sir."

R.J. and I sat in the office pondering the judge's ruling. Neither of us seemed to have anything to good say about it.

"You let Andy out already?"

"Yes. Before he corrupted me further with alien stories."

"Did you send word we needed to see Jack James?"

"Yes. It was easy. They said he was down at the feed store picking up grain."

"Do you happen to know the woman who works at Candy's saloon?"

"The attractive one? I've spoken to her a few times. Why?"

"Parth thinks he knows her from somewhere but can't remember where."

R.J. let out a short laugh. "Attractive women will do that to you."

The door shimmied open. Jeff James stepped in. He was a commanding figure. Hat set straight. Leather vest. Long barreled six shooter tucked into a tied down holster. He wasn't the type to smile. You'd need to have a real good reason to pick an argument with him.

"You wanted to see me, Sheriff?"

"Jack, nice to see you. Want to grab a seat?"

James looked like he was too busy but sat anyway.

"How you doing, Jack?" asked R.J.

Jack nodded. "Just fine, deputy. What's this about?"

I tilted forward in my chair. "We got word somebody was prospecting on your land illegally."

James interested peaked. "When?"

"Probably a couple weeks ago. Just before R.J. and I got called out of town."

"Where?"

"Somewhere in the hills southwest of your place."

"Who? Who was out there?"

"The man's name was Jace Dooly. But we know that's a fake name because he signed two documents and spelled it differently each time."

"How do you know about this, Sheriff?"

"Parth Sharma reported this to me after the man turned in core samples for analysis."

"Guess I owe Parth a drink or two. Where is this guy now?"

"We're watching but there's been no sign of him."

"Did he find something out there, Sheriff, that I ought to know about?"

"According to the judge, as county assayer, Parth can't release any information until the man is brought in and charged and a warrant is issued."

"I guess I'd better take a ride out there. I appreciate you calling me in, Sheriff."

"Wish I could do more, Jack. But I will keep you informed."

James rose, tipped his hat to us and left.

"That went well," said R.J. "I was afraid he would go gunning for the guy."

"There's a famous old saying, *day ain't over yet*."

The door rattled open. Fantasia peeked in and entered. "Let's go have lunch at Candy's."

"Really?" I asked.

"I'll be safe there with my own sheriff and deputy."

"Not sure about the food."

"We'll find out."

"You want to go check out Diya."

"I'm starved. Let's go before someone shows up at my office with their rheumatism acting up."

R.J. and I grabbed our hats and followed her out.

Candy's was slightly busier than usual. The perpetual poker game members waved to us as we entered. Alien Andy was seated at bar's end. Hugh looked surprised at the sight of Fantasia. We gestured to him, removed our hats, and took seats at a table out of the way. Hugh lifted the bar gate and came to us. "Doctor Tarn, it is truly a pleasure to see you ma'am."

"Good afternoon, Hugh. What's on the menu?"

"Grilled steak and eggs, ma'am."

"I believe we will all have that, and coffee please."

"Yes ma'am. Right away." Hugh dashed off.

R.J. said, "Someday they'll have more than one item on the menu."

There was a sudden wave of commotion at the swinging doors. A group of trail dusted cowboys pushed in. They were all wearing chaps and rain-worn hats. They all had handguns strapped to their side. They ambled up to the bar and spread out. Hugh came out from the kitchen, grabbed his bar towel and spoke, "What can I get you boys?"

I switched my badge from my belt to my shirt pocket. I was careful not to look at the group but listened carefully. One in the middle had already noticed Fantasia.

"Whiskey, bartender. And just keep fillin' 'em."

The drink tipping began. They each downed two or three. The tallest of them looked back at us and pushed away from the bar to head our way. R.J. flinched and under the table unsnapped his gun for reassurance.

Trail bums all look the same after too much time pushing cows. This one was no different. He came up to the table and to my relief tipped his hat to us.

"Sheriff, I'm Sal Kenden. My boys and I are moving a herd to Westend. They are parked just south of town. We'll be out of your hair in a couple hours. Just need some supplies for the chuck."

I reached out and offered a hand. His handshake was genuine. "If there's anything you need, Sal, feel free to ask."

"Mighty obliging of you, Sheriff. Sorry for the interruption." He tipped his hat to Fantasia, turned, and went back to the bar.

The drover who had been paying too much attention to Fantasia straightened up to collect himself. He took a step in our direction. The man next to him noticed, reached out and caught his arm to pull him back to the bar. There was a brief exchange of words. Drinking resumed.

R.J. said, "It's so nice when you don't have to shoot them."

I said, "There are five of them. If it had gone the other way, I believe we could have taken out four of them between us, but the fifth one would have been a bitch."

Fantasia perked up and said, "Perhaps not. I have a pocket pistol in my purse."

I straightened up. "What?"

She smiled, "Silver with an ivory handle."

R.J. laughed then said, "I think you mean grip, Fan. It has an ivory grip."

"Yes. It does."

I asked, "Fan, where did you get that?"

"From the gunsmith's display cabinet. He gave me ten percent off because you are the sheriff."

I persisted, "You didn't need a gun to protect yourself, Fan."

"It is not to protect me. It is to protect you."

"What do you mean?"

"The day may come when there *is* a fifth, as you call it. It is so I will not need to stand by helplessly if that happens."

R.J. smirked at me. "I'm not seeing a comeback for that, Adrian."

"Have you fired the thing, Fan?" I asked.

"No. I thought perhaps you would give me some lessons out behind the jail."

"When were you going to tell me about this?"

"As soon as an opportune moment arose such as the one we just had."

R.J. smirked again and stifled a laugh. "It's awful when they're smarter than you, isn't it?"

Diya arrived with a large tray stacked with food. Hugh was behind her with coffees. Diya kept her floor length, bland dress out of the way as she placed our food. Hugh reached around and set coffee cups then hurried back to the bar to wait on the cowhands. Diya had to pause to push her long dark hair behind her. The small features of her face were delicate and tan. She had a smile with dimples even when she was not smiling.

Fantasia said, "Diya, I'm Doctor Tarn, the Sheriff's wife. I have been wanting to meet you."

Diya looked up with a curious expression.

Fantasia continued. "We have a mutual friend I believe. Parth Sharma has mentioned you."

Diya paused and looked up again. "Parth? Parth mentioned me to you?"

"Yes. He mentioned what a nice person you are. We wanted to invite you to dinner with us."

Diya finished placing the food and stopped. "I am very shy with new people."

Fantasia was not about to give up. "But you know Sheriff Tarn and Deputy Smith, and I am the town doctor. You and I should get to know one another. Come to our house for dinner tonight."

Diya took a long thoughtful pause. "Alright. I will come."

Before Fantasia could respond, a rather slinky blond-haired buxom woman dressed in a loud gown suitable for dance-hall girls charged in. Her makeup was exaggerated. She walked with a prance.

"Diya, there is stock waiting to be unpacked. It will not unpack itself."

"Yes, ma'am," replied Diya and she scurried off.

"Sheriff Tarn, Deputy Smith, and Doctor Tarn, we have not been introduced. I'm the new owner, Candy Shrack. It's a pleasure to meet you."

We nodded. I reached over and shook her hand. R.J. gave a wave. Fantasia gave a forced smile.

"Well, please enjoy your meal and come in again. We will be expanding the menu and I have the Colton brothers clearing out a back room. We will be reworking the small stage for entertainment a couple nights a week."

As she spoke, a loud crash came from the room where the Colton's were working. Candy winced, looked regretful, but quickly switched to a practiced smile.

I shook my head approvingly. R.J. stared blankly. Fantasia gave a forced smile.

Candy Shrack moved on to the gambler's table where her husband Bert seemed to be doing well though I do not know how. Even from where I was sitting his comically short crop of black hair sticking up always seemed to bristle when he drew a good hand.

The food was fairly good. Hugh refilled the coffee before we could signal for it. We ate, kept a side glance on the cowhands and finished up without any problems. I left the money on the table and we took our leave.

On the boardwalk Fantasia said, "I'm not sure I like that woman."

I asked, "You mean Candy Shrack?"

"Of course. Diya seems wonderful."

R.J. said, "It takes a special kind of person to run a saloon."

I added, "Yeah, hours of noisy chaos with moments of stark terror."

"People need a release from their troubles," said Fantasia.

I hooked an arm over Fantasia shoulders. We traded smiles.

Fantasia said, "I need to stop in the assay office a moment."

"You're going to invite Parth over tonight also, huh?"

"I certainly am."

"Fan, are you trying to match-make two married people?"

"I do not know Diya well, but I am sure Parth would never go back on his vows. There is no reason those two can't be good friends."

"Risky business," said R.J.

Fantasia sounded surprised. "Why R.J., how enchanting! You so rarely give your opinion about such things. I'm intrigued."

We waited outside while she went in. She was out a moment later.

"Is he coming?" I asked.

"You had doubt?" she replied.

"Silly me."

Dinner was fried chicken and potatoes. R.J. arrived early with a book on mysteries he had drawn out of the town library. He wore a white shirt with suspenders which was formal wear for him. Parth also arrived early looking very proper in a black vest and tie carrying a bottle of fine

156

wine. It forced me to ask Fantasia if I should change. She was concerned Diya would not have fancy wear and did not want to make her feel uncomfortable so we stayed in our casual clothes.

We milled around making jokes, too tempted by the wine not to open it. Just about the time we were all doubting Diya's attendance she knocked on the door. She wore a floor length dress with a flower pattern and looked quite beautiful in it. We sat, gave thanks, and devoured Fantasia's chicken. Stuffed and slightly dreamy we moved to the fireplace area to finish off the bottle.

"So you must tell us about yourself, Diya," said Fantasia.

"I fear it is a dull story," she replied.

"Where are you originally from?" persisted Fantasia.

"I am from the coastal city Oldear. I came to Oldtown to meet my husband. He is an engineer who travels often. After I arrived I was notified by telegram of a loss of track for the connecting rail from the coast. My husband could not make the trip. I am waiting for the connection to be reestablished so that I can return. I have been here almost four months waiting."

"What did you do in Oldear?" asked R.J.

"I taught history when not working as an archeologist on site somewhere."

R.J. perked up. "History and archeology? So, Diya, I have this book on mysteries. There's a reference in here that puzzles me. Look at this word. Do you know what it means?" R.J. opened his book to a certain page and pointed as he held it out to her.

Diya took the book and studied the print. "Do you mean Tirumalai?"

"Yes, that's it."

"It is a very interesting reference. Tirumalai was a legendary city of the Gods. It was not a part of our planet. A special magic doorway was needed to go there. But if you could, it was said to be a place of wonders beyond imagination. But that is just legend. Does the name somehow hold special meaning for you?"

R.J. wrinkled his brow as he considered the question. "I guess it does but I don't know why really."

I asked, "Diya have you ever heard any of Alien Andy's stories?"

Diya smiled, "He is a very imaginative man. But in the town library in the documents section there are other stories by people very much like Andy's."

R.J. straightened up. "Diya, is there anything describing what is beyond the southern far mountains?"

Parth refilled Diya's glass.

Diya answered, "The geography books say that area is a long stretch of barren desert and is particularly dangerous. It should not be crossed even on horseback. Apparently, the desert will suck the water from your body faster than you can replace it. Those who have ventured out there have not returned."

R.J. said, "Sounds kind of mysterious to me."

Diya said, "There is one written story by a man named Jeck Higgs who claimed to have found a tunnel system in those western far mountains. He claimed to have followed the tunnel all the way to the other side and saw what was beyond those hills. He claimed he saw a strange city in the far distance. A city made of glass and metal."

R.J. said, "He's also the one who claimed a door in the ground opened up and a cow was taken down into it."

Diya answered, "Yes. Before the claim about the distant city, Jeck was famous for his hollow planet theory. He claimed the planet is hollow and there are cities beneath us with many people living there."

Parth asked, "You have now sparked my curiosity, Diya. Whatever became of this man?"

"Shortly after claiming he had seen the distant city, he sort of disappeared. That was just a few weeks ago, actually. It was said he took the train back home. A warning was issued soon after that indicating highly venomous snakes had been seen on the western range. No one has dared explore it since."

R.J. raised his glass. "Here's to Jeck and those of us not afraid to explore mysteries."

We all laughed, clinked our glasses, and drank.

Parth said, "Diya, is there any chance you and I have met before, somewhere other than Oldtown?"

"I have had that same feeling Parth but for the life of me I cannot remember where. Have you spent time in the coastal cities?"

"Only for school. I do not even recall much of that period."

"I don't mean to be inappropriate but you remind me a great deal of my husband."

Parth sipped and nodded. "I have had the same feeling. The four of us must have met in passing somewhere."

"Perhaps that is it. I seem unable to stop trying to remember that. It has become almost like a hobby of sorts."

We went on to discuss Oldtown politics and history with Parth and Diya both continually glancing at each other trying to fill in the blank spot. R.J. and I drank too much wine. We broke up the gathering late with Parth walking Diya back to her room. R.J. slept on the couch, dreaming about the land beyond the mountains.

## Chapter 14

We had two blissful weeks without shootouts in the street, bank robberies, or full-scale brawls in either of the saloons. Fantasia became the busiest woman in town. Besides the medical clinic she had picked up two more underfed horses for nearly nothing and at night she was working on her automatic typewriter telegraph which she'd nicknamed typeomatic.

R.J. and I finished going through the afternoon release of wanted posters and headed out the door for our Main Street patrol. I waited for him to cross over and we started down opposite sides of the street. As I passed the general store a mischievous–looking youngster came bolting out from between buildings, gave me a quick ·worried look and kept going. I signaled to R.J. and headed into the alley.

Halfway through the alley I started hearing muted cries of "oh, oh, oh...."

I drew my gun and held it pointed toward the ground. As carefully as possible I eased up to the rear of the building and slowly peeked around the corner.

Behind the bank, President Melda Nick was holding her long office dress up around her waist while the bank janitor Saul Brell, his trousers and suspenders down around his ankles, was repeatedly boosting her against the wall. It was clearly a unified effort.

I jerked back, winced, and felt sincere regret that it was an image I would never be able to get completely out of my mind. I tucked in my gun, quietly made my way back to the boardwalk and gave R.J. a disgusted wave ahead.

Rounds completed, we headed into Candy's.

R.J. pushed through the swinging doors, looked back at me and said, "We'd better take a table. We need to talk."

We sat off to one side and waved to Hugh.

With coffee in front of us, R.J. said, "What was all that behind the bank?"

"Saul Brell was attending to bank president Melda."

"You mean…."

I nodded.

"Oh my God, you're kidding! She's got twenty years on him."

"I know it's not in his job description."

"I would bet that Judge Nick does not know a thing about that."

"Agreed, and we must keep this to ourselves."

"Absolutely."

R.J. stared down at his coffee. "I wish my story wasn't worse than yours."

"Oh, boy."

"Yesterday Luke James and Mae came into town with their wagon to pick up grain because the feed store was out the day Jack was here. They backed the wagon up to the feed store big doors out back and went in to load the stuff. I happened to be in just the right spot across the street that I could see them. Inside the storehouse they were at it like newlyweds."

"Luke with his brother's wife?"

"Neither of them having any second thoughts about it, if you know what I mean."

"I am really sorry to hear that."

"And like you say, we can't breathe a word of this but it's like a fuse set to burning."

I sat back and shook my head. I couldn't think of a single appropriate thing to say. I sipped my coffee and as I did the swinging doors opened and a stranger entered the saloon. He was heavy set, too much of it gut. The stage wasn't running and the train wasn't due so he had to have ridden in but had cleaned up somewhere first. Gray standard hat. Gray shirt with a pocket. Big belt buckle, slacks, and boots. Gun with a heavily worn grip in his holster. He did not look friendly.

He went to the bar, ordered whisky, leaned in and turned to look over the place. No eye contact.

R.J. and I exchanged looks.

R.J. said in a low tone, "He's here for a reason."

"I wonder what."

"Somehow I think we'll find out soon enough."

I left my badge pinned to my belt, a test to see if he was anxious for trouble. He finished his drink and clapped the glass down for a refill. Turned to face the bar, using the bar mirror to watch the place.

R.J. said, "My guess is he's fairly quick with that thing but he's the type that would prefer a sucker shot."

"Why is he here? That's the question."

We extended our coffee break. People came in, had their drinks, and left. A couple took a table and had lunch. Stranger kept getting his drink refilled and he took close notice of everyone that came in.

"Okay, he's looking for someone," said R.J.

"Very good. We know what he's doing. Now why?"

"You don't want to go up and ask him?"

"I don't want to get off on the wrong foot."

Stranger finally took a last look around, still avoiding eye contact with anyone. He threw money on the bar and walked casually out.

"One of us should tail him," said R.J.

"That would be you."

"Right. I'll meet you back at the office."

R.J. showed up at the office a half hour later. He plopped down in his seat and pulled out his pipe. "Ren Shuner. Registered at the hotel. Paid cash up front. Didn't say why he was here. Didn't say where he was from."

"Well, at least we have a name."

"Sometimes paying cash up front is so you can make a fast exit."

The door rattled open. Fantasia entered. She pulled up a chair and sat with us. "What are you two up to?"

R.J. replied, "New gun in town making us nervous."

"Name?"

"Ren Shuner. Heavy man," answered R.J.

"Well, if he shows up at the clinic I'll let you know."

R.J. added, "If he shows up at the clinic it will probably be because one of us sent him there."

Fantasia drew her little mystery magic box out of her purse. "This thing is so crazy. It reads you, dear and you, R.J., but it does not read children. It does not read horses and it does not read all adults, only some. It is truly a mystery box."

R.J. leaned in for a closer look. "Where'd you get it?"

"I found it in my pants leg pocket when we got off the train. I don't know how it got there."

"It's a kid's game, I think."

"A kid's game that can read someone's temperature and blood pressure without touching them."

164

"Really?" replied R.J. "See what I mean about Oldtown being a weird place. Maybe it belonged to one of Alien Andy's strange beings."

"Oh, no; you've set him off, Fan!"

"Maybe he's right!"

"Where are you off to, Fan?"

"A final check of my old office, then it's officially closed and the new medical clinic is formally open."

"God, what an improvement!" declared R.J.

Fantasia stood and smiled as she left.

We kept covert eyes on Ren Shuner for three days. He visited both saloons often. Sat in on poker games sometimes. He did not look for work. He would ride out of town frequently and be gone for several hours, sometimes at dusk.

On day four of his visit something unpleasant happened.

As we stepped out to do our afternoon patrol, Jack and Luke James arrived on a wagon pulled by a team. Jack motioned us over. There was a pack mule tied off to the back of the wagon. In the wagon was a body covered over with a dirty blanket. Jack hopped down and pulled back the blanket for us to see.

It was a gray-haired old man with a beard. The heavy lines in his face formed a perfect expression of death. Jack pulled the blanket down to the man's waist. There was a bullet hole surrounded by blood in the center of his chest.

"R.J. would you go fetch the undertaker and Parth?"

R.J. took a long last look and turned away.

I looked at Jack. Luke watched over us holding the reins.

"What's the story Jack?"

"We went looking for anybody prospecting on our land. This morning we found him stretched out next to a dead fire not far from the south side of the ridge line. We never heard any shots, never saw anybody around who didn't belong with us."

Parth Sharma arrived.

"Is this him, Parth?"

"Yes, Adrian. That's the prospector who brought in the samples."

I asked, "Have you ever seen this guy before, Jack?"

"No. He's a complete stranger to us."

The undertaker came trotting down the boardwalk with two assistants. They took positions at the rear of the wagon.

"I appreciate you bringing him in, Jack." I nodded to the undertaker. "Don't do anything with the body until we've had a chance to take a close look but you can take it."

They pulled the body off the wagon and carried it away. R.J. untied the mule and took it to water.

"You need anything else from us, Sheriff?"

"If we do I'll come out to your place. I'll let you know what we find out about this guy. Thanks again."

Jack climbed back up, took the reins from his brother, and slapped the horses on.

R.J. returned with the mule and asked, "How do you want to handle this?"

"Let's take the mule over to the office, unload everything, then have the livery kid feed and brush him down. We'll have to sort through all this stuff as evidence."

R.J. added, "There's no doubt about cause of death."

I nodded. "Yeah, we have a murder on our hands."

As we were dragging the prospector's packs into the office, Fantasia showed up.

"I saw that wagon. Does someone need medical attention?"

"Not anymore," replied R.J.

"What happened?"

I paused and looked at her affectionately. "He was shot."

"Oh my."

R.J. grunted lugging a sack up onto the boardwalk. "Nothing you can do for him."

"Perhaps I should go and remove the bullet if it's still there."

I said, "The undertaker can do that okay. You don't have to do that."

"But there's a way to identify bullets and guns now you know, by the scratches on the base of the bullet."

I stopped loading. "How do you know that?"

"I read it somewhere but it's just common sense. You find two bullets with the same scratches and you know they came from the same gun. But I'd better go remove the bullet so the undertaker doesn't add scratches to it."

I stood wondering why I hadn't known that and said, "Okay."

"The undertaker will have everything I need. I'll go right now."

I helped Fantasia step up onto the boardwalk. She dashed off.

I looked at R.J.

R.J. said, "She is so smart sometimes she scares me. You ever hear of bullet matching before?"

"Maybe but I can't remember where. Believe me, she scares me too."

We spent two hours sifting through the prospector's gear. Aloysius Pen was his real name. He had family in the coastal cities. They would have to be notified by telegraph. There were no clues in his tools and clothing, no hint as to why he was shot.

"Maybe he went ahead and began carving silver out of that hill and somebody killed him and took his silver," suggested R.J.

"Motive one," I replied. "Got any others?"

"He didn't have a dime on him. Maybe standard robbery?"

"Motive two."

"You're trying to get me to say somebody from the James ranch killed him for trespassing, but I'm not going to say that."

"There's nobody at the James place who would do that."

"Bard Coverton?"

"He's mellowing with age. He wouldn't murder an old man."

"Questions will be asked," said R.J.

I stood and poured coffee. The door rattled open. Fantasia stood in the open doorway. I went to her.

She held up a shot glass for me to see. "Here it is. Bring me bullets from other guns and I'll tell you if any match."

I leaned into her ear and whispered, "I love you so much it hurts."

"Oh, my! I'm all flustered now." She backed out, smiled mischievously, and shut the door.

R.J. asked, "What'd you say to her? I might need to use it someday."

I asked, "Suspects?"

"Just one."

In unison we said, "Ren Shuner."

R.J. added, "He shows up in town wearing a well-used handgun and a few days later there's a murder. Bit of a coincidence wouldn't you say?"

"Fantasia's bullet was from a handgun. I'd sure like to have one of his spent bullets."

"We'd never get a warrant from Nick with what we've got."

"I'm inclined to agree."

R.J. said, "Maybe we can be devious."

"Oh, we're definitely devious."

"He's got to sleep sometime."

I nodded, "Even if we somehow pulled that off it couldn't be used as evidence."

"Yeah, but I if we knew for sure, we could get another bullet the legal way."

"Getting his gun while he's asleep is a bad idea. We'd have to take it out, shoot it, and then put back. Too high a risk. I have a better idea. From now on, anyone playing poker has to check their gun belt with Hugh. New safety regulation."

"I like it."

Three days later we got our chance. With Hugh's help we rushed the gun away from under the bar counter, fired it into a water trough, replaced the spent shell, cleaned the barrel, then replaced the gun in its holster.

An hour after that, Fantasia informed us Shuner's gun was not the murder weapon.

I said, "You realize this means we have to go get samples from every handgun at the James' place."

"Won't we be popular," replied R.J.

That fiasco took all day and was punctuated by different versions of a sour look underlined by off-color mumbling.

Twelve bullet comparisons later, we were informed none of those guns were the murder weapon.

Back out to the James place to make them show us where the prospector's body was found. The campsite was still there. Burro tracks led to the hillside. Tracks from a second lone rider approached the site from the other direction and stopped short, but the sand was so loose they were just smudge marks with no identifiable detail.

In the office we sat contemplating our lack of evidence.

The front door rattled open. It was Judge Nick.

He pulled up a chair and sat at the desk with us. "Okay, boys; what have you got so far on this murder?"

We went through all the steps we'd taken.

"Okay, then, here's what you're going to do. You're going to go out there and arrest Jack James. He's going to stand trial. If he's innocent he'll get off. If he's not I'll take it from there."

I had to contain my anger. "Judge, there is no evidence at all that Jack James did this."

"Oh no? James finds out this man is trespassing on his land and stealing silver and few days later the man is found shot to death. And who brings the body in? Jack James. That's plenty of evidence in my book."

R.J. tried to be reasonable. "Sir, that is all circumstantial. If he was guilty would he have brought the body into town? He could have hidden it and nobody would be the wiser."

Nick persisted, "Or that was to make himself look innocent rather than take a chance on the body being found later on his land."

I held my temper. "Judge, we know Jack James. He didn't kill anybody."

"That's my decision. Now you go out there and pick him up. There will be no bail set."

I shook my head. "I don't think so, Judge."

"You're disobeying an order of the court?"

"I'm obeying the rule of law. There is no evidence that the man is guilty."

"Alright. I'll make other arrangements." The Judge stood, put his hat atop his angry red face and marched out.

170

R.J. looked at me. "What other arrangements?"

"Your guess is as good as mine. But we need to quietly warn Jack James."

# Chapter 15

Three days later we had our answer when a district marshal stepped off the train. He wore a black suit and hat with a vest and tie. His sidearm was partly hidden by his matching jacket. His badge was clipped to the vest inside the jacket. He had a black beard and mustache which went well with dark eyes. He was a killer.

His first stop was to check in with the judge. His second stop was to book a room at the hotel. His last stop was in my office.

"Why did I have to come all the way out here to do your job, Tarn?"

"I'm doing my job. I'm protecting the innocent."

"Tarn, you got motive, means and opportunity. Didn't they teach you anything in sheriff's school?"

"None of those are connected to Jack James. You don't even have the murder weapon."

He smiled. "You mean *you* haven't found the murder weapon. What I have is this search warrant from the judge to search the James property. We'll see, then; won't we? I'm going to need that bullet you took out of the prospector when I get back."

He turned and marched out the door.

R.J. looked at me and rolled his eyes.

"If he finds something out there, I'm going to start smelling a rat."

"He forgot to introduce himself."

"Oh, he introduced himself alright. He just didn't give his name."

R.J. said thoughtfully, "We'll I'm glad some unidentified individual accidentally warned Jack."

"I'd better go get that bullet. Don't want that guy anywhere near my place."

I retrieved the murder bullet from Fantasia and placed it on the desk, still in its shot glass. At dusk there had been no further sign of the district marshal so we closed up and knocked off for the day.

In the morning the badge in black met me at the office door.

"Well lookie lookie what I found. Tucked in between two bales in the James barn but real easy to get to in a pinch. Funny, Mr. James wasn't around anywhere."

He held up a sock with what looked like a six gun in it. I opened the door to let him in. He saw the shot glass and bullet, stepped in and grabbed it.

"Off to the assay office. More trustworthy there I think."

I never said a word to him. He just walked off with his heavy sock and bullet.

Fantasia came up behind me. "So that's him."

I nodded to her. "Do we have any way to be sure he doesn't switch bullets?"

"Yes. I drew a diagram of the bullet's markings. I'd know if they used a substitute."

R.J. joined us. We stood on the boardwalk and watched the district marshal disappear into the assay office.

"I find I am not fond of that man," said R.J.

"What's to like?" I added.

Before I could step back inside, a voice called out, "Sheriff."

We all looked. To my surprise it was Bard Coverton on horseback headed our way with Riley Kit riding alongside him. They pulled up in front of us.

"Sheriff, have you seen Jack in town?" asked Bard.

"No, Bard; I have not."

R.J. shook his head.

"We're a little concerned. Now don't tell that I let on about this but Jack and Luke had a knock down drag out fight last night. Still don't know what it was about. I haven't been able to catch up with Jack ever since. I gotta know if we're still gonna move those cows this week. If you see him would you tell him I'm looking for him?"

"I will, Bard."

"Thanks, Sheriff."

The two rode on.

Fantasia grabbed my arm. "I'm on my way to the general store for a few things, then I'm going to drop this book off for Diya. Do either of you need anything?"

We shook our heads. Fantasia hugged me and headed off. In the office we sat in silence considering everything that was going on.

R.J. said, "Maybe we need to step back and look at this from the bad angle."

"I'm listening."

"Jack James goes looking for the prospector illegally on his land. He's either alone or with somebody from the James Ranch. Eventually he finds the prospector camped out on his property with prospecting tools. He tells the prospector to get off his land. Prospector tells him he's filed a claim, even though he hasn't. They argue. The old man is stubborn. He's got that rusty old long barrel six shooter we found in his stuff. He grabs it and starts waving it around at Jack. Jack tells him to drop it. The old man gets more ornery and tries to scare Jack with the rusty old gun. He levels it at Jack like he's going to shoot. Jack draws and fires. They load up the old man's body, tie off his mule and gear, and bring it in to us."

We sat in silence again.

"If all that happened, all Jack would have had to do is say the old man drew down on him and he was forced to shoot. If he had a ranch hand with him he'd even have a witness. There'd be no reason to lie and cause a murder investigation."

The door rattled open. Parth entered.

"Parth, did that district marshal pay you a visit?" I asked.

"Yes, Adrian. And the death bullet was a match for the gun he found. He's declared the gun he found in Jack's barn was the murder weapon. He left and headed for the newspaper office to have wanted posters printed up for Jack James."

R.J. asked, "How much is the reward?"

"I don't know. He didn't say."

I looked at R.J. "This is what you do when you *want* someone to be guilty whether they are or not."

Parth added, "There does seem to be a rush to judgment here."

R.J. said, "If I was Jack James I sure as hell wouldn't turn myself in."

Parth said, "I've got to get back. If I can be of any help in this please let me know." After a last worried look back, Parth shut the door behind him.

R.J. shook his head in disgust. I rubbed my eyes in frustration.

R.J. said, "We'd better do our walk around."

"Yes. We need to stop in the Bucking Horse. Sal Breva is a good friend of Jack."

We did our patrol and at the south end of town stopped in The Bucking Horse. There was an eternal poker game going on there also and to my surprise the black suited Bert Shrack was sitting in this particular game. It seemed odd the husband of the owner of Candy's was here playing but the group seemed in good spirits and friendly.

At the bar, Sal nodded his greeting. "Coffee for you two?"

"Yes please, Sal."

Sal brought the order and stood by wiping glasses.

"Sal, have you seen Jack James recently?"

"Nope. No sign of him."

R.J. said, "If you happen to see him tell him now's not so good a time to be turning himself in."

Sal kept wiping but replied, "He knows Judge Nick has it in for him and he knows the district marshal is working for the judge."

I said, "We know that gun was planted in Jack's barn but we can't prove it."

Sal said, "Jacks got quite a few way stations out on the open plain for watching over herds. He'd be hard to find right now."

I added, "If you see him, tell him we're working the other side of this scam. Tell him we'll keep you informed."

"Kinda risking your neck and your badge, Sheriff."

"Just doing my job, Sal."

Before he could respond a wide-eyed kid came charging into the saloon. "Sheriff, sheriff, shooting over at Candy's!"

R.J. and I hurried out. Bert Shrack quickly cashed out and followed us but his weight prevented him from keeping up. We passed through people hurriedly leaving Candy's and relocating to the Bucking Horse. A few people were still in front of Candy's.

Inside the scene told the story. On the floor a man in a plaid suit lay dead. A pool of blood still was flowing from his neck area. An ace of hearts was half in and half out of his left sleeve. A two shot mini pistol attached to a spring mechanism was extended out from his right sleeve. The poker players had grouped at the bar staring in repulsion at the scene. I spotted the second gunman almost immediately. His firearm was holstered. He was clean cut in jeans and a work shirt with a dark leather jacket. Short black hair. Blue eyes. In his twenties. He was leaning against the bar staring at the dead man. He was nervous.

I went to the gambler's group and took one aside.

"Tell me about it."

"I can't hear you too good, Sheriff. My ears are still ringing. Damn guns went off right in our faces."

"Who did what?"

"The guy on the floor was dealing under the table. We all knew it. He tried to take a big hand but that fellow over there stopped him and asked him to pull up a sleeve. The cheater told him to go to hell. The young guy wouldn't drop it. He kept insisting. The cheater finally started to figure he wasn't going to get away with it. He stood up popped that little gun out of his sleeve and fired one shot but missed. It was a two shot mini-gun. The young guy drew and fired. *That's* how it all ended up like this."

"Thank you."

I went to the young shooter. R.J. stopped talking to witnesses and joined me. "I need to see your gun, mister."

"It was self-defense, Sheriff."

"I know, but I need to see you gun for the record."

He drew out his handgun. R.J. took it and smelled the barrel and nodded. He opened the cylinder and spun it. "One bullet, Adrian."

"What's your name?"

"Del Travin. Am I in trouble, Sheriff?"

"Doesn't look like it, Del, but you've got to come over to the office with me so I can fill out the paperwork. R.J. will bring your gun with him."

"I didn't have any choice, Sheriff."

"The witnesses seem to agree with you. There was supposed to be a rule that you check your guns at the bar to play poker."

"That lady over there said she was quitting that rule, Sheriff. Nobody checked guns. It's a good thing. That sleeve shooter would have gotten me."

I looked around the room. Candy Shrack was holding tightly to one of her hired hands for comfort. Bert Shrack spotted them and went to her. She broke away from her supportive employee and hugged her husband. I went to them.

"Candy, why did you quit the gun check rule?"

"It was bad for business, Sheriff. Some players don't want to be without them."

"I'm guessing blood on the floor is going to be bad for business too, Candy. There'll be an investigation about this."

Bert Shrack said, "There was no bad intent here, Sheriff. It was what the customers wanted."

I motioned Del Travin to follow and headed out. R.J. stayed to finish talking to the witnesses.

On the way to the office I said, "You know what you should have done, Del?"

"I'm listening, Sheriff."

"As soon as you knew that guy was cheating you should have sent for me. I would have made

178

him pull up his sleeves. He would have gone right to jail. No shots fired."

"I didn't expect him to pull a gun, Sheriff. I didn't think he even had a gun. I thought we were just arguing about the cards up his sleeve. Then it all went down so fast there was no time to think."

"Next time, Del."

"Yes, sir. Next time."

"Now you got to live with a notch on your gun for the rest of your life. Believe me that never goes away."

Del Travin went silent.

We sat in the office filling out the forms. R.J. returned, handed me Del's gun which I handed over to Del.

R.J. said, "I dug the mini-gun bullet out of a planter across the room. It's a miracle it did not hit you, Del."

"I heard the thing whizz by my ear."

"The closest witness said the first shot made the mini-gun jump so badly in the guy's hand that he fumbled it. That's why he didn't get off the second shot."

The door rattled open. In walked Bert Shrack. He handed Del Travin a satchel with money in it. "I spoke with those guys. They tallied up the game. They said you would have won that last hand after the sleeve cards were thrown out. It's twenty, nothing to sneeze at. We're sorry about all this, Sheriff. We'll try to do better."

"Well, thank you for that, Bert."

Bert nodded and left.

"So do I have to hang around, Sheriff?" asked Travin.

"Normally they'd ask you to stick around until all the evidence is looked at but in this case I don't see a problem there. You in a hurry to leave town?"

"I can't stay here. People will be looking at me like I'm a gunslinger."

"Another reason to stay out of gunfights if you can. Remember what I told you about next time, Del."

"I'll remember, Sheriff. There won't be a next time."

# Chapter 16

The district marshal posted wanted signs for Jack James all over town. If seen contact District marshal Ty Ringo. Ringo tried to organize a posse to search but no one would help him. A week later three men rode into town wearing guns along with long rifles attached to their saddles. They looked hired. They booked into the hotel and relaxed at the 'Bucking Horse.

I sent the paperwork on the Travin shooting to the judge. He never said a word about it. Instead he sent down documents proclaiming the James property assets were now frozen by court order until Jack James had been apprehended and a trial held. He also advised us in writing that three contract district deputies had been hired to assist Marshal Ringo and they were not to be interfered with.

The following morning the three were seen at a table in the Bucking Horse having a long chat with Ren Shuner, the gunslinger we'd been keeping an eye on. They rode out of town shortly after in the direction of the James place. R.J. and I watched them head out during our walk around.

Back at the office I was summoned immediately to the bank for some sort of disturbance there. Inside I spotted Luke and Mae James having a meeting in Melda Nick's office. The voices were loud.

I winced and forced myself to step into it.

Luke James looked at me with a pleading expression. "Sheriff, this is absolutely outrageous. We cannot withdraw any cash from the ranch business accounts."

Melda Nick gave a flat smile. "As I've explained to them repeatedly, Sheriff, the judge has put a freeze on all ranch assets in the event Jack James is found guilty of a crime and incurs fines or civil penalties."

Luke raised his hands in frustration. "It's ridiculous, Sheriff. If we need equipment for the ranch we can't draw out the money to buy it. What are we supposed to do?"

Melda was not swayed. "You have accounts with all the merchants in Oldtown, Mr. James. You can charge anything you need until this matter is cleared up."

"But we can't pay the drovers. We can't pay bills that are due."

Melda interrupted. "That's not true, Mr. James. All ranch expenditures can still be paid. Your drovers just have to bring in their wage due statement and sign a receipt. It's the same with your bills. You bring in the bill and the bank will pay the appropriate amount out of your account. This is to stop someone who might be guilty from drawing out all their assets before a verdict is reached."

Luke looked at me and held up his hands for help.

"I sympathize with you Luke, but I'm not in the loop on this. All of this was done without consulting me. I have no say in any of it. You'd have to bring this directly to the judge."

"Oh, great. Try to find *him*." Luke stormed out of the bank dragging Mae with him. I shook my head and left. I stepped outside in time to see Luke and Mae driving away. They were seated as far apart as possible for the show of it.

R.J. walked up, looking back at the departing carriage.

"Trouble in paradise?" he asked.

"Where'd you pick up that phrase?" I asked.

"I think I just made it up. You want to head for Candy's?"

"Sure. It's that time."

We walked the boardwalk checking on all the stores and alleys. It was a busy day of riders and wagons coming and going.

R.J. said, "You know I miss the stage coming in more often."

"Yeah, the railroad made it unprofitable."

We turned into the saloon, paused to check the place out, and took a table out of the way.

Two drovers I recognized, still wearing their chaps, were at the bar celebrating a successful drive. They were cross-country on their way home with money in their pockets. They were drinking some of it.

R.J. said, "I've been going over this James deal in my head. I think there's more to it than just a rush to judgment, as Parth put it."

"You too?"

"First, Parth reports the illegal prospecting and the big silver find. The judge is consulted. A few days later this Ren Shuner guy shows up. Next thing you know the murdered prospector's brought in by Jack. The judge immediately goes after Jack. He doesn't pay any attention at all to Ren Shuner. The judge orders you to arrest Jack. You refuse. A few days later the judge brings in District Marshal Ty Ringo. Almost immediately Ringo finds the murder weapon practically hidden in plain sight. A few more days and three contractor guns show up and are deputized by Ringo. They start hunting for Jack. What do you want to bet if they do bring Jack in, the judge will see to it that it's not a jury trial? He'll turn in the verdict and sentence himself."

"If you're going somewhere with all of this you have my full attention."

"The judge is the common denominator in all of it."

"You think the judge killed the old prospector?"

"No. I think he brought Ren Shuner in to do that."

"I'll play along. Why?"

"Luke and Jack own the ranch and land together, fifty-fifty. All of a sudden now, the bank all but owns Jack's fifty percent of that ranch and land, or at least the bank controls it. What happens if Jack is brought to trial and is found guilty? His assets are subject to fines and civil suits all controlled by the judge and the bank. I think this is all about the silver found on the James' land. I think Judge Nick has a plan to eventually take possession of it. Jack is found guilty. Luke can't pay his bills. A lien is placed against the ranch and land. Closed bidding takes place under the scam that it's to pay off creditors. Judge Nick announces the winning bid. The winning bidder is secretly an associate of Judge Nick. Nick suddenly owns the James land."

"You have a devious mind."

"Thank you. And you know what the worst part of that story is? Most of it is perfectly legal."

The two drovers at the bar interrupted with a, "Yah-hoo!" just for the sake of celebration.

R.J. looked over at them and in a low tone said, "Please be friendly drunks. Please...."

"So how would we screw up the judge's plans?"

"I'm having trouble with that. First, if we could prove Jack was innocent the whole plan would go up in smoke."

"That's a tough one. What else you got?"

"If we could prove Ren Shuner killed the prospector that would be the same thing."

"We'd need a witness or a confession."

"Yes, a witness who saw Shuner shoot the prospector or even a witness who saw Shuner plant the gun."

"There may not be any witnesses. You got anything else at all?"

"If we could find some dirt on Ringo. Or maybe check Shuner out. That would probably slow things down."

"Yeah, I've been thinking of asking Fantasia to go to the library and find me the best government office to wire for information about those guys."

"That might be a start."

The saloon doors swung open. In walked Bard Coverton and Kid Riley. Coverton came to our table. Riley spotted the two drovers and went to the opposite side of the bar. He ordered a beer. Hugh looked at me for approval. I nodded.

"Can I sit for minute?" asked Coverton.

R.J. pulled out a chair.

Coverton rubbed his beard stubble. "It's really getting out of control, Sheriff."

"Where is Bard?" I asked.

"Yesterday at dusk Jack sent a message to Luke to bring him some supplies. Luke is all pissed about something and wouldn't do it. Late that night Jack comes riding in from the darkness, ties off at the supply shed, and goes in with his saddlebags to get some supplies. Luke sees the light and comes out still all pissed off. He goes in and they start yelling at each other. Luke's real mad cause his name's not on the ranch cash account. Jack is yelling back that he's got more things to worry about than Luke whining. It goes on and on. The two of them get to fighting. It's an all-out brawl. It goes on for a good ten minutes or so. Finally Jack knocks Luke out. Jack fills up his saddle bags and rides away. About an hour later these three hired guns show up looking for Jack. Luke tells them he doesn't know where he is. It's too dark for tracking. At first sun the three of them are back. They ride off following Jack's trail. I don't think it will get them anywhere. Jack's way too smart for that."

One of the drovers, in too loud a drunken voice, distracted us. "He must be skipping school!"

The two drovers laughed loudly.

R.J. said, "Oh, brother. Here we go."

The first drover replied, "If his mama knew he was in here he'd get a whippin'."

They both laughed again.

One of them added, "Is that right, boy? Will your mama tan your hide if she catches you in here with the real men?"

Riley continued to drink his beer and ignore them.

R.J. looked at me. "I think it might be time."

Coverton's eyes were locked on the drovers. He started to stand. I put a hand on his shoulder and pressed him back down. "We don't want to make this look like we're rescuing the kid."

R.J. said, "I see your point."

I pushed my chair back to get up, but not in time.

"Does your mama even know you're here, little boy?"

Riley had enough. He turned to face the loudmouth and to my dismay replied, "Nope. But yours does."

The entire saloon went silent. Hugh became a statue holding a glass and cloth. The poker game froze. The silent expectation was that the drovers would laugh it off. Riley looked dead serious. It took the drovers a good full minute to

186

understand what Riley had just said. It gave me time to get halfway there.

As I held up one hand stop the confrontation, the first drover's face turned bright red. He slapped at his gun and started to pull it. There was a echoing bang and a puck mark appeared in the drover's chest. The second drover flinched and drew. A second loud bang made everyone jump again in their seats. A bullet mark appeared in the shoulder of the second drover. It snapped the gun out of his hand. It bounced on the floor and turned in place. The man grabbed his shoulder. Red appeared between his fingers. The first drover slowly slid against the bar and settled to the floor.

No one said a word. Keeping an eye on the kid I went to the man on the floor. He was dead. As I stood, Riley tucked his gun back in the holster. The poker group started cashing in and leaving. Hugh nervously resumed cleaning glasses. R.J. came alongside. Coverton went to the kid and spoke to him in a near whisper.

The drover with the bullet in his shoulder was now wide awake and dazed.

I looked at R.J. "Want to take him to Fantasia?"

R.J. nodded, took the man by the good arm, and led him away. I picked up both guns from the floor.

Candy Shrack appeared in a back doorway. Her face quickly turned bright red with anger. Her husband Bert left the card game and went to her.

I went to Riley and Coverton.

Riley asked, "Is he dead, Sheriff?"

"Yeah, he's dead, Riley."

"Should I have drawn on him?"

"I had a clear view of it, Riley. He would have shot you dead if he could have."

"I didn't think he'd go for his gun. I thought we were just bad mouthing."

"You gotta come down to the office with me. I've got to fill out a crap load of paperwork."

"Am I in trouble, Sheriff?"

"Only your reputation is, Riley."

"How do you mean?"

"You just outdrew two drovers and neither one of them even got their gun all the way out of the holster. That story may follow you around some."

Riley looked at Coverton for support. Coverton slapped him on the arm and said, "Nothing here to be ashamed of, son."

I gestured Riley toward the door. Coverton followed close behind. At one point he leaned in and said, "Holy crap. You were right."

As we headed for the office Riley said, "Maybe I could have walked out of there."

"I don't think they would have let you walk away, Riley. They were bar room brave," said Coverton.

"That man was stupid, Sheriff."

I nodded. "He didn't think you had any chance against him."

"I need an outhouse bad, Sheriff."

"There's one down that alley behind the lawyer's office."

We went to it. I stood outside and listened to the sounds of someone being sick.

Riley came out still wiping his mouth. We walked.

"This wasn't your first gunfight was it?"

"No. But it's the first one somebody died."

"What happened last time?"

"Big guy said he was going to spank me in front of the whole town for wearing a gun. I told him another step and he'd be limping home. He went for his gun. Bullet caught him in the hip. He was okay. Never did bother me again."

"There will always be those kind, Riley."

"How do you keep out of it?"

"You do your best and sometimes you can't."

"What will you do about the other guy, Sheriff?" asked Riley.

"My guess is he'll be getting on home leading his friend's body along behind him and wondering all the way why they did what they did."

"What do you think I ought to do?"

"I'd say just lay low for a while until this blows over a bit."

"Trouble sure can have a way of finding you."

"Yep."

## Chapter 17

For the rest of the week we watched the Ringo gang joined by Ren Shuner head out on horseback, in search of Jack James. On one or two occasions they took overnight gear and did not return until morning. New wanted posters went up around town. This time the reward was two thousand.

R.J. and I sat in the office trying to come up with ways to stop the travesty of justice that was happening right in front of us.

"Who the heck put that kind of money up to bring Jack James in?" asked R.J.

"It worries me to think about it," I replied.

"It must be the judge himself. He figures he'll get it back later."

"Not much we can do until we get word from the coastal city offices about that gang."

A discordant noise began to leak through the poorly hung front door. It grew louder and louder. We rolled over in our chairs to look out the windows.

A three-piece marching band whose members had probably not learned to tune their instruments together went high stepping by in ragged band clothes. A scattered following of townspeople were close behind. They were all headed for the train station.

R.J. looked at me. "We gotta go check this out. It's bound to be good."

We stepped outside and watched from the boardwalk. When the street was clear we followed them.

At the station, smoke from the approaching train billowed above the treetops. The band took a position on the platform and played continuously although one of the overweight members seemed to be running out of breath. The engine passed us by, slowed, and crept to a stop. A conductor hopped down the steps and turned to help what promised to be a VIP off the passenger car.

Four attractive young women in blossoming hoop skirts squeezed out the compartment doors and lined up in front of the crowd. They synched up with the out of tune music and began kick dancing for the crowd. There was cheering and a single person throwing confetti.

Candy Shrack pulled up with a two-horse wagon and motioned to the girls. They line danced over to the carriage and climbed in. The band played to applause as Candy drove the girls away toward the saloon. After a few more discordant notes the band broke up. The crowd scattered.

Throughout the afternoon the town became busier than normal. With monumental effort a banner was strung up by the Colton brothers that read, "DANCE HALL NIGHT AT CANDY'S." An elixir salesman in a banner-covered wagon rolled into town for the event. A few people started drinking early and ended up missing the show. This first event was advertised as free but the bar was open. No less than three bartenders were on hand, one of which was Candy, dressed as a dance girl. We had to bring in four extra deputies. Two inside and two at the door. It was easy to find volunteers. It was like a free ticket to the show.

Tunes from the new piano rang out late in the afternoon. People were showing up from quite far away. R.J. and I tried to take the whole thing in stride. Fantasia set up the medical clinic to receive patients late.

The evening show began to thunderous applause and cheering. Dance hall girls kicking high to loud piano. There were two celebratory gun shots into the ceiling. The offenders were taken away to jail. It was a riotous but successful town party with Fantasia treating overdoses and superficial wounds from falls and brief fights.

The next morning the town was very quiet with very little activity. It would take two days to clean up the trash.

R.J. and I walked the boardwalks the morning after. As we neared the trash in the street, a rider appeared in the distance heading into town. He rode past us without acknowledgment. He had an expensive saddle and bridle. Long gun with an engraved stock attached to his saddle. His clothes were dusted but new looking. A Bandana hung from his neck. His hat looked equally high quality. His six gun had a black pearl grip. He tied off at the hotel and went in.

R.J. crossed over. "He missed the party."

"I don't think that's why he's here."

"Bounty hunter?"

"Good guess now that the reward is jacked up to two thousand."

"God, what a circus. There's something else, too. On some of these wanted posters I've been seeing DOA at the bottom. Dead or Alive."

"Yeah, I don't think the judge has the authority to do that."

"What can we do?"

"I'll send another wire off to the District Manager's office but by the time that gets through the bureaucracy it'll probably be too late."

Back at the office R.J. asked, "You want to let the ceiling shooters out?"

"Yeah, they're as hung over as the rest of the town. They started early."

R.J. unlocked the cells and ushered the two out, handing them their gun belts as they went out the door. As R.J. sat, the door rattled open again.

The town's newest bounty hunter entered. "Sheriff, name's Dude Banks. Any idea where I might find this man?" Banks dropped a wanted poster for Jack James on my desk.

I replied, "A district marshal has been here looking for him for weeks. Does that answer your question?"

"I tend to be luckier than most, Sheriff."

"He's probably a hundred miles from here, traveling."

"He's got a ranch and wife here, Sheriff. Patience is part of this game."

"If I were you, I wouldn't put too much stock in the DOA on that poster, Mr. Banks. It hasn't been sanctioned."

"I appreciate the warning, Sheriff. Makes my job a little tougher though, don't it?"

Banks nodded to R.J., turned, and left.

R.J. said, "He must be pretty successful all decked out like he is."

"I would bet he doesn't live a long life. Someday he'll catch up to a wanted man whose gang is still together and they'll be wanting that fancy saddle and hardware."

The door rattled open.

The telegraph operator stepped in. "Sheriff, I got an answer to that telegram you sent asking about district marshal Ringo. It's a funny answer." He placed the telegram on the desk.

### 'WITH REGARD TO TY RINGO LAW ENFORCEMENT STATUS (stop) PLEASE SEND BADGE NUMBER. EOM'

I nodded to the operator. He nervously exited.

R.J. leaned over and read the message. "He's right. That's kind of strange. They must *know* his badge number."

"How the hell are we supposed to get his badge number? Walk up and ask for it?"

R.J. thought for a moment. "I'll bet he takes comfort with ladies of the night sometimes."

"Are you sure? The man is like a robot."

"I shall make a few discreet inquiries."

I shook my head. "I wish I knew what this telegraph means."

"Something is up at the home office. You can bet on that."

We both stared down at the message trying to see something more in it.

R.J. said, "You know, maybe we should send a letter directly to the ruling council and tell them what Nick is up to."

"I've thought about that. But we'd be telling them this long ugly story of what we think Judge Nick has planned with no evidence and with him not having done anything illegal. All that would do is make us look bad."

R.J. rubbed his chin thoughtfully. "Well, I'm going to get that badge number somehow. I'll tell you that much."

We sat in thought.

I said, "It was a hell of a celebration last night. I'll say that much."

R.J. laughed. "The gossip was flying."

"Like what?"

"Well, Candy Shrack danced and sang and was carried off stage by two cowboys, waving her handkerchief to the crowd as she went while her husband Bert was in the back room working on the books."

"Might still be innocent...."

"Luke and Mae James sat together trying to look apart but apparently it wasn't working."

"God, while her husband, an innocent man, is out on the run."

"Yeah, and Melda Nick was there with the bank janitor who was supposed to be acting as her personal assistant except he was getting way too familiar. The Judge did not attend."

"Of course the Judge wasn't there. He's got other things going on."

"Oh yeah, fast gun Kit Riley was there not wearing his gun and being held onto by one of the young dancers. They left the place together later on."

"You really do get all the gossip, don't you?"

"It's easy. All you have to do is listen carefully."

"So what else can we do about this frame-up of an innocent man?"

R.J. shook his head. "I thought about us bringing him in and locking him up for safety, but Judge Nick could override anything we did at that point. We'd probably be signing his death warrant."

"So we'll have to get that badge number and hope there's a flaw in Nick's little arrangement."

"I'm sure Grace at the hotel will be willing to help us."

I said, "We'd better act fast. This thing is dragging on too long."

"Now might be a good time to take our walk around. I know the Ringo gang rode out early this morning. It should be clear."

So we took another Main Street patrol walk. At the entrance to the hotel I waited outside while R.J. went in. The street was still dead. Payment for partying. As I waited, I caught sight of Sal Breva, the Bucking Horse saloon bartender, headed my way. He walked up and looked around nervously.

"Sheriff, we got a problem."

"What do you need, Sal?"

"I saw Jack James last night. He was waiting for me at my place. Took a real big chance comin' in here."

"Yeah, he did."

"He took a rifle bullet in the shoulder trying to lose Ringo's men. A shot in the back. He needs the doctor."

"Where is he?"

"He's holed up in the far south hills. There's a cave there. He's got it all set up. He blocked it in with stones so no one can see it. He's asking if you'll bring the doctor out there. He'll be watching and will signal you with a mirror when he sees you."

"Why didn't he just come to the medical office?"

"Ringo's men think they may have hit him. They're watching the doctor's place."

"I'll take care of it, Sal. Thanks."

Sal gave a long worried look and hurried off.

R.J. returned. "Apparently Ringo does not employ ladies of the night. Damn strange. But Grace said the cleaning girl will help us. Ringo leaves his gun and badge on the dresser at night. She thinks if she cleans early she can get a look at the badge."

"So maybe tomorrow?"

"With a little luck."

On the way back to the office I filled R.J. in on Sal Breva's visit.

R.J. said, "Damn. Now he's being hunted with a bullet in him. How you going to get Fantasia out there without being seen? You got Ringo, his gang, Ren Shuner who's probably the real killer, and now fancy pants bounty hunter Dude Banks. We are getting real outnumbered here."

"I have a plan."

"You always do."

"I've got that sea captain's spyglass in my desk. I should be able to clear the open desert before turning toward those hills. They're watching the medical office and our place so we can't use our own horses. We want them all grazing peacefully in the pasture. You go quietly down to the livery and give the kid there a full silver to keep his mouth shut. Tell him if he talks we'll return to take the money back. Have him saddle up two horses and take them out the back way. Bring them around back of our office and tie them off. I'll have Fantasia walk down to the library. She spends hours there sometimes. You and I will go out back to the shooting range. I'll take the horses along behind the buildings to the library. You start your target practice. Use two different guns make it sound like there's two of us shooting. When she's sure there's nobody watching, Fantasia will come out the back door where I'll be waiting with the horses. We'll ride out to the east until we're out of sight of the town then zigzag our way toward the south hills. When we're close enough I'll begin clearing around us with the spyglass. We'll keep zigzagging until we pick up Jack's mirror signal. We'll come back the same way."

"And you accuse me of being devious."

"Some of you must be rubbing off on me."

"You going now?"

"No choice. He could be bleeding out. You head back to the office. I'll go fill Fantasia in."

"I'll try to have the horses waiting when you get here."

Fantasia was in the medical office. She listened to the plan intently. "We need to go now. You understand that, don't you?"

I asked, "How can we bring your medical kit along without being obvious?"

"I'll simply put it in my book bag."

"You know who to look for to see if you're being watched?"

"Of course."

I stepped close to her and kissed her. "I'll see you behind the library."

"That's not quite payment enough."

"IOU?"

"I'll collect later."

I waited in the office for R.J. to show. He entered from the back.

R.J. said "I found an old set of long saddlebags in the closet back there. I've packed them with all the supplies I could find."

"Are we ready?"

"Horses are back there waiting."

"Okay, don't start shooting until I've walked them away. We don't know those horses."

I took a minute to fill the empty bullet loops in my gun belt. We checked out the front door for anyone coming then went out the back. The horses were cinched up. I mounted the buckskin gelding and left the bay mare for Fantasia.

R.J. looked up at me and said, "Pray you don't run into Melda Nick and her janitor out behind the bank again."

"Please don't ever put that image back in my head."

R.J. laughed and checked his revolvers. He handed me the lead line for the mare and stepped back. I turned my horse toward the back of the next building and urged him on. When we were far enough away I heard R.J.'s target shooting begin.

There was no one behind the bank or the feed store. There were crates and other obstacles to wind around before reaching the library. Glimpses down alleyways leading to Main Street showed no one out and around. Behind the library I leaned back and held the lead line, waiting.

It was a twenty-minute wait. Fantasia finally appeared and gave me a wink. She tied off her book bag to the horn on her saddle, vaulted on, then tied off the lead line and adjusted her reins. I pointed eastward and with a little distance between us and the library we went into a canter.

When the trees and brush cleared, Fantasia came up beside me and we cantered in unison together. The worrisome, somewhat desperate ride somehow suddenly became pure joy. A rocking horse canter with a beautiful woman running alongside me. We reached out and held hands just to prove we could do it. The horses seemed to pick up on the pleasure of it and stayed in synch.

The horses made the decision when to slow to a walk. I pulled out the spyglass and did my best to check behind and around us without stopping.

Fantasia asked, "How bad was he?"

"I don't really know. He must have been able to make the long ride to Sal's to ask for help, but at the same time he must need help pretty badly to take a chance doing that."

"Is it just a shoulder?"

"That's what I was told. What are his odds?"

"No way to tell. He could have a nicked artery, broken shoulder bones, or both. He can't be bleeding too badly to have made it that far."

We made our zigzags, getting closer to the far hills with each leg. Stops at the end of each leg to study behind us gave no indication we were being followed. We kept on running roughly parallel to the hills until we were as close as I dared to get. On the third eastern leg Fantasia spotted the glint of a mirror.

After a last careful spyglass check we rode fast to the light reflections. Up a shallow embankment covered by scrub brush brought us to Jack James, standing in front of a partially opened cave entrance. He motioned us to bring the horses inside the cave with us.

The cave looked more like a tunnel system. It was large enough to drive a covered wagon through. The entrance had been covered over and concealed a very long time ago. Only a portion of it had been opened up to gain entry.

Jack had set himself up quite well for long-term hiding. He had lanterns, supplies, his bed roll, and a water and feed bucket for his horse. His arm was in a sling. He looked a bit ragged. It looked like he had been clipping his beard to keep it short.

Fantasia went right to work while I unpacked the fresh supplies.

She had him sit on a flat stone while she removed the sling and he wrestled out of his shirt.

"I broke this arm a while back cause of a bad-mannered cow on the end of my lasso."

Fantasia gently removed a sloppy bandage Jack had wrapped around the wound. "Oh, yes, I see."

"How bad is it, ma'am? It hurts like fire."

"Just hold on a second." Fantasia drew her magic box from her bag and pointed it at the wound. She made a "Tsk," sound and put it away. She pressed all over Jack's shoulder and studied his reaction carefully. "You may not believe this Jack," she finally said.

200

"The bullet's in there and bone's broken somewhere right?"

"No on both counts," replied Fantasia. "It's just a long flesh wound. The bullet nearly missed you completely. It just barely passed by your shoulder blade and cut though a three–inch line of epidermal layer. It's not very deep but this kind of wound is like being skinned alive. It is more painful than a direct bullet wound and it bleeds like a deep cut."

"Are you saying I'm not hurt bad? I been carrying on like a stupid child?"

"I wouldn't say that. You couldn't get a good look at this being on your back as it is. All you knew was great pain and bleeding. If we hadn't come the chance of you getting an infection from this would have been high. You could have ended up with a high fever or worse. It's a deep enough cut that I need to stitch it. But there do not appear to be any breaks in your shoulder or arm, so that should do it."

Fantasia began laying out tools on a cloth next to Jack.

"What is this place, Jack?" I asked.

"Your guess is as good as mine, Sheriff. I knew about it from Jeck Higgs before he left town. Old Jeck had a lot of wild-ass stories but this cave wasn't one of them. This thing goes way the hell into the hill. I don't know how far. It's an escape route for me but I've never been down it."

Fantasia asked, "Okay, are you ready, Jack? I need to sterilize this wound. It's not going to feel good."

"Doctor it can't feel much worse than it already does."

Fantasia tipped her bottle onto cloth and began dabbing Jack's gunshot wound. He winced repeatedly but refused to groan.

"Okay, now I'm going to give you a couple shots to numb the area before we pull it together and stitch it up. Here goes."

Jack did some more wincing.

Fantasia said, "Adrian, rinse your hands in this alcohol and come be my clamps."

I took the bottle from her and knelt beside her. "I have not clamped before."

"You just have to squeeze the skin together to close up the wound. Hold it tight and I'll put in the sutures."

"If this hurts, don't hold it against me Jack," I said.

"I give you my word," replied Jack.

I squeezed. Fantasia stitched.

Between winces, Jack asked, "So what's the story out there, Sheriff? Am I as good as hung?"

I brought him up to date and added explanations of why it was all happening.

"This is a nightmare, Sheriff. I few weeks ago I was running a successful cattle ranch. I had a beautiful wife and a good place to lay my head. Now, almost overnight, suddenly my damn brother wants to sue me for control of the ranch. My wife is cold as ice. And, I'm a wanted man for something I didn't do and I can't even turn myself in 'cause I won't get a fair trial. How does this happen? It's like I went to sleep and woke up in a different world."

"It's greed, Jack. That prospector found a pure vein of silver on your land. We weren't allowed to tell you about that. That's what all this is really about."

Fantasia said, "All set, Jack. You're stitched. Let me just clean this up and bandage it and you're good to go."

I said, "We're working on this crap, Jack. Somehow we'll bring all this out."

"If they don't hang me first."

"I'll turn outlaw before I let that happen, Jack. Count on it."

Fantasia asked, "Jack, do you want us to try to make a few more supply deliveries to you out here?"

"No thank you, ma'am. It's much safer for me to go get them. More chance of two riders being seen coming out here, than me sneaking out. I'm set up pretty good. Only problem is I got enough grain and water for my horse but he's not getting any hay or grass. I'm worried about him comin' down with colic but there's nothing I can do about that now. Anyway you two have done more than you should have. I'm in your debt."

Fantasia began packing her medical kit.

"Jack, I'm going to step out and do a thorough check of the area with the spyglass. If it looks okay, we'll pull the horses out quick and run along the ridgeline a ways before turning north."

"That should cover me, Sheriff. I'll be packing stone back into the opening once you're out."

"Yeah, this place is impossible to spot from the valley. We'd never have found you except for the flashes."

"I'm counting on that, Sheriff."

We cleared the horizon and made our dash away from the hidden cave. When we were far enough we walked to cool the horses.

Fantasia said, "That cave is not a natural formation."

"You're right, too smooth and well formed."

"They must have been planning to run the railroad through there but changed their minds."

"That death valley beyond must have been too much even for the railroaders."

Fantasia thought for a moment. "I'd sure like to see that stretch of desert."

"Well, once this mess is all over we could come back and follow that tunnel through to the other side."

"That would be fun."

We made our way back to the rear of the library. Fantasia slid off, grabbed her bag, and handed me the lead line. She gave a last wave after checking inside the back door to be sure the coast was clear. Through the alleyways I could see the town was slowly coming back to life. Behind the jail I tied off the horses and went inside.

R.J. was reading a book and smoking his pipe. He sat up at the sound of the door closing. "How'd it go?" he asked with great interest.

I looked around to be sure we were alone. "It was a bad flesh wound. Needed stitches."

"How is he holding up?"

"A little beat but okay considering what he's going through. Anything happening here?"

"They're all still too hung over or party weary. It's been quiet."

"You want to sneak those horses back so I can get cleaned up?"

"Sure thing."

"Pay the livery kid to give them a good brush down and some feed, okay?"

"Okay."

Later that afternoon we started thinking about closing up early. The town was still running slow.

R.J. said, "I need to return this book to the library. Time to find another one on Oldtown mysteries."

"Take your time. I'll close up here in a little bit."

I cleaned up and started clearing my desk and locking away private paperwork, wondering what else I might do to help with Jack James' plight.

The door rattled open. It was the town's visiting bounty hunter, Dude Banks.

"Sheriff, I need a moment of your time."

I sat back and folded my hands together.

He leaned forward at the desk and in a flash a hand came up and sprayed a mist in my face and kept on spraying. I managed to grip my chair armrests to stand but the world went black.

When my eyes opened I was still in my chair but my hands were tied tightly behind me, fastened to the back of the chair. Banks was seated opposite me using his side of the desk to play solitaire. He looked up and noticed I was awake.

"Ah, finally. I gave you too big a dose."

My voice cracked as I asked, "What the hell was that?"

"Dentist vapors. They use it to knock you out for a bad tooth."

"Why?"

"Well, I told you I was luckier than most, but really it's that I'm smarter than most."

I carefully tested the ropes. They were tight. The knot was tight. He had been careful. But one of the wooden slats in the chair back had been fractured in a fight with a prisoner long ago. I could just get my fingernails into the crack and work at it. I managed to peel it free which left me with a small, pointed stick to work on the knot with.

Banks continued celebrating himself. "Word is James was wounded by Ringo's goons. So I paid a couple kids to keep an eye on your place and the livery. The kids never saw any horses leave town, but one of them said two horses were getting brushed down and fed for some reason. There'd only be one reason to do that, Sheriff.

Those horses must have been run. And who would want to sneak out of town like that? Only one I know would be the doctor going out to treat Jack James. And why would she take two horses? Only cause her old man was riding with her for protection."

I could get the point of the wood chip into the knot's joint. It was loosening. It had to be done very carefully so as not to break the wood. Appearing to be motionless was equally difficult.

"I don't know anything about any horses. Mine are back at the ranch. You got the wrong guy, Banks."

"No, no, no, Sheriff. There's fresh hoof prints out back of the jail. No sense in denying it. I could maybe follow those but I'm betting you would have made that too hard."

"What do you want, Banks?"

"Oh, come now. I'm giving you a break. I could have gone to your place and gotten this information from your betrothed, sir."

A flash of anger made me pause to collect myself. "I asked you what you want."

"I'll bet there's blood on bandages in her medical kit. She wouldn't be able to deny it either."

Extra motivation pushed the wooded piece through the joint in the rope.

"Where is he, Sheriff?"

"I tell you that and you're just going to walk out of here and go get him?"

Banks gave a flat smile. He shuffled his cards. "Not exactly, Sheriff. You're going to be accidentally killed cleaning your gun. Where do you keep your cleaning kit by the way?"

A few more levering movements were needed on the knot.

"So why the hell would I tell you if you're just going to kill me?"

"Because Sheriff, if you don't tell me I'll kill you anyway and get the information from your wife after which I'll have to kill her also. This way she gets to live on thinking her husband was accidentally killed cleaning his gun. It happens all the time."

I could just barely get one fingertip inside the knot. I realized my gun was still in my holster. Vain men make mistakes.

"How would you explain her death?"

"Suicide from the loss of her one true love."

The knot opened up. I twisted it apart and quietly lowered the rope to the floor. My hands were free. I kept them behind me.

Banks continued to shuffle his cards feeling like he had the world on a string. His gun was still holstered.

It would have been awkward to try to draw my gun while still seated. Instead, as he looked down at his cards, I put one hand on the armrest and stood, keeping the other hand on my holster.

With my first inch up from the chair, Banks jumped to his feet and exclaimed, "Shit!"

We were now face to face six feet apart. If I drew on him he'd be forced to reciprocate.

I said calmly, "Unbuckle your gun belt and let it drop to the floor."

"Sheriff, you don't think I'd leave a loaded gun in your holster, do you?"

It was his only play but it was a bad one. If I gave up he'd already told me he was going to kill me. So if my gun was empty I'd die either way but it wasn't going to look like any gun cleaning accident.

Still trying to keep the situation calm I said, "Even with a bullet in me I'll come over this desk and be all over you, Banks. Drop your gun belt."

"So I have two choices, Sheriff. Go to prison for sure, or kill you and stay free. It's an interesting gamble isn't it? I kill you then I find out where James is from your wife. You kill me and the James' hideout stays a secret. Yes, an interesting throw of the dice indeed."

"You just told me my gun's loaded, Banks. Drop your gun belt and I'll let you live."

He went for it.

My hand and arm jerked up with a deafening bang. My draw was too quick. The shot went slightly high. A small black spot appeared on Bank's throat. His gun fired into the floor. We stood in a frozen moment of ears ringing. He stared at me trying to understand his condition. He opened his mouth. I think it was his intention to make some sarcastic compliment. A choking noise was all that would come out. His knees buckled and he went straight down and ended up in a hunched sitting position against the wall, his head resting back against it, his gun still lying in his open hand.

I sat back down. For some reason I gathered up the piece of rope on the floor and put it in the desk drawer. No reason for someone to trip on that.

Oddly enough, the gunshots did not attract anyone. All that target practice behind the jail.

I sat for a long time trying to get my heartbeat back to normal. The man who had once been Dude Banks and I had a long silent conversation about the value of life and someone trying to take yours from you. His eyes were frozen open staring right at me. They say when you die the last looks you get are very important to you. When the faint tremors in my chest had faded away, I had to get up and walk to the undertaker's place. He was uplifted by the offer of more new business. He gathered his two cohorts and raced out ahead of me. I called to him to lock up after they cleaned up the place.

I went home.

## Chapter 18

I got up late the next morning, making sure not to wake Fantasia. I took my time cooking eggs, bacon, and toast and served it to her in bed. There was still some subconscious fear way down deep from the threat Banks had made. She devoured her eggs but kept looking at me with a narrow stare, knowing something had happened. On my walk down the street to the office R.J. met me in front of the East Inn. We walked and talked.

"What the hell happened yesterday and how did I manage to miss it?"

"Believe me, you were in the right place."

"What happened?"

"There's an old saying but I don't remember where I heard it. Somebody left the door open and the wrong dog came home."

"What does that mean?"

"Dude Banks picked up on our little excursion yesterday and wanted to cash in."

"You mean with a gun?"

"Yep."

"Is James' secret safe?"

"It's in the hole with Dude Banks."

"Holy crap. So the undertaker has cleaned up?"

"Yep."

"I thought the place smelled like pine. That means the whole town knows."

"Yep."

"You gonna tell me what happened?"

"Soon as my heart drops back down out of my throat."

"So it was a bitch?"

"It got personal."

"Well, one less asshole to deal with. That leaves the Ringo five."

"For some reason I'm starting to get the feeling we're going to be facing off with those guys before this is over."

In the office I plunked down at the desk. R.J. stood looking around for signs of death.

"So where?" he asked.

"Just about where you're standing."

"He get a shot off?"

"Look down."

R.J. searched and found the new hole in the floor. "I'll dig that out later." He looked up at me with a fretful stare. "You want to at least tell me why it was personal?"

"If I lost the draw, he was going to kill Fantasia."

R.J. expression turned to dark anger. He went to the storage shelves in the hall and began straightening up. I fidgeted with blank incident forms.

The front door rattled open.

Judge Nick entered. As usual his dark vest was close to popping buttons. "They've taken the body away already?"

I nodded.

"That man had some expensive hardware. We need to gather that up and turn it over to the town treasury. Make sure you see to that, Sheriff."

I narrowed my stare. "Judge, I donated the shit. Find one of *your* grunts to do the dirty work."

His expression turned from curious to stolid. He opened the door and marched out.

R.J. said from the hall, "Didn't even ask why it happened or if you had any new holes in you."

R.J. came back to the desk and read over my shoulder as I documented the incident. "What did you tell Fantasia?"

"Only that someone needed shooting. Let's leave it at that, okay?"

"Absolutely."

The door rattled open. One of the Colton brothers stuck his head in. "Sheriff, the elixir salesman has been taking too much of his own medicine. He hooked a wheel up on the boardwalk and turned his carriage over. It's blocking Main."

"Thanks. We'll be right there."

R.J. said, "You want me to handle this? You need a break."

"I don't think it's all that safe for us out there. Anything could be a setup these days. Let's go."

But the Colton brother had it right. The elixir wagon was on its side with the horse still in harness standing there kind of looking annoyed. The elixir salesman was walking around with frequent staggers moaning, "Oh, the injustice of it."

I went to unhitch the horse and paused to look him over. "When's the last time this horse was out of harness?"

The horse suddenly took notice of me. The salesman looked over and yelled, "Oh, the injustice of it."

I started unhooking the horse and waved a couple kid onlookers over. "You boys help me take the harness off this gelding, then you take it down to my place put it in a stall and tell the doc it needs looking at right away." I flipped them both a coin. A few minutes later we had the harness on the ground and the horse being led away by a rein thrown around his neck. He seemed happy to be out of the leather and happy to be going anywhere else.

The salesman came up to me to speak but seemed unable to form words. He swayed a little and just stood there in defiance.

I said, "You're under arrest, sir."

He managed, "Why?"

"Drunk and disorderly and maybe later animal abuse."

R.J. grabbed his arm and hauled him away.

I helped right the carriage. Kids picked up the harness and stuck it in the back. The Colton brothers pulled the thing into an alley. Elixir was leaking out everywhere. Oldtown life returned to normal.

Back at the office R.J. and I regrouped to do our daily walk around.

"R.J., it's time we started keeping an eye on the upstairs windows."

"You mean to watch for the errant rifle barrel?"

"Exactly."

"You want the left side or the right side?"

"Your choice."

We walked the boardwalks. Oldtown was bustling again. The dressmaker was unwinding material for a customer in the front window of her store. There was a line waiting at the feed store. The general store was too busy for the single cashier. Two carriages with women driving went by. Tired trail hands rode in and tied off at the Bucking Horse only because it was the first saloon they came to. The hazy sky cast thin, double shadows. No upstairs curtains had been pulled back for the purpose of sighting a rifle.

We went into Candy's for our daily dose of coffee. Candy was no longer bartending. She was now dressed as a dance hall girl. She was seated on the lap of one of two cowboys at a middle table. Bert Shrack was not far away, his back to her, his focus on the cards in his hand.

Candy spotted us, jumped up and came to me. "Sheriff, you protected us from another bad man. How can we ever repay you?" Candy's voice had suddenly taken on a strong musical accent. She pushed up against me and grabbed one arm. "There must be some way to reward you, Sheriff."

I tried to ease back but she stuck like glue. R.J. began to smirk and went to a table to sit. I gave him a pleading stare for help. He smirked some more.

"Sheriff, we should put a special table in back just for you with no one around to bother you."

The thought of being trapped alone with Candy frightened me. I gently took both her arms intending to separate us. It was at that particular moment Fantasia came waltzing through the swinging doors and spotted me holding Candy tightly against me.

R.J. broke out in loud laughter.

Fantasia huffed at us and her expression changed to one of determined anger.

Candy saw Fantasia and eased away, quickly taking refuge back on the lap of the cowboy.

R.J. laughed out loud again.

Fantasia came to me and without saying a word demanded to know what was going on.

"I was abducted against my will."

She took my arm, led me to R.J.'s table and we sat.

"What brings you here at this most entertaining of moments, Fan?" asked R.J. still smirking.

"Diya wants to return my book. I'm inviting her to dinner with us tonight. You, too. R.J., Candy is not invited."

R.J. snickered.

In desperation I said, "I'm completely innocent. Ask R.J."

"Oh, I wouldn't go that far," replied R.J. and though he tried to choke back a laugh he couldn't.

Candy crossed the room and took a seat on the lap of one of her husband's playing partners. Bert seemed to pay no mind to it.

To my relief Hugh brought the coffees.

I sipped dutifully.

Fantasia remarked, "What a flirtatious spirit. I see she's cheating on you already."

"She's not cheating on me. There is no me."

R.J. snickered.

"Oh, will you stop it! You know what happened. Tell her."

R.J. teased, "Who am I to destroy a budding romance?"

"Oh, for God's sake."

Fantasia finally said, "It's alright, dear. We'll talk about this later tonight."

R.J. raised his eyebrows and sipped.

Diya appeared from the back carrying a book. She came to us and placed it gently on the table. "Thank you so much, Fantasia. It was very interesting."

"I'm glad you liked it. Come to dinner tonight so we can discuss it."

"I'd love to but I want to come early and help you in the kitchen."

"Fine. Whenever you can make it."

We could all feel Candy giving Diya the evil eye.

"See you all tonight," said Diya and off she went.

R.J. said, "That woman knows all the gossip but it's not easy getting it out of her."

"Like what?" I asked.

"Like yesterday, Mae James came into town alone to visit the bank. She had a long conversation with Melda Nick about rights to the James' place if and when Jack is convicted of the crime he didn't commit."

"Well that makes me a little sick to my stomach," I said between sips.

"Any other good tidbits?" asked Fantasia.

R.J. replied, "Oh yeah, Saul Brell is no longer the bank janitor. He's been officially promoted to the position of Melda's executive secretary, whatever that means."

We sat quietly for a moment. We all knew what that meant.

R.J. asked, "So what do you want to do with the elixir salesman, Adrian? He'll be sobered up by this afternoon. You want me to let him out?"

Fantasia sounded defiant, "He's not getting that horse back, I'll tell you that much. It had leather burns and was underweight. He's been in that harness most of his life. You guys better not give him another horse either or I'll make protest signs and march on the sheriff's office."

"Wow!" said R.J.

They both looked at me.

"Well, I can't have the sheriff's wife marching on town hall, can I?"

R.J. persisted, "So do I let him out?"

I thought for a moment. "I have a feeling that horse is that man's only family. The old man is getting too old to run that rig anyway. We need to find a niche for him here in town so he gets to keep his horse but doesn't have to be on the road until he keels over. Fan, why don't you work on that instead of protest signs?"

A faint flash of guilt seemed to pass by Fantasia. She drank her coffee, put the cup down very slowly and very carefully and said, "You're absolutely right, my love. I was so angry about

216

the horse I didn't stop to think about the man. You leave him to me. I have an idea."

R.J. smiled. "Oh, this is going to be good."

A loud argument broke out at Candy's previous cowboy table. There was a scraping of chairs and curse words usually reserved for the trail.

R.J. looked at me for a cue.

I held up my hand for Hugh. He hurried over.

"I want to buy those guys a couple drinks, Hugh."

Hugh understood. "Right away, Adrian."

In less than thirty seconds Hugh was dishing out drinks to the two and talking to them. They looked over at us and nodded. The saloon was again quiet.

R.J. said, "Sheriff, you are a man of great wisdom."

"Any chance not to get bruised up," I replied.

"He's right, dear," added Fantasia. "In twenty-four hours you shot a badman, saved an old man and avoided a barroom fight. No wonder I love you."

I held up my cup. "Here's to me. The luckiest guy in Oldtown."

Fantasia stood, clinked cups with me and drank. She put the cup down, grabbed her book and turned to leave but looked back and said, "Just see that you stay away from Candy."

R.J. howled with laughter.

I sneered at him. His expression begged forgiveness.

R.J. finally said, "There is good news by the way."

"I'm not sure my heart can stand it."

R.J. reached in his shirt pocket and drew out a slip of paper. He pushed it across to me. It was Ringo's badge number.

"The cleaning lady?"

R.J. nodded. "She was quick. Apparently, the district marshal is not well loved."

"Got that right. So our next stop should be the telegraph office."

"After you, sir."

We made our way past the train station to the telegraph operator's little shack and answered the request for Ty Ringo's badge number, then headed back to the office just in time to meet Fantasia.

"I'm here for my prisoner, Sheriff."

I smiled and we went in.

The three of us gathered at the salesman's cell and looked in on him. He was sitting on the bed hanging his head. He looked up pitifully.

"What do I have to do to get out of here, Sheriff and where's Bucky, my horse?"

"What is your name, sir?" I asked.

"Bernar Hall, Sheriff."

"You have two choices, Bernar. You can stay locked in until the judge decides if he wants to charge you or I will release you into the custody of this lady here, Fantasia Tarn."

"I need some food from my wagon."

Fantasia said, "Don't worry. Bernar. There will be food."

Bernar stood and took a minute to get his legs under him. "I've really gotten myself into it this time. Where are you taking me, lady?"

"Your horse needs brushing, Bernar."

"Fine. I want to see my horse. I need some water."

We led him out of the cell. Fantasia kept one arm on him for stability. She took him out the front door.

"He may want to go back in jail when she gets though with him," said R.J.

At the end of the day we gathered at the ranch, Parth, R.J., Diya, Bernar, Fantasia, and I.

Diya and Fantasia had made stew. We sat around the table seldom speaking because the food was so good. When we had finally overstuffed ourselves, wine was passed around to numb the pain. Only then did the stories start.

R.J. asked, "So, Diya; any good new mysteries in your bag?"

Diya thought for a moment. "I have not told you about the Minors family. It was last month. Davie Minors was working on his roof and fell from the ladder. He hit his head and was injured badly. They brought him to the bedroom where his wife watched over him. He did not regain consciousness. According to his wife, she fell asleep watching over him but awoke later to find two people in white suits doing something to her husband. They saw her watching them and she doesn't remember anything after that. When she awoke again there was a message on her kitchen table saying her husband had been taken to a hospital in Pomona. There was a train ticket included for her to come immediately to assist in his care. She took the train the next day and neither of them were ever heard from since."

R.J. asked, "So where were these people in white suits from?"

Diya answered, "No one knows."

Bernar jumped in. "Perhaps she was dreaming."

R.J. persisted, "Then who took her husband away?"

Bernar replied, "It must have been medical people from the doctor's office."

Diya answered, "We did not have a doctor at that time, only a horse vet. He treated more people than he did horses."

"It is a mystery, then," said Bernar.

R.J. asked, "Bernar, how many towns have you visited?"

Bernar hesitated, "Oh, so many I've lost count. I am generally thrown out of them."

"Well, what was the last town before Oldtown?"

"Truffington, to the west of here," replied Bernar.

R.J. looked at me. "You ever hear of a town called Truffington?"

"Maybe. I'd have to look through the wanted posters."

Bernar said, "I am extremely thankful for your kindness, Fantasia and Sheriff. I've never experienced this kind of helping hand before, ever."

Fantasia said, "Bernar, Adrian is away during the day most of the time and I am often in the medical office. Our ranch could use someone to care for the horses and generally keep things in order. There is a storeroom attached to the clinic which has water and power. Would you be interested in working for us? Room and board could be included. It would be something you could try for a time to see if it suits you."

"Ma'am your kindness has no limits. I would be honored by that."

We moved to the living area by the fire and traded stories. Parth took a seat next to Fantasia and me. He leaned in to speak. "Adrian, I have some information you should be aware of."

"Well, you'd better tell me before I have any more of this wine, Parth. You need a refill?"

"I have friends and contacts in the judge's office and at the bank. None of them are happy with some of the proceeds taking place. I am told the judge is filing paperwork to establish a new law enforcement position. It will be called District Marshal of Oldham. It will replace the position of Sheriff. Judge Nick intends to appoint Ty Ringo to that position and deputize his hired guns, including that man Ren Shuner. One of their first assignments will be to evict you from the Sheriff's office and take over there."

Parth's story sobered me up. "When will all of this happen, Parth?"

"Apparently he is getting the town council to sign off on this new legislation by letting them think you will occupy the new position. Once they have approved it, they will learn the judge is entitled to appoint anyone he chooses."

"Can you guess how long all this will take?"

Parth shook his head. "Not long, Adrian. Maybe a couple of weeks for them to quietly post the required message of public notice."

Diya came to us with a fresh bottle and refilled our glasses. Next there was dessert. None of us had room for it but we ate it anyway. The voices around me became a friendly drone in my ears. I sipped my wine and discovered it no longer had an intoxicating effect. I stared at the flames, cold sober.

## Chapter 19

It took a week to hear back on our telegram. The message dazed us.

**District Marshall Ty Ringo body recovered (stop) All possessions stolen (stop) Individual in Oldtown an imposter (stop) Two District Marshals will arrive Oldtown in two weeks to apprehend. (EOM)**

We both had to read the message several times to believe it. R.J. sat back in his chair and said, "Did you see the look on the telegraph operator's face?"

"That guys reads everything."

R.J. made a "Tsk," sound. "That means the whole town is going to know."

"I'd say we've got a serious problem."

"You think? A fake Ringo with a gang of four backing him up set to take over the sheriff's office?"

I added, "They think they're sending two marshals to take care of it. They don't know what they're up against."

R.J. said, "From reading this I'm wondering if they expect us to throw Ringo in jail and have him ready to go when they arrive. It's either that or they expect us to keep this under our hats until they get here. Like a telegram is not going to be spread all over town like wildfire."

"They're not stupid. They decided they had to let us know there was a killer with a borrowed badge in town even though word might spread. They are hoping we can handle it somehow."

R.J. added, "And then there's the judge."

"A corrupt judge giving orders to a killer and his gang."

"Could this get any worse?"

"Believe me. It will."

R.J. thought for a moment. "We are in our right to go arrest the fake Ringo right now if we want."

"The two of us against five professional guns?"

"We need some back up."

"We can't endanger the lives of Oldtown citizens against professional guns. If the two district marshals were here, I'd be willing to buy into those odds."

R.J. nodded. "The five of them rode out this morning still looking for Jack James. Until they find him that will keep them busy for a while."

I said, "Let's walk Main and stop in Candy's. Maybe we can see how far the telegram gossip has gotten."

We stepped outside and stood on the boardwalk for a minute scouting out the town.

I looked at R.J. "We still need a careful eye on those upstairs windows."

R.J. nodded.

Before we could move, a commotion and dust cloud appeared farther down Main Street. It was a wagon being run haphazardly toward us. As it neared, I made out the reckless driver and passenger. It was Luke and Mae James. Luke pulled up in front of us, out of breath. Mae looked angry and frightened from the ride.

Luke called out too loudly, "He's in the back, Sheriff."

In the back of the wagon was body covered over by a blanket.

I looked up and asked, "Who is it, Luke?"

"It's Jack. He's dead."

R.J. stepped around the wagon and pulled back the top of the blanket. Jack James cold white face was staring at the sky, eyes still open.

R.J. pulled the blanket farther down and said, "Two red spots on the chest, Adrian."

Luke climbed down nervous and fidgeting. "I had no choice, Sheriff."

It took me a few seconds to fathom what I was being told. "You shot your brother?"

"He came to the ranch again demanding money and supplies we couldn't spare. We got into a bad argument. He tried to take the stuff anyway. I tried to stop him. We fought. It ended up he drew on me. I had no choice."

Mae James remained seated in the wagon with her husband's body behind her. She kept looking away as though she didn't want to be a part of what was happening.

I said, "Luke, Jack was pretty good with a gun. Are you saying you outdrew him?"

"I don't know. Sheriff. It all happened so fast. It don't matter anyway. He's a wanted man. I'll be wanting that reward at least."

R.J. checked under the blanket and said, "He's not wearing a gun, Adrian."

"We took it off him when we checked him over," said Luke.

R.J. covered Jack's body back up. He and I exchanged looks of disbelief.

I opened my mouth to ask R.J. to get the undertaker but when I looked the undertaker and his helpers had already come out of their shop and were headed our way.

"Can we just get this over with, Sheriff?" said Luke. "I need to get back to my ranch."

"Get what over with, Luke?"

"The reward. I need that money."

It took me a moment to gather my feelings as I stared at the body of the man we had been helping to avoid false charges made against him. Now his brother was asking to be paid for killing him, and his wife hadn't shed a tear that I could see.

Technically I had no choice, but the words were difficult to say. "The bank has to issue the reward, Luke. You'll need an affidavit from me. Step into my office; we'll both need to sign it."

Luke's hand was still shaking as he signed.

"I'll have to go to the bank with you to verify it."

We stepped outside. The undertaker's crew was sliding Jack's body off the wagon. The three of them carried it away. Mae James jumped down and followed us to the bank. R.J. came along.

Half dazed, I led Luke to the bank followed closely by Mae James and R.J.

Inside, we went straight to Melda Nick's office. Everyone in the bank watched as we went by. Melda was seated at her desk shuffling documents. She looked up with a curious stare. I placed the affidavit on her desk in front of her. She appraised me for a moment then read the account.

She looked up with a doubting expression. "Jack James is dead? Where is the body, Sheriff?"

"Undertaker."

Melda quickly wrote a note and turned her attention to a courier outside the door. She waved the girl in and handed her the note without speaking. The courier took off.

Melda returned to the affidavit. "Well, this looks in order. Let me stamp it." A large rectangular ink stamp was made. We both had to sign it. Melda stood and said, "This way."

Melda went to a teller at a desk and said, "Please draw two thousand from the James ranch estate."

It took Luke a full minute to grasp the statement. "Wait. Why are you drawing the money from the ranch accounts?"

Melda looked at him as though she was confused that he didn't understand. "It's the reward for bringing him in."

"Yes, I understand that, but why are you taking the money out of the ranch account?" asked Luke with great exasperation.

"The reward was posted by the ranch estate," replied Melda.

"Wait, you're using my money to give me the reward?"

Melda seemed genuinely willing to explain. "You don't understand, Mr. James. When the ranch property was frozen, Judge Nick held power of attorney for the asset. The judge determined the ranch should post a reward to aid in the conclusion of the case. So it was the ranch estate offering the reward."

Luke was beside himself, "This is insane! You're giving me my money as the reward. It was already my money."

Melda shook her head. "Until the case is closed, the ranch assets are under the control of Judge Nick, no one else. The case must be formally closed to determine who is entitled to what."

The teller handed Melda the two thousand. Melda handed it to Luke.

"Now if you'll excuse me, I must get back to work." Melda turned and walked away.

In silence the four of us left the bank.

Outside the bank Luke stood and stared down at his own money.

Mae James tapped him on the shoulder. "I now own half the ranch. Half of that money is mine. Give it to me."

Luke looked up glassy eyed. "What?"

"Half of that money is mine. Give it to me."

Without thinking, Luke counted out half and gave it to her. "Let's get going Mae. I want to get out of here."

"I'm not going with you, Luke. I'm going to get a room at the hotel and when I'm ready I'm taking the next train back to the coastal cities."

Luke looked up, still stunned by everything that was happening. "What? That's not what we planned."

Mae James was adamant. "That's not what you planned, Luke. I never agreed to any of it. I now own half the ranch. I want that in cash. Make the arrangement to buy me out. I'll be waiting."

Luke complained, "What are you talking about? We're in love. What about us?"

"I was never in love, Luke. You were a fun pastime in a dull dreary life. I'm going back to the coastal cities. Either pay me off or sell the ranch and give me my half. If you don't, I'll send a lawyer out here to make sure you do."

Mae James stepped off the boardwalk and headed for the hotel, counting her money as she went.

Luke stood staring out into nothingness. A few bills escaped his hands in the breeze. He quickly jumped down and began picking them up from the street.

R.J. and I left.

On the way back to the office R.J. said, "I'm getting tired of this job."

"The worst isn't over yet."

At the office the empty wagon was still there, horses waiting.

Inside R.J. asked, "Coffee, or whiskey?"

"Coffee. I could sure use a drink after that but we need to keep clear heads."

"The whole thing is making me sick to my stomach."

R.J. set a coffee down in front of me.

I said, "We can't even charge those two for shooting him."

"Talk about a stab in the back." R.J. poured for himself. "Our fake district marshal can stop looking for his innocent man."

I tested the coffee. It was still a touch too hot. "But he won't be leaving town."

"He *thinks* he's going to be taking over your job."

"The irony is when the judge hands him a badge, he actually *will* be an Oldtown district marshal," I said.

"Along with his deputies."

I sipped my coffee. "You know they're going to come for us before those two district marshals can get here."

"You think they'll just waltz in here and demand our badges?"

"No, they won't risk a confrontation in such a confined space. The judge will issue warrants for our arrests. The final report will say we were shot while resisting."

"So we call in our sniper crew?"

"I'm not really comfortable with that. If we lose the battle, those hired guns will kill those guys. I'm not sure we should put them at risk just to try to save our skins."

"It would be tricky to set up too. How could they be in the right place at the right time? But what have you got? We can't face off five against two."

"The only thing I can come up with is to let them think we're going to walk into their trap, but at the last minute change the deal."

"Ah, that famous saying; the best way to block a punch is not to be there when it arrives."

"We'll meet them in the street, but before we're in range we'll drop aside to safety where we can shoot and move, shoot and move."

"Yeah, use the alleyways to sucker them into a no cover position."

"It's the best chance we have."

"We'll get at least some of them for sure."

"You know, you could just ride out of Oldtown. They wouldn't care if you were out of the picture."

"That's kind of insulting."

"I had to mention it."

R.J. said, "We should map out the town, figure out shoot and run routes then hide weapons along the way which are easy to get to."

"I wish I had thought of that."

"We can't both be geniuses."

"Very funny."

"What will you do about Fantasia?"

"I want to put her on the train, but she'll never go willingly. I'm going to have to teach her to use that mini gun she's got. Won't that be a surprise to any of them that go after her."

R.J. gathered up old wanted posters and together we mapped out the town and planned shoot and run routes from various points up and down Main Street. From the confiscated weapons locker we brought out every shootable handgun and serviced each. We plotted the best places to have backup weapons available, then one at a time went looking for spots in those areas to hide them. It took most of the day. Near sundown, the Ringo gang rode back into town, weary from searching for a dead man. They headed straight for the Bucking Horse.

As darkness fell, we closed up for the day. It was decided R.J. would sleep at my place for the time being. At the ranch we set up tin can and string alarms in the most likely places for intruders. From that point on we had to bide our time. R.J. and I sat around the fire considering our odds.

R.J. asked, "How do you think they'll set this up?"

"I can only guess but I'll bet we'll get called out to a disturbance somewhere and it will be them waiting for us."

"Ambush?"

"They'll need to make it look legal."

"Like, drop your gun, but when you try to, you get shot?"

I nodded. "Good guess. That's one way. I'm expecting they'll all be wearing shiny new badges for the town folk to see."

"They'll have to try to do this in the street. There's too many of them to be inside."

"That's my bet."

"We'll have to break to the right and left to separate them."

"I agree. Come down the street on separate sides on the boardwalk planning for cover all the way."

R.J. thought for a moment. "You know, as bad as all this is, I kind of feel good about the hit and run. I've got the cover points and hidden weapons in my head pretty good."

"The longer we last, the better our odds."

R.J. asked, "So you're good with the ranch then?"

"Bernar has been very reliable now that he's sober. He knows how to use a gun. He's given me his word anybody that shows up here will have to get through him to get to Fantasia."

R.J. leaned back. "So that's it. We're ready. All we can do now is wait."

## Chapter 20

The next day the mood in the town became ominous. Everyone knew just about everything. The Ringo gang stopped hunting Jack James and began hanging out around town. People tended to leave when any of them arrived. Main Street traffic fell off noticeably. People conducting business in town were nervous.

We couldn't tell about the damning telegram. There was no way to know if the Ringo group had heard the rumor that district marshals were on their way to arrest them and no way to know if Judge Nick was aware.

For three days we stayed ready and kept our routine, patrolling Main Street and stopping in Candy's. The Ringo group remained in the Bucking Horse. An invisible line had formed between the two saloons.

Once the paperwork was stamped off and signed and shiny new badges handed out, everything changed. The Oldtown business leaders did not understand why there was a new Marshal. One gunman from the Ringo gang was stationed outside the Judge's office to dissuade dissenters. Shop owners were advised the morning Main Street patrol would soon be discontinued and all calls for law enforcement should henceforth be made to Ringo or one of the new deputies.

R.J. and I sat in the office waiting for the telltale summons. I repositioned my chair to keep a better eye out.

Shortly before noon, Ty Ringo surprised us. Spurs jingling, he came walking up the boardwalk, opened the front door and entered. R.J. stood and went to the storage shelves pretending to look for something.

Ringo gazed down at me with a half smile, his thumbs in his belt. "Tarn, don't you think it's about time you vacated this office peacefully?"

"Why would I do that? I'm an elected official. I haven't received any notice of my position being eliminated."

"Oh, it's been eliminated, believe me. I'm just trying to avoid any conflict breaking out between you and the boys."

"Well now, they wouldn't break the law would they, being deputized and all?"

"They will enforce the law, Tarn. You included."

"Have I done something illegal?"

"You need to vacate this office."

"Again, no paperwork from the town council directing me to do that."

"I'm just trying to do you a favor Tarn, but I see I'm wasting my time."

Ringo opened the door, looked back at R.J., and left.

R.J. returned and sat. "Holy crap. He doesn't know."

"What?"

"He doesn't know he's been found out and those marshals are on their way here."

I thought for a moment. "I don't believe it! The whole town knows and not one person passed it on to them."

R.J. added, "And that probably means the Judge doesn't know either or he would have warned them."

"How could Melda Nick not know? She hears all the gossip in the bank."

"Either she's so wrapped up with her new personal assistant Saul Brell that she's not paying attention, or nobody told her either."

I shook my head. "I can't believe this whole town is keeping that secret."

"They're backing us, Adrian. If we end up out there, we may have more firepower behind us than we expect."

"There's no if about ending up out there, buddy. That visit from Ringo was an ultimatum. I've been watching the street. There's not a kid in sight."

Almost in fulfillment of my prophesy the front door opened. Mars Jenks from the leather shop stepped in. "I gotta let you know, Sheriff. Two of that bastard gang just robbed the general store. I say robbed but they just walked in and took whatever they wanted. A box of cigars and some other stuff. Just walked out. They're wearing badges. They were headed for the Bucking Horse when I last saw them. I thought you should know."

"Thanks, Mars. We'll take care of it."

He left with a strained look on his face.

R.J. asked, "Well? Is it time?"

I shook my head. "Not yet. We need something more than shoplifting. But don't worry. It won't be long."

R.J. lit his pipe and sat back. I swiveled in my chair. Thirty tense minutes passed.

Something completely unexpected happened.

The door rattled open, causing R.J. and me to sit up straight.

In walked Bert Shrack still in his black gambler's clothes, vest, and white shirt, but no jacket. He was now wearing a round-rimmed black hat pulled down low. With the hat his beady eyes suddenly made him look like a hard cold killer. He was carrying a short double-barreled shotgun and a pistol stuck in his waistband.

He pulled up a chair and sat with the shotgun in his lap. R.J. and I stared in surprise.

"It's time, Sheriff. Two of them just pulled Matty Dern's daughter into a back room of the Bucking Horse. I've been told she did not want to go."

"You know how to use those, Bert?" I nodded toward his guns.

"They will be heading for Candy's next, Sheriff."

I looked at R.J. He stared back speechless.

I said, "I agree with you it's time, Bert. But are you sure you want in on this?"

"Time's a wasting, Sheriff."

I pushed up and stood. R.J. rose. I tucked my spare gun in behind me. R.J. did the same.

The front door rattled open.

In walked Riley Kit, bearing arms. "We'd better get going. They're getting ready to leave the Bucking Horse to head for Candy's," he said matter-of-factly.

Bert Shrack stood.

I said, "Riley, if I didn't know how good you are with that gun I'd send you home. But these guys aren't drovers. They're city guns. You sure you want to line up against a group of city guns?"

"Wouldn't miss it, Sheriff. I got a girl in Candy's now. I'm with him." Riley pointed his thumb toward Bert. "By the way Sheriff, Bard was coming but he's bad sick. I had to take him to your place. He's got a bad fever. The doc's looking at him."

I said, "Gentlemen, it would be an honor to stand with you." I opened the door and held it.

As R.J. went by he said, "So much for shoot and run."

We walked the street. We spread out so as not to be one big target. R.J. and I took the center. The kid on our left. Shotgun Bert on our right. Just about every curtain was pulled back with eyes staring out. There was not a horse, wagon, or human in sight. Boardwalk displays had been taken back inside. The silence was so unusual it was unnerving. The lack of dust made the air smell fresh.

We spotted four of them far in the distance walking the street toward us, heading for Candy's just as Bert had predicted. They saw us about the same time we saw them. It was Ringo and his three hired guns. Ren Shuner wasn't with them. As we neared Candy's saloon a disturbance broke out at the entrance. Ren Shuner backed out the swinging doors pulling an angry Candy Shrack by one arm. She was fighting him like a wild cat.

We stopped just short of the saloon. Bert stepped up onto the boardwalk. Shuner spotted him and let go of Candy. She charged back inside. Before I could even consider the situation Bert flipped up his shotgun and blasted both barrels into the chest of Ren Shuner. The boom made us all jump. Shuner flew backwards off his feet, slammed down onto the boardwalk, slid a few inches, and did not get back up.

The Ringo bunch had of course seen the entire affair. They were still out of pistol range. They came the rest of the way to the saloon as Bert cracked his shotgun open, dropped in two fresh shells and snapped it shut. He stepped back onto the street and took his position with us. I no longer saw Bert Shrack as a gambler.

The Ringo gang stopped at the opposite end of Candy's. There was a heavy moment of silence. I sensed Ringo had prepared a short speech but the Shuner incident had ruined the moment.

This was point I was obligated to tell them they were under arrest and to drop their guns.

To hell with that.

We stood in cold silence. Someone had just died. The eight of us appraised one another. If anyone was going to back out of this, now would be the time.

It was now four against four. Four professional guns against two professional guns, a ranch hand kid, and a gambler. I had Ringo in front of me with one of his gunmen to his right in front of the kid. The two others were in front of R.J. and Bert. I had a moment to decide whether to try to protect Riley or R.J. I couldn't protect both. Subconsciously I had already chosen R.J. Besides, the kid was so fast he probably would end up protecting me.

The finality of the standoff had reached the awkward stage.

Ringo flinched.

Eight men went for their guns. Instantly it became adrenalized slow motion.

To my utter amazement, the Kid put bullets into his man *and* Ringo before either of them got off a shot. But he had fanned the shots so unfortunately neither was accurate enough to be fatal. The first bullet stunned Ringo just enough to let me place a second shot in his gut. In unison the kid fired a third into his man. Bert's first two booming barrels hit his man square and also caught R.J.'s opponent in the shoulder and face. At the same instant R.J.'s first shot hit him in the opposite shoulder. Bullets from all of them were whizzing by us. One passed between my legs and tore my pants. From the corner of my eye I thought I caught sight of R.J.'s upper sleeve slapping back from a hit. The kid's opponent was dying on his feet but still managed a shot into Riley's upper leg before his eyes glassed over and he fell. Bert's man was sprawled out dead. R.J.'s man was on the ground on his side with his face and shoulder full of buckshot, digging holes in the street with his boot heels. Riley's man stayed down and did not move. Ringo was still standing, bent over holding both hands and his gun against his stomach, unable to gather himself enough to continue to shoot. We waited with our smoking gun barrels still leveled in case there would be more. R.J.'s man kept digging with his feet and groaning. The amount of blood coming from Riley's leg worried me.

Ringo staggered to stay on his feet, still hunched over. He refused to drop his gun. He looked up at me holding his stomach. "Hick town lawmen, kid, and a fat slob gambler. No way."

Ringo fell down dead.

I tucked my gun in my holster and began visually checking everyone for bullet wounds. R.J.'s hit was just to his shirt. My pants leg was just the pants. Bert wasn't hit at all. I took a nervous wobbly step toward Riley but a young girl from the saloon brushed by me and began tearing strips off her slip to wrap Riley's leg. It was then I spotted Fantasia marching out from the nearest alley, her little gun in one hand, her med kit in the other. She looked mad.

R.J. spotted her and said, "Uh-oh."

I said, "Yeah, she's scarier than they were."

"Did you really think Bernar could keep me at home?" yelled Fantasia.

I tried to come up with the right answer but only stammering came out.

"Who's hurt?" she asked and it sounded like an order.

She searched, saw the girl wrapping Riley's leg, then saw the groaner on the ground and went to him. Bert hurriedly picked up the man's gun and tucked it in his belt.

I looked more closely at R.J.'s torn shirt. "The town will pay for that, you know."

He looked down at the wide tear in the inside of my pants leg. "That just missed the long arm of the law."

The undertaker joined us and began poking the bodies with his cane.

Hugh the bartender came out. "We're bringing a wagon around, Sheriff. What do you need?"

"Riley and the guy on the ground need to get to the doctor's office fast."

"We're on it, Sheriff."

Up and down the street people began to appear in their doorways.

The undertaker came up and asked, "Can I take them away, Sheriff?"

"Please do take them away, sir."

He signaled his associates and dashed off.

A photographer's flash bar went off making us all jump.

Candy Shrack came flying out of the saloon crying. She charged Burt, jumped him and with her arms and legs wrapped around him sobbed into his neck. Shotgun still in hand he carried her into the saloon.

A horse drawn wagon was brought up. We helped Riley and his girl up into it. Then four of us lifted the unconscious gunslinger onto it. Fantasia climbed into the back with him. The driver headed for the medical office.

Crowds were now forming in front of shops. As I scanned the area, I spotted Judge Nick with an upstairs curtain pulled back to watch the melee. He saw me looking and let the curtain close.

All his doing.

The last gunman died a few days later. Just before his death he confirmed Ren Shuner had killed the prospector. The charges against Jack James were dismissed.

Ever so slowly the town reverted to its natural state from before the gunman had been brought in. Judge Nick was never seen around town. He would not take visitors or appointments. The James ranch was released from litigation and formally became the property of Luke and Mae James. Mae left on an afternoon train soon after. Luke remained in his room at the ranch drinking full time. Bard Coverton fully recovered from his illness and was now running the ranch with Riley's help.

We thought we had weathered the storm. The real district marshals were due in soon. R.J. and I sat in the office, marveling that it was still ours, and drinking coffee that tasted better than ever before. We had pinned a copy of the front page of the week's newspaper on our bulletin board.

### *Oldtown Crier Special Edition*

### *SHERIFF 'S TEAM PUTS DOWN GUNMEN*

### *Group brought in by Judge Nick were criminals*
### *Judge not available for comment*

The article was anything but kind to the judge. It was like the anger of the town was now on him. The editor had done his best to keep direct castigation out of the story but what was written between the lines was so damning it was hard to read.

We sat back thinking it was time to relax a spell.

The front door rattled open.

240

Bank Vice President Peal pushed inside and looked at us. He was out of breath. "Sheriff…." He held up one hand to pause and breathe. "You're not going to believe this!" He had to take another moment. "Melda Nick just robbed the bank."

## Chapter 21

I looked at R.J. "He didn't just say that Melda Nick robbed the bank, did he?"

R.J. looked away. "I didn't hear a thing."

Peal persisted. "Her and Saul Brell."

I rubbed my eyes. "Mr. Peal, did you just tell me that Melda Nick robbed her own bank?"

"Her and Saul Brell."

"How do you know this?"

"When I came in this morning to open the bank two kids were sitting on the boardwalk laughing at me. They said Nick robbed the bank. I thought it was just a joke they were playing. I went inside and found the safe open and all the paper money missing and the safe deposit boxes opened and emptied. I went back out to get you and asked those kids how they knew. They were out last night going through the shop owners' garbage looking for anything they could get their hands on. They saw Melda and Saul at the back of the bank with a covered wagon, loading up trunks. I asked them why they didn't report it and they said they did but no one would listen."

I looked at R.J. "Apparently we have to get up."

"It would seem so."

"I haven't even finished my first coffee."

"Nor I. This is a travesty of a morning rite."

We stood, stretched, and gestured Peal to lead us on.

At the bank, a crowd had already formed outside. People were concerned about their deposits. As we approached, they all tried to talk at once. I made an overt gesture of plugging my ears with my fingers as I passed by.

Inside the bank everything was as Peal had described. The teller drawers were all open and empty. The safe door was ajar. A few bills had escaped to the floor in a path that led to the back entrance. The shelves in the vault were cleaned out except for some gold bars, too heavy to bother with. Paper documents were scattered everywhere.

R.J. and I stood staring at the violated vault.

"He's right. I think we've been robbed," said R.J. sarcastically.

"There *is* evidence to support your theory, sir."

"I suppose we should be serious about this in front of the depositors."

"Or we could just go out the back."

"Better idea," answered R.J.

Behind the bank there was a large, disturbed area in the dirt where the loading had taken place. Narrow wagon wheel tracks led behind the buildings and eventually onto the street. Tracks from the heavy wagon pointed north.

"My guess is they went south," said R.J.

"Knowing those two that's a good guess."

"You're thinking we're going to have to ride out after them, correct?"

"Although we've had our excitement for the week I see no way around it."

"My ass is already feeling sore."

"I believe elixir salesman Bernar has some lotion for that."

"And if it doesn't work we can always drink the elixir."

"Let's go pack the saddlebags with food, and fill the canteens."

"If we must."

It seemed like the entire town was outside watching us as we walked our horses down Main Street. They were now a solemn bunch. Outside of town we broke into a slow canter and held it for about a half an hour. Past the James place we stopped and debated our strategy.

"This has got to be the stupidest robbery I've ever seen," said R.J.

"So they're staying off the main roads which puts them in the softer sand with a heavy wagon. They're running slower in that stuff. The question is, have they gone to the east or the west? We've got to pick up their tracks before we go any further. There's always the possibility that they did actually go north."

"No way," replied R.J. "I'll take a straight line to the east, you go west. When one of us picks up the wagon tracks, fire off one shot and we'll regroup."

"I like it. They couldn't have gotten too far."

We split up and watched each other shrink into the distance. It didn't take long. I was the lucky one. I found deep wagon tracks with dragging brush marks heading west. I could have followed the brush drag as easily as the wagon wheel trenches. They had been trying to cover their tracks by dragging the brush behind the wagon but the weight of the wagon made their tracks too deep for that. I stared down at the ridiculous trail, shook my head, and fired off a shot. I dismounted and stretched my legs while waiting for R.J.

Almost an hour later R.J. came plodding up and stopped to appraise the sneaky yet stupid-looking trail that had been left.

"Did I mention that this is the dumbest robbery I've ever seen?" he asked.

"Yes, but that goes without saying."

We headed off on our pursuit. We cantered for a bit and walked for a bit. It took another hour to spot the tiny silhouette of a covered wagon far in the distance.

"Nothing like hiding out on a wide open plain," said R.J.

I drew out my sea captain's spy glass for a better look. "I do believe these sly burglars have become stuck in the sand."

R.J. leaned forward on his saddle horn. "They've probably worked those horses past the point of no return and they're too far out to walk back. They probably would have died out here if we hadn't come after them."

"Don't give me any ideas. I still haven't had my first cup of coffee."

We rode up to the runaways and found them sitting in the shade of the covered wagon next to their money. Their two horses looked at us with expressions which could only mean, "Thank God."

As R.J. had guessed, there was no way those horses were going to pull that wagon back to Oldtown. We unharnessed them, hooked up lead lines, tied the hands of our two bank robbers and boosted them onto their horses bareback. R.J. commented that at least we wouldn't be the only ones with sore asses.

The pair wasn't speaking, to us or each other. After several hours of riding we finally led them down Main Street to a chorus of reluctant cheers, jeers, and foul language. There was also the occasional question, "Where's our money?"

We put them in jail. Melda begged they be kept in the same cell. We separated them. Vice President Peal came charging into the office intent on questioning them but abruptly realized he did not have questions to ask.

I said, "Mr. Peal, do you know exactly how much was taken?"

"Down to the penny, Sheriff."

"Good, then here's what you're going to do. Three of my special deputies are going to take you out to that wagon with a fresh team of horses. You're going to check the money and stay with it while they bring that wagon back. Then when you get here, you and your staff can put everything back into the vault. Got it?"

"You want me to ride all the way out there, Sheriff?"

"There's no other way, Peal. You're in charge of the bank. You have to be there to make sure nothing disappears."

"Could I take a carriage?"

"I wouldn't. Not in that sand. You get stuck you might be there a very long time."

Peal nodded reluctantly. He left, looking slightly dazed.

We got Candy's to feed the prisoners. A crowd lingered outside the jail. Judge Nick never showed his face. A telegraph to the regional office was answered quickly. The prisoners were to be transferred by train in two weeks so that a regional judge could handle the case. It meant another prisoner transfer for R.J. and me.

### Oldtown Crier Special Edition

### BANK PRESIDENT ROBS OLDTOWN BANK

### Former bank janitor an accomplice

### Sheriff and Deputy track robbers down

### Judge Nick recused from case

As usual the story was somewhat embellished in our favor and coldly antagonistic toward the robbers. It was dusk before the wagon and money came rolling back into town. There was cheering and cursing. Vice president Peal's crew would be up all night putting things back in order.

R.J. and I sat in the office with the door to the cell area closed for privacy.

"It's about time to lock up," said R.J. "You think those two will be okay back there? Adjacent cells may not be enough separation, if you know what I mean."

"Better leave the lights on."

R.J. added, "It seems like Melda doesn't really care about what she did."

"I think all Melda cares about is Saul Brell, and Saul seems to be wondering how he got where he is."

"Led astray for the love of a woman."

"A married woman."

"On paper only, I think."

"What do you think will happen to Judge Nick when the full investigation is over?"

"He may spend a good deal of time in prison, or at least be disbarred."

R.J. shook his head. "It was the Judge who got Jack James killed."

"No other way to see it."

"Led astray for the love of silver."

"Yeah, wait till Mae James finds out about that."

"They are a sad bunch."

"Do we have any loose ends on the James case, R.J.?"

"I thought about that. We should probably ride out to that cave Jack was holed up in and bring back whatever personal possessions he left out there."

"Good point. I forgot about that. Let's ride out there tomorrow."

Early the next morning we saddled up after coffee and rode out while the town was still waking up.

Walking his horse alongside me R.J. said, "You know, I've always wanted to ride out to those far south mountains but I just never felt like making the effort."

"Really nothing to see except the cave Jack held up in is not natural. It's man-made. Fantasia figured the railroad was going through there at some point but the desert beyond made them change their minds."

"That hiding place worked so well for Jack. It's a shame his family didn't."

"Yeah, you'd never find the place if you didn't know where it was."

Outside of town we cantered side by side. We rested the horses with period of walks. We watered them halfway there from our canteens.

As we approached the distant ridgeline we hung to the right side. No need to conceal our destination this time. The bad deed had been done.

At the base of the hills R.J. paused to study them. "Wow! We call these hills but they're only hill halfway up. It's practically sheer cliff on the upper half. You'd need climbing gear to get to the top."

"Yeah, climbing gear and probably all day. The cave is over there sealed up to look like rock fall."

We dismounted and went to the pile of fallen stones. I put on gloves and began pulling stone away from the top of the entrance.

"It's big enough to drive a cart through," said R.J.

"Oh yeah. He kept his horse inside with him."

The top portion of the cave entrance became a big black hole. We kept expanding it until we could enter without crawling. Inside, R.J. lit a pipe match and held it up.

I said, "He left lanterns. You see them?"

"I got it," said R.J. and he pulled two down and lit them.

We each took a lamp and looked around. Sleeping bags, food stores, a little bit of ammunition, bucket of grain and another bucket for horse water. A stack of dirty laundry. Other miscellaneous junk.

"All that's left of an innocent man," remarked R.J.

We packed it all up in long saddlebags and stood staring into the tunnel's darkness.

"Adrian, we got to see where this goes."

"To be honest, I really don't feel like it."

"Me neither but when will we ever be standing here with oil lamps again?"

"That's true. Okay. Let's go a ways in and see how it is."

Twenty minutes later we were deep into the cave. There was not a thing to see except smooth cave walls cut by man. We both considered quitting but we'd gone far enough that the opposite end should not have been far.

It was a forty-five-minute walk behind smelly hand lanterns. Finally a glow of light appeared in the distance.

"Thank God," said R.J.

We trudged along with the distant oval of light growing larger and larger until the cave opened up to a dull sunlight and a hazy sky.

It took our eyes time to adjust. We had to shade them with our hands. We both looked out at the horizon and tried to focus.

"What the hell?" exclaimed R.J.

As my eyes adapted I saw what he was referring to. About a mile away there were buildings, strange buildings.

"I must be going crazy," said R.J.

"Then we both are because I see them too."

"They're close enough to walk to."

"Let's not."

"The big one looks like it's made entirely of glass. You ever seen a glass building before, Adrian?"

"I'm not sure."

R.J. stammered, "There isn't any long stretch of desert here. It's buildings. What is this place?"

"It's making me dizzy."

"Me too. Must be from stepping out into the sunlight."

"I don't think so. It's getting worse. Maybe we'd better get back."

I tried to turn back into the cave but went down on one knee. R.J. dropped onto both knees. I braced one hand on the ground and watched R.J. lay over onto his left side. He managed to set his lantern upright and off just before passing out. I switched mine off, set it down and tried to look back at the desert that wasn't there. The lights went out.

I awoke with half my face buried in sand. Had to spit some of it out of my mouth. I pushed up and looked back at the new buildings. They were the structures we had discovered after first entering the dome. I could see the general point where we had entered and wondered if our belongings were still there.

R.J. groaned and half sat up on one elbow. He wiped sand from his face and shirt. He looked at me in total confusion for a moment. He adjusted himself into a sitting position.

"Adrian, beyond that fake forest, that's where we came in."

I sat in the sand and nodded. "I think I understand what's happening."

"Fill me in."

"We must be outside the town limits. Remember they said if you go outside the town limits the implant dissolves. We've lost our implants. We know who we really are."

"Holy crap!"

"Are you with me?"

R.J. said, "Oh my God! We couldn't stop them from putting the implants in. We've been living with false computer-generated memories!"

I nodded again. "We thought Oldtown was real."

"Holy crap, it seemed so real!"

"To us and everyone else it was."

"What are we going to do?"

"I think we need to sit here awhile and think this through."

"Good. I need to stare at those buildings a bit so I can believe this is really happening."

I said, "We found Diya. We just didn't know it."

"I wonder if anyone knows our implants are gone?"

"I bet if we play along with the charade they won't realize it, at least for a while. This whole thing is run by computers."

"We've got to bring the others out here. Get rid of their implants."

"I agree."

"We could make a run for those buildings and be out of this place pretty quick."

"That might not be the way to go. They'd know we were suddenly missing. That would probably set off a mad scramble to find us."

"You're right. They'd come after us. It would screw up Oldtown, that's for sure."

"Yeah, and we can't tell any Oldtown people about this all being a simulation. They waited a long time to get on the list. We'd be ruining their one chance to be here."

"I agree. We have to play along."

"At least that seems like the safest way to go. How much time do we have left here?"

R.J. did the math in his head. "They said a three-month stay. If I'm figuring right, we have a little less than two weeks left. Oh my God! That's why we got the order to move prisoners. They're going to take us out of Oldtown on that train ride just like when we came in."

I said, "Well, at least we know now bullets can't kill us."

"Now you tell me."

"Are you feeling a little sick to your stomach?"

"Yes. Must be the shock of all this. Adrian, you know what? We haven't actually killed anyone."

"Not a one, I'd say."

R.J. smiled. "And, Jack James isn't dead."

"Thank God for that."

"That undertaker. He doesn't bury anybody. He lowers them down below for repair or removal."

"That would be my guess."

"Wow! This is all too much."

"Shall we start back?"

"Oldtown is not going to be the same."

"You got any more matches?"

Within the shadow of the cave R.J. relit the lanterns. We walked in silence trying to reconcile everything that had happened.

I said, "You know, I think there are glitches in the Oldtown science from time to time."

"Why do you say that?"

"I think that flesh wound Jack James received was real. I think the smart bullet expected to miss him but at the last second he moved into its path. I'm pretty sure Fantasia put real stitches in his back."

"Yeah, I noticed a slight bruise on Candy Shrack's arm where Ren Shuner tried to pull her out of the saloon.Shuner had to be an animatron, I think."

"So it's not all perfect."

R.J. replied, "Just pretty close."

I said, "No wonder Alien Andy and the others were seeing strange beings."

"And I've been saying that all along. We need to cover this cave entrance back up. We don't want any Oldtown people having their vacation ruined by coming here."

After closing up the cave entrance we gathered up our saddlebags and went out to the horses.

R.J. shook his head and exclaimed, "I don't believe it. This horse is obviously robotic. It's plain as day. But I sure didn't see that this morning."

We checked the cave entrance from a distance, went back and covered it up even better than it had been with artificial scrub brush. We mounted our horses expecting them to fall over but they did not. We even trotted down to the main road and headed for town.

R.J. asked, "So why'd they take Jack out of the simulation? Why not just make him wounded so he could heal up?"

I said, "I can guess the answer to that one. Jack was intentionally hurt by his brother. If they left him in the simulation his brother might have tried again some other way."

"You're right. The whole town is a simulation but man, some of the stuff that happens here is too real."

"We've got to be really careful in town. Try not to look surprised by anything."

"Adrian, I've been sensing Elachia the entire time we've been here. She's been looking for us."

"You should empathically let her know we're okay."

R.J. continued, "But you know what this means? According to Fantasia, that ship brought us to a different dimension. That means the links we have with Elachia and Fantasia connect us even when we're in other dimensions."

We cantered and walked our mechanical horses. On the outskirts of town we passed by a distant ranch to the north. Suddenly I could see that the place was simply a prop. There were no actual people there. The buildings were empty. Every other time I had seen it the place had been busy.

Oldtown was a completely different place. Kids were still running around everywhere but not one of them was human. They were all animatrons. One or two of the shops were storefronts only with no actual building attached. But over the months I had seen people coming and going. As we walked Main Street, suddenly all the people we had come to be close to were animatrons. R.J. and I kept exchanging glances of hidden disbelief. The animatrons were all very fond of us. We had saved animatron city from some bad gunmen. The bank was now back in order and open for business. We rode up to the office, pulled down our stuffed saddlebags and went inside. We stored everything and took our seats at the desk. R.J. began to speak. I held up one hand for silence.

I flipped over a wanted poster, grabbed a pencil and wrote;

*Only normal conversation. Prisoners in hearing range.*

He understood immediately.

"Coffee?" asked R.J.

"One gallon, please."

He laughed and lit the wood burning stove, rattled the coffee pot to be sure it was still filled, then came back and sat down.

I said, "We should invite Diya and Parth over for dinner. I think Bernar is busy tonight."

"I wouldn't miss it. I'll be there."

I added, "I've been thinking. It's been too long since we all went for a ride together just to get away from things. Fantasia has been asking to go back to the cave to explore it."

"That sounds great to me. We could ride out south and maybe show them where the stolen money ended up. We could have lunch out there in the cave."

"Yeah, after everything that's happened just a peaceful day away."

"That'll work."

Later I walked down to Candy's. There were many compliments from bystanders along the way. Saloon business was slow but the poker game was in full swing. Four animatrons holding cards and one human, Bert Shrack.

I went to the table and stood looking down at Bert. He looked up with a new friendly expression.

I said, "Bert, thank you."

He understood and gave a brief smile. "Sheriff, we should all thank each other. How's Riley?"

"He lost quite a bit of blood but bed rest and pampering by his girl seem to be doing wonders."

Several men at the table laughed which for the first time amazed me.

I went to the bar where Candy was wiping. She too looked at me with great affection.

"What'll it be lawman who saved my ass?"

"Can we borrow Diya for tomorrow?"

"A day off for Diya? For you I'd give her the week with pay, Sheriff."

"Just tomorrow will do. And please ask her to come to dinner with us tonight. Fantasia needs some help with a book she's reading."

"Sure you don't want a drink on the house, Sheriff?"

"IOU?"

"You got it."

R.J. made sure Parth would be there. Just the mention of Diya assured that. Those two did not know who they really were, but they had instinctively bonded. The temptation to make it physical must have been overwhelming.

We gathered for dinner. The three of them were their casual selves; R.J. and I were not. We kept glancing at each other, knowing what the others thought was reality. With our stomachs full we sat around the table discussing the past week's events, good and bad.

When the time seemed right, I proffered our offer. "By the way, R.J. and I would like you three to ride out to the south with us tomorrow morning. There's something we came across and would like to show you."

Diya sounded sympathetic. "Thank you for such a nice offer, Adrian, but Candy would probably fire me if I did not go in tomorrow."

I tried to sound innocent, "I've already spoken to her and she has given you the day off tomorrow."

"What!?"

Fantasia said, "He has a way with women but he's supposed to stay away from Candy!" Fantasia gave me a stern look.

They laughed.

Fantasia asked, "What is this about, darling? What do you want to show us?"

I tried not to be evasive. "It will be a surprise."

R.J. murmured, "That much is certain."

Parth asked, "Is it a long ride? Could Diya and I take a carriage?"

I smiled, which seemed inappropriate somehow. "We will be crossing some hilly areas. We'll all need horses."

Parth shrugged. "I'm not much of a rider but I suppose with a friendly horse I could manage."

R.J. mumbled, "Oh, the horses will be friendly alright."

I gave him a warning stare.

"What time shall we do this?" asked Fantasia.

"Everyone should come here for breakfast and we'll leave from here. R.J. and I will have the horses ready to go."

R.J. opened his mouth to make another glib remark but a look from me silenced him.

We drank wine around the fire until we were too tired to be sociable. Diya and Parth left, followed by R.J.

"I'll bring three saddle horses with me in the morning," said R.J.

"I'll pack lanterns and food and water," I replied.

"I'll pick out the friendly horses," added R.J.

Neither of us laughed.

Later in bed with Fantasia she became restless. "So what is this all about, darling? Where are we going?"

"I don't want to bias you. I want you to see it without any preconceptions."

"See what?"

"Just trust me on this. I'll explain everything tomorrow."

"Okay, but mysteries intrigue me something awful. I'll try to wait."

## Chapter 22

The three of them were ready to go right on time looking half awake. R.J. and I were wide awake. We fed them and brought them out to the corral where the horses were patiently waiting. Perth made an ireful comment about horses so early in the morning. We got him up and with all five of us in the saddle went around the town rather than down Main Street. Diya and Parth paid no mind to it but Fantasia immediately became more suspicious than she already had been.

The ride out became pleasant. We cantered and walked. Diya and Parth held hands during one canter, another indication the morality barrier between them was breaking down.

As the far south hills grew near, Fantasia's curiosity became difficult to manage.

"We're going to the cave because I said I wanted to explore it," declared Fantasia.

I nodded.

"So that's where you were yesterday! Did you go all the way to the end?"

"I'm not telling."

"That's okay. I'll get to discover it myself." Fantasia turned to the others. "We're going to a cave in the mountains."

R.J. replied, "Technically I do not believe they are mountains, just tall hills."

Diya called out, "Oh, I love caves! I always think they hold a secret I might find if I explore them."

R.J. looked at me, bit his tongue, and rolled his eyes.

We rode up to the base of the Jack James' section of hill and dismounted. There were a number of, "Wows," and comments about the steepness of the upper portion of the hill face. We led our guests to the pile of rocks and brush covering the cave entrance and with gloves began to clear the opening. They marveled at the secrecy of it. When the black hole was big enough we beckoned them in.

They became quiet as we lit the lanterns.

Parth finally asked, "How far in are you taking us?"

I said, "You've all come this far. Trust us."

Diya said, "I know what you're doing. You're going to show us the long stretch of desert on the other side. This cave must go all the way through the mountain."

Fantasia said, "This cave is not natural. It's man-made."

Diya added, "This is a little spooky. I feel as though I could lose myself in there."

R.J. bit his tongue and rolled his eyes.

We led them into the darkness. There was little conversation since the bare walls provided little to talk about. Far into the tunnel Parth looked like he was having doubts. When the tiny spot of light finally appeared in the distance, Diya cheered.

"I was right. It's the other side," she declared.

We emerged into the daylight. They struggled to help their eyes adjust.

Fantasia was the first to see. "What!? There's no desert! That building shouldn't be there! Is that made of glass?"

Diya said, "I don't understand. What are you showing us? Where is this place?"

Path said, "Things are not at all as we've been led to believe."

I stood close to Fantasia and put an arm around her waist.

She looked at me and said, "This is all making me a little dizzy."

Diya held on to Parth's arm. "I'm feeling dizzy too."

Parth swayed. R.J. caught him and stood by.

Ever so slowly the three of them bent at the knees and gradually lowered themselves to the ground. We took care that no one was harmed, and watched them fall asleep.

R.J. looked at me. "This is having a little more emotional impact on me than I expected."

I nodded.

We positioned our friends to be comfortable and took seats to wait for them to awaken to a new, old life.

R.J. said, "You know, this is a little bit like killing them. They will never be the Oldtown people they were, ever again."

"Relax, we are scheduled to be taken out of Oldtown in a few days anyway."

"I know, but still…."

"It was another life we never signed up for, R.J. We were just accidentally incarnated into it. We forgot who we really were."

R.J. thought about it.

Fantasia was the first to begin to awaken. She groaned and held on to me. She looked up and her eyes fluttered open. She looked at me in a long recovery stare. I could practically see the memory flowing back into her mind.

"Oh my!" she said weakly.

"Are you okay?" I asked.

She looked over at Parth and Diya still unconscious. "It's Diya!"

"Yes, we found her," I said.

She pushed up with one hand and looked out over the landscape. "Where we came in."

"Yes. Our stuff should still be outside waiting for us."

"Adrian, what happened to us?"

"They injected implants in us. We weren't expecting it. We couldn't stop it. We became Oldtown citizens."

"Oh my!"

"Are you okay?"

"Two sets of memories."

"Yes. It's a crazy feeling."

"R.J.! You've been through it too."

"Yes, Fan. I know who I really am."

Fantasia sat up and brushed herself off. "How long have we been unconscious?"

I replied, "About twenty minutes."

Fantasia climbed to her feet, went to Diya and Parth and lifted their eyelids to check their eyes. "They're coming out of it."

Parth stirred first. He let out an irritated groan. He sat up by pushing both hands behind him and looked at us in confusion. Still sitting he looked out over the landscape. "Adrian, R.J., where are we?"

I pointed to the glass building. "That's where we came in, Parth."

"Oh my God! We've been in Oldtown all this time!"

Diya jerked up abruptly and looked around in a daze. Her eyes focused and the first thing she saw was Parth. "Oh Parth! I'm so glad to see you. How did you get here? Where are we?" Diya hurriedly looked around. "Oh God! I remember. But how...?"

Parth embraced her tightly. She held him in her arms. "We've been searching for you, Diya."

Diya pulled away and looked him in the eye. "But how could you have found me here? It's impossible."

"It is a long story, Diya. I too have just remembered who I am. We must allow our minds to sort all of this out. I will tell you everything. I promise," replied Parth.

I stood and brushed myself off. "Is everyone well enough to walk? It's a long hike back. We should probably get started."

Fantasia was standing next to Parth and Diya. She came and wrapped one arm around me. Parth and Diya stood and brushed off. We all looked at each other with new eyes. R.J. relit the lanterns and handed me one. He gestured into the cave and we slowly started walking.

Diya commented, "We passed through a dark tunnel and came out of a dream."

Fantasia added, "It *is* very much like waking up."

Diya asked, "What can we do now?"

I answered, "We think it is important to play along and pretend we are still Oldtown citizens."

There was a long period of silence. We kept walking.

Parth said, "It is possible they may know our implants have dissolved."

R.J. replied, "There's just too much happening in Oldtown, Parth. It has to be computer controlled. We think if we act normally they may not notice."

"It is a fair guess, R.J."

"Do you have a plan for our escape?" asked Diya.

I said, "We think if we act normally they will simply take us out of Oldtown at the intended time which is only a few days from now. That would be better than trying to suddenly disappear from the town."

Fantasia said, "I agree. Leaving now would cause too much confusion. They would search for us. It would be better to let them think everything was proceeding as expected."

R.J. asked, "Can you put up with Candy for a few more days, Diya?"

"Oh, my God! I am a barroom cleanup maid!"

R.J. snickered.

Diya added, "This is quite a strange way to meet Parth's friends. I already know all of you but I am just now meeting you."

"Yes, it is nice to finally meet you too, Diya," said Fantasia.

Diya asked, "I am assuming you came to this dimension the same way I and my associate did."

Parth asked, "Where is he, Diya?"

Diya had to gather herself before answering. "He was shot and killed in the last city before this place. He delayed a gang so I could get away on a bicycle. I will always be sick about it."

Fantasia asked, "So you found the dome and came through it like we did?"

"No. Many workers came out of the dome to do maintenance. I was out of food and water. I followed them back in as though I were one of them. I went to the underworld with them. It is an endless place. Everywhere you go down there is like the inside of an elegant English manor. There are sports arenas and theaters. In many places food and supplies are free to be taken."

"How long were you in the underworld?" asked Parth.

"I do not know. Eventually I wanted to see if there was any way to get back to Earth. I needed to go to the surface to see what might be done. I managed to blend in with a group going up to Oldtown. I didn't know what it was about. Apparently when the ship jumps from one dimension to another it emits a pulse that erases computer memory. I was able to slip into the Oldtown group because their databases had been corrupted. I thought Oldtown was just a way to get to the surface. I did not know what I was getting into."

I asked, "Diya, if we could get back to the ship, could you operate it?"

"It is not necessary. In our studies of it we found this planet had already been programmed in and once here, a return trip is automatically set up in the navigation system. I doubt we can ever return, however. A special crystal is needed to activate the power systems in that craft. We took the crystal when we exited it to explore this world. John, my associate, had it in his boot. When he was killed it was lost. Besides, it would be impossible to walk back that far though territory inhabited by surface dwellers. They kill anyone on sight."

I said, "We have a way to get back, Diya, but what about this crystal key for the ship you mentioned?"

Diya looked over at me through the shadowy light of the cave. "You have a way back to the craft? How would you do that?"

R.J. said, "We have a vehicle hidden away in a barn near here. What kind of a key is it?"

"It is a crystal about the size of an almond. But I have never seen any type of crystal here. They must be rare. This particular crystal has special properties. It fits into an indentation in the ship's navigation console. Unless we could find something that might work there would not even be any sense going out into the surface world."

A beam of light appeared ahead. We walked in concerned silence the rest of the way. We climbed out into the daylight and stumbled down to our horses. R.J., Parth, and I went back to reseal the cavern.

"I don't believe it. My horse is not real!" said Fantasia as she inspected her horse.

Parth laughed. "I have always been afraid of horses."

Diya added, "What marvelous engineering."

We packed our saddlebags and took turns helping each other up. I turned my horse machine to North and led the way.

We walked the horses to start.

"So we are all on the same page here, right?" I asked. "Back in Oldtown, Parth is still the assayer, Fantasia is the town doctor and Diya is a barmaid. Everybody's got that, right?"

There was a kind of compliant silence.

I continued, "And Parth and Diya, even though you are married you cannot let on that you are."

Diya looked at Parth. "We must sneak around like school children, Parth."

Parth smiled.

R.J. said, "Adrian and I have already received notice to take the train for the Melda Shrack prisoner exchange next week. We think that is how they will extract us from Oldtown. You both will probably be receiving a notice and train tickets to go somewhere also at that same time as will the other Oldtown people in our group."

We rode around the west side of Oldtown to stay out of sight. As we approached the ranch I gave one final warning. "Remember now, don't let slip that we know in front of Bernar or any of the other townspeople."

The others gave me annoyed looks.

Bernar stood waiting for us as we approached the corral. We dismounted and tied off to the fence. Bernar waved us away and began taking care of the horses. We grouped together and headed for the ranch house and lunch.

As we sat around the table eating thick sandwiches made from home-baked bread, Diya began to giggle for no apparent reason. We all looked and waited for an explanation. Her giggle broke out into a full laugh.

Fantasia stopped eating and finally asked, "What!?"

"I'm a barmaid. Eight years of college and I ended up a barmaid."

Fantasia let out a muted laugh.

Parth said, "I specialize in interplanetary science but I'm a rock person now."

Diya laughed at him as well.

R.J. said, "Adrian and I are starship officers and we're hick town lawmen."

Everyone laughed.

Diya said, "Fantasia, at least you're still a doctor."

Fantasia's eyes opened wide. "Oh my God, I've been trying to figure out what my medical scanner is for months."

We all stopped eating and laughed.

Drinking wine by the fireplace had now become a daily routine. We gathered there and sat musing our unexpected fates. It was agreed Oldtown had become a part of our lives forever.

## Chapter 23

R.J. and I sat in the office trying to prepare mentally for a very different Oldtown experience. We had only a few days to go but we were still the town sheriff and deputy. We still had to take care of Oldtown.

The front door rattled open.

Bank Vice President Peal stuck his head in the door and entered. He looked nervous as usual. He held his black derby hat against his chest and tried to see into the back where Melda and Saul Brell were being held. It was suddenly clear to R.J. and me that Mr. Peal was an animatron.

"What can we do for you, Mr. Peal?" I asked.

"May I close that door to the back?" he asked.

R.J. got up and shut the door to the cell area.

"Thank you. I was uncomfortable discussing bank business with Melda there," he said.

"Is there something we need to know about, Mr. Peal?"

R.J. brought up a chair while trying to keep the smirk off his face.

Peal sat. "It's about the bank, Sheriff. As you know I am running it. However, Judge Nick has stepped in and feels he should be acting as president because he will eventually inherit all his wife's holdings."

"Has he issued an arrest warrant for his wife yet?"

"I believe he has recused himself from that proceeding and is referring all those matters to the next circuit judge."

I looked at R.J. "I don't see him having any claim at all to the bank, do you?"

R.J. answered, "Not a one."

I looked back at Peal. "If Judge Nick tries to impose himself on the management of the bank, tell him you have a direct order from the sheriff he has no jurisdiction there until the circuit judge passes the necessary rulings on that property."

Peal squirmed nervously. "I will do that, Sheriff, but I'm afraid Judge Nick has already set himself up in Melda's old office and will not listen to reason."

R.J. said, "Well, it had to come to this sooner or later."

I ruffled the papers on my desk. "I have a cease and desist blank here somewhere."

It took a few minutes to find it and fill it out.

I stood and grabbed my hat. R.J. joined me. The three of us marched down the boardwalk to the bank and pushed inside. The place came to an immediate standstill. Every person in there stared as we headed for Melda's office. Peal followed but hung back.

Peal and most of the bank patrons were animatrons. A few were real citizens who were not from our group. At the door to the office we found Nick coasting around in his wife's chair, merrily organizing paperwork. He stopped and looked up as we entered. The expression on his face was suddenly one of worry.

"Yes, gentlemen. What can I do for you?"

"I have a cease-and-desist notice for you, Judge. You are to vacate the bank immediately and are to have no further interaction with the bank staff."

"How dare you! You can't do that. I'm the Judge here in Oldtown. I make the law!"

"No sir. You do not. And unless you comply with this order, we will escort you to the jail where you will reside with your wife until the circuit judge arrives."

"This is preposterous."

"You will also turn over any keys you have before you leave."

"This is atrocious, not only am I the judge in this town, my wife owns this bank outright."

"She did, right up until she robbed it."

Nick stood, red faced and came out from behind the desk, ready to leave. "You're going to be in a lot of trouble for this, Sheriff. Just you wait."

"Judge, you don't realize how much trouble you're already in, do you? You put out an arrest warrant on an innocent man. You hired an outlaw gunman to find him. Your actions resulted in his death. You're the one who's in trouble here. Don't you get it?"

Nick made a loud, "Humpff," sound and marched out. Peal came out from hiding outside the door.

"Thank you, Sheriff."

"Let us know what he was up to in here, Mr. Peal."

R.J. and I left. I thought I heard a smattering of applause as we exited.

Back in the office, we took our seats and poured more coffee.

R.J. said, "Once again fake Oldtown is pretty real."

I glanced around to be sure the door to the cell area was still closed.

"I checked already," said R.J.

"You're right, you leave your guns behind but your deeds follow you home."

The front door rattled open.

Animatron Hugh stepped inside. He stood in the doorway with the door still half open and said, "Sheriff, two men just rode into town.

They're at my bar. One of them claims to be the brother of Dude Banks. He's saying he's here to gun down the men who shot him."

"Where's Bert, Hugh?"

"I think he's upstairs with Candy."

"Please let Bert know right away and tell him I said to stay out of sight until we deal with this. And Hugh, give those guys free drinks but don't tell them they're from me. Let them drink their fill."

Hugh gave a machine-like nod and left.

R.J. sipped and said, "Well at least we know they can't kill us."

"Don't forget about the shoulder wound Jack James accidentally got. We can't be too nonchalant about this."

R.J. said, "You know, I just realized I've developed a fondness for some of these animatrons. Like even though I know they're not real people they still seem like friends to me. Hugh, Sal, Bard Coverton; they have real personalities, you know?"

"You're right. I wonder if any humans who come here actually fall in love with an animatron?"

R.J. thought for a moment. "Must be a trip waking up to find you've fallen in love with a robot."

"I have almost felt that way about some spacecraft."

R.J. added. "We've got a human and an animatron back there in our cells who have been carrying on."

"I can't imagine how that's going to play out."

"So when do you want to go take care of those guys down at Candy's?"

"If I was the old Sheriff Tarn I'd say let's wait and let them drink."

R.J. replied, "Too bad we can't let them get staggering drunk and then just arrest them."

"That's a problem. They won't have broken any laws and even if we did bust them when they sobered up they'd still want to kill us."

"What a nuisance."

I glanced out the window and spotted the Colton brothers pulling their wagon by. As I watched, a back wheel began to zig-zag then fell off its axle. The wagon flopped down to the ground on one side. The Coltons began gesturing and arguing at each other.

R.J. had leaned over to see. "I'm going to miss those guys."

We watched a comical half hour of the Coltons trying to get their wagon going again. Eventually they fitted a wheel and dragged the buckboard away, but I for one would not have wanted to ride in it.

We sat around the office the rest of the morning expecting Banks' brother to show up and call us outside. Nothing happened.

"It's time to do the patrol if we want to look normal," said R.J.

"They may be waiting to bushwhack us."

"Yeah, but we know they can't kill us."

"Unless the gods of Oldtown decide we need to be taken out of the simulation early."

"What'd you want to do?"

"Let's walk Main Street and visit Candy's for lunch."

"And watch the upstairs windows and alleyways really close."

"Yep."

Outside we split up and took either side of the street. We walked the boardwalks slowly and methodically. No sign of our mechanical bandits.

But Oldtown had grown quiet again. Not much retail being done. No horses or carriages passing by. There was definitely something in the air.

At the end of Main, R.J. and I met up.

I said, "I've been thinking. Change of plan. I'll go in and have lunch. You circle around and come in the back door and stay out of sight and cover me."

"You're baiting them."

"There's a trick I saw in an old Clint Eastwood movie. It might work pretty good here."

"That why you have a second gun tucked in behind you?"

"Let's go."

We split up. At the saloon I pushed slowly through the swinging doors and checked the place. No patrons, no poker game. I took a seat at a table near a wall where nobody could get behind me. I took off my gun belt and draped it over a chair back so anyone could see my gun was still in the holster. I took a seat and as Hugh approached I slipped the second gun out from behind me, cocked it, and let it rest in my lap under the table, my finger just outside the trigger guard. Moved my badge from my belt to my shirt pocket.

Hugh placed a folded menu in front of me. "New menus, Sheriff. Candy's latest idea." Hugh leaned in and whispered, "Haven't seen them for the past hour." He headed back for the bar.

I sat with one hand holding up the menu, the other hand on my lap gun.

It was less than five minutes before I caught a glimpse of someone looking in a front window at me. Despite knowing this was all a simulation, it still made me tighten up.

The two of them pushed their way through the door and paused to look around. I spotted the Banks' family member immediately. Big guy,

272

a little too heavy, same corrupt aura, similar facial features. It made me wonder if down below they had just dressed up Banks himself differently and sent him back into the simulation. His partner was a little younger, lacky, self-assured. The partner went to Hugh, ordered a drink, and leaned against the bar looking back at us. Banks wasted no time. He came up to the table but stayed back the appropriate amount for a draw and fire move.

"You won't be needing that menu, Sheriff."

"Do I know you, sir?"

"You will. You shot my brother down. I know it's true cause I had a long talk with your undertaker. You may need a new undertaker by the way, yours is pretty beat up."

"You shouldn't have told me that, Mr. Banks. Now you're under arrest."

Banks gave a short laugh. "You gotta be an idiot Sheriff, coming in here alone. You make one move toward that gun and you're quick dead."

"Your brother was trying to kill me, Banks. I had no choice."

"You would'a been better off leavin' town, Sheriff. I'm a lot faster than my brother was."

"You going to let me put my gun belt on then? I mean to make it a fair fight."

"Your gun's fine just where it is, Sheriff. Make your best move."

"I'm law enforcement, Banks. I can't make the first move."

"Okay. I will."

Banks slapped at his holster. I squeezed the trigger. Muffled bang from under the table. The bullet caught him low in the groin. There was a big look of surprise. Slightly bent over he finished his draw. I fired again, hitting the same area. This time it bent him all the way over.

Banks' partner jerked up, sending his drink into the air. He reached for his gun just as R.J. stood up from behind the bar and raised his gun to the man's head.

R.J. clicked back his gun's hammer and said, "If you want to live don't take us both on."

Banks partner froze.

Banks, still bent over, fell to the floor. His face slapped against the floorboards. Drool came out his open mouth.

Two machine kids were staring in the front window wide-eyed. I got up, leaned out the front door and waved them over. I flipped a coin to one of them and said, "Run to the doctor's office and tell the doctor the undertaker needs help bad." The kid took off. I flipped a coin to the second one. "Find the Colton brothers and tell them we need them to take a body to the undertaker's." The kid charged away.

I turned back in time to see R.J. gently lift the gun from Banks' partner's holster. R.J. came around, took the man by one arm and together we led him to the jail.

I said, "We'd better get back there and get Banks' gun and wallet before somebody lifts them."

R.J. nodded. "I'm sure Hugh has put that stuff away."

Halfway back to Candy's we saw the Coltons had already loaded Banks' body into their wagon, leaving his legs to dangle off the back. With great effort they were pulling the wagon along even though the back wheel was still doing a wide in and out wobble. As we approached, Bert Shrack came out of the saloon heading toward us with a stern look on his face. I had a feeling he was about to complain he was left out of the latest showdown. The saloon doors swung open again behind him as Candy charged out to catch up to him. Quite a few townspeople, machine and human, had come out onto the boardwalks to watch and gossip.

Banks' body was being jostled around something terrible. As the wagon passed by, his right arm slipped off his chest, fell over the side, and went in between the spokes of the errant wheel.

The wheel ripped Banks' arm completely out of the shoulder socket and threw it in the street. Tubing, harness, and white goo flowed out of the torn arm.

The Colton brothers stopped. As we stared at the mess on the ground, Banks' body abruptly sat up, looked around with a jerking motion, straightened up and regained his feet in the street. He began marching around mindlessly less one arm, looking here and there, bumping into the wagon only to bounce off and continue stomping along in no particular direction.

R.J. and I knew what was happening. No one else did. A few shrieks broke out from Oldtown citizens. Banks banged into a post at the boardwalk, veered off and kept going in a Frankenstein walk.

I thought to shoot him again but doubted that would work. As I considered my slim options, something else equally bizarre took place.

Every animatron in sight suddenly froze in place and became dead eyed, except for Banks. Humans up and down the street buckled at the knee and slowly settled to the ground, unconscious. Bert Shrack went down on his side. Candy Shrack fell atop him.

I thought I understood. I motioned R.J. down and we stretched out in the street and pretended to be asleep.

Ten minutes of absolute silence and stillness in Oldtown. My only fear was that Diya, or Parth, or Fantasia would come charging out asking what was going on, which would blow our cover.

As we secretly watched, a cigar-shaped object appeared in the sky above Oldtown. It was gun metal gray, the size of a bus, and it lowered down to the street and hovered a few inches above the ground. A door opened. Two men in white suits exited. One was carrying what looked like a cattle prod. They went to the still wandering Banks, took position and jammed the prod into him. He stiffened and fell to the ground. With great effort they lifted him up and dragged him inside the craft. One of the white suits hurried back out and collected the dismembered arm. The door shut. The vehicle raised up and disappeared.

We continued to pretend we were asleep. Animatrons began to wake and move. When the first humans began to rouse, R.J. and I got up.

R.J. said in a low tone, "Well, that's not something you see every day."

Everyone began rising. The animatrons went back to what they were doing before the interruption. The humans seemed to focus more slowly but gradually just shrugged the whole thing off. I had the feeling none of them remembered anything that had happened.

The Coltons gathered themselves and pulled their wagon away. The fact that the body had disappeared was of no concern. Bert and Candy Shrack got up, brushed themselves off, spotted us and headed our way.

"Sheriff, really, I should have been involved with that guy. I'm the one who shot his brother after all."

"We were hoping maybe we could take them both in without any bloodshed, Bert. And Bert, you've already done way too much. I'll always be in your debt."

Candy grabbed Bert's arm and tried to coax him back to the saloon. Bert reluctantly went with her but stopped to look back, "Next time, Sheriff. Next time I'm in."

R.J. and I nodded and waved.

R.J. said, "The man has true grit."

"I'm such a bad judge of character."

R.J. laughed.

We stopped off at the assay office on our way back. Parth was inside staring out his window. "What was all that about?" he asked.

We explained.

I said, "Why don't you grab Diya and come over for dinner again Parth? We need to talk some more."

"We will be there."

R.J. and I headed for the ranch to check on the undertaker. Fantasia was in her office still dressed in white, a few blood stains added.

"How is the patient?" I asked.

"It is quite amazing," she replied. "When he was brought in, he appeared to be near death. But as I treated his superficial wounds they began to clear up right in front of me. I know had I been under the influence of the implant that all would have seemed natural. Only now can I tell there is artificiality at work here."

"What happened during the shutdown?"

"What shut down?"

We explained.

"My, my," she answered. "What an incredible simulation."

We gathered for dinner. Jokes were made to relieve stress. After dinner we went into a long discussion about what to expect over the coming departure from Oldtown and how to handle it. It was unanimously presumed we would all receive train tickets and reasons to use them just as Fantasia, R.J., and I already had. In fact, we assumed everyone in our original Oldtown group would suddenly have reason to take the train. R.J. and I were scheduled to transport Melda Nick and her animatron lover Saul Brell to Pamona. We also suspected that at some point on the train ride we would all be put to sleep. It was a troublesome thought but for us to escape dome world without attracting attention it was a gamble we would need to take. When we had exhausted all the possibilities both good and bad, and finalized our plan, we moved to the fireplace and sat together drinking too much wine and nervously making more poor jokes. We were scheduled for a train ride to reality.

## Chapter 24

The days before departure were mercifully uneventful. On departure eve we brought out the original clothes we had worn to enter Oldtown. Fantasia packed her medical scanner in the same pants leg pocket which had allowed it to slip by inspection. We sat outside for a while to take a long last look at Oldtown, the place we never intended to visit and would now never forget for as long as we lived.

The morning was filled with arcane duties. The train came in, stack smoking, right on time. R.J. and I had to handcuff Melda and Saul Brell for the move to the train. We kept stealing glances at each other trying not to laugh. Melda had the look of a woman scheduled for the gallows. Saul Brell seemed unconcerned. On the train we locked them in a compartment and went back for our meager luggage. Stepping off the train, I spotted Judge Nick sneaking aboard farther down near the engine. It was obvious he thought he was making a grand escape. R.J. and I passed Riley Kit also boarding but we did not have an opportunity to speak. We did run into Bert and Candy Shrack boarding to visit a sick relative in the coastal cities. To remain in character, R.J. and I wore our guns. Fantasia carried her medical kit. We met up with Parth and Diya on Main Street. The five of us climbed on together and found a comfortable compartment. We threw our packs on the overheads and sat looking at one another nervously. The train's five-minute warning horn made us all jump.

We finally jerked to a slow roll, picked up speed, and watched the artificial world race by. That was the last thing we remembered.

I awoke to a bright florescent kind of light, in a sterile smelling white room. I was unable to lift my head but I could scan the room pretty well just from eye movement. We were all there. There had been twelve of us going in. There were now thirteen counting Diya. We had all been carefully positioned on reclined seats. Several attendants in white lab coats moved from one patient to the next.

The man I remembered as Chancellor Doun entered on the left. He was still dressed in his red drake vest with a white long sleeved collared shirt. He smiled continuously. "My fellow Oldtown citizens. Welcome back! What an adventure you've had! I realize you are not yet fully recovered but I know you all can hear and understand me, so let me do our short reintegration summery while you continue to recover. As specified in our contract you all are being withdrawn from your Oldtown personality at the same time. There were one or two unusual circumstances during this visit. Mr. Jack James had to be taken out of the simulation early for safety reasons, and Mrs. Mae James elected to leave Oldtown early so she too was an early extraction. Both Mr. and Mrs. James have been kept in stasis sleep so that revival from Oldtown would be uniform as promised. All in all this was a very good episode of life in the old settlers' country. We hope you are all pleased with the experience. When you are fully recovered, the door to my left will take you to the checkout area where you will find a locker with your name on it containing all of your belongings. Please take your time collecting those, then you can just follow the signs to the tram system which will return you to the Underworld. My thanks for your participation. Perhaps some of you will consider another visit in the future."

People began to move. There were low groans here and there. For me, adrenaline gave an advantage. I pushed up from my seat and looked around. As soon as I did the seat automatically moved me up to a normal sitting position.

I found Fantasia on my right. She smiled and nodded. R.J. was on my left. He made a smug expression like there was nothing to it. I pushed up with my arms and stood. My circulation seemed to even out. My head cleared. Fantasia and R.J. both were rotated upright. Parth and Diya were across from me. They were laying back holding hands.

The others began to sit up and focus but instead of celebration, social warfare broke out.

Jack James was standing beside his seat staring down at Luke still sitting. "What the hell did you do, Luke? You shot me dead, you bastard! You didn't even give me a chance to draw. I turned around and bang two bullets in the chest. You are one sick bastard. Kill me for a two thousand reward? What the hell are you, you bastard?"

Luke looked around as though he did not believe it was all happening. He sat up straight and tried to sound sympathetic. "It wasn't real Jack, none of it. It was all faked. Nothing really happened!"

"Bullshit nothing happened. And what's the deal with you and Mae? You're sleeping with my wife and then you kill me to get her and the money?! You sick bastard!"

Mae James sat up and looked around like she wasn't part of the conversation.

Jack James pointed at Mae and continued, "So you're with him now, right? Fine by me. Take the ranch and all the reward money you two didn't really get and have a nice life. You two are made for each other."

Luke tried again. "Jack, come on, none of it was real. It was all make believe!"

Jack wasn't convinced, "You two have a great life together. You've earned it. I'll have my lawyer send you both the appropriate papers. I don't ever want to see either of you again, ever!"

Jack James looked around to get his bearings and marched passed Chancellor Doun. The Chancellor watched him go and shrugged.

Luke James looked at Mae. "We still have each other."

"Luke, you shot your brother and tried to steal his ranch. I'm not with you."

"But it was your plan! I only did the stuff you talked about. You can't put this all on me!"

Mae James stood and straightened her clothes. She had no good answer and was embarrassed by the public revelation. "I'm going!" was all she said and with a glance at Chancellor Doun, she walked briskly to the door and out.

Luke was bewildered for a few moments. Finally he stood and hurried after her. "Mae, it was all fake! It wasn't real! We can be together!" He disappeared out the door.

Before we had time to react, the former Judge Roy Nick stood and scanned the room for the quickest exit. He looked down at Melda still waking up, mumbled, "I'll meet you outside," and hurried past us without looking up from the floor.

Melda's eyes fluttered open. The first word out of her mouth was, "Saul?" As she sat up she searched the room. An expression of fear and anger came over her face. She called out again, "Saul!" She stood, straightened herself up, and searched even more, then focused on Chancellor Doun.

"Mr. Doun, where is Saul Brell?"

The Chancellor stepped over to her and tried to sound compassionate. "Mrs. Nick, Saul Brell is an animatronic character in the Oldtown simulation. He is not a real person."

"I would like to see him, please."

"Mrs. Nick, that isn't possible. The Oldtown program continues to run as guests come and go. Saul Brell is still playing his part in Oldtown. He can't be taken out of it for any reason."

"No, no, no. If I discuss this with him I'm sure he will want to leave with me."

Doun exhaled exasperation. "Mrs. Nick, Saul Brell has no life outside of Oldtown. He is programmed to be a citizen there. He could never function here in the real world. He is the property of the Oldtown Corporation."

"Very well, I would like to buy him."

"Mrs. Nick, once again, Saul Brell is an intricate part of the Oldtown computer system. He would not operate if taken too far from it."

"Can't he be reprogrammed?"

Doun rubbed his forehead. "I believe you are asking if an animatronic system could be set up in your residence to support an animatronic companion. Yes, that is possible but your animatron experience would not be enhanced by the use of implant technology. A complete reprogramming would be needed on Saul Brell even if you could remove him from the simulation. That reprogramming would erase all of Saul's memory."

"Then I could have a second Saul Brell manufactured and a copy of this Saul Brell's memories implanted in the new Saul Brell."

"All of that may be possible, Mrs. Nick but you must realize the huge undertaking you are suggesting."

"Chancellor Doun, which way to your corporate offices?"

Doun looked emotionally fatigued. Melda looked determined.

Doun said, "When you are done with your locker, do not follow the signs to the trams. Instead you will see a directory on the wall. It will show you the way to the business office. That would be your starting point, Mrs. Nick."

"Thank you," barked Melda, and she headed out the door.

Riley Kit came up beside us.

Doun turned and looked at us. He smiled. "I must say. The six of you contributed greatly to the success of Oldtown. We are issuing special passes for each of you should you wish to return for a follow-on visit. Mr. Tarn and Mr. Smith, you were the best law enforcement we ever had, animatronic or human. Mrs. Tarn, you were an exemplary Oldtown doctor. Mr. Sharma and Mrs. Singh, the same to you both. Mrs. Singh, we apologize for your unexpected extended stay in Oldtown. We have still not corrected the damage from the mysterious pulse that has so decimated some of our files. We hope you found some merit in that extra time."

Diya nodded, "Oh, believe me I did, Chancellor." Diya cast an affection stare at Parth.

I looked over at Riley and held out my hand. We shook.

I said, "Riley, we stood side by side facing down those guys. I now consider you a friend. Call me Adrian from now on, okay."

Riley laughed. "It was a pleasure, Adrian."

"Me as well, Riley. It's R.J. to you."

Riley nodded and smiled.

I added, "You're a special person, Riley."

Riley answered, "Yeah, all that practice with my computer fast draw game paid off."

"He's means you're a special person in there *or* out here, Riley," said Fantasia.

Riley stepped back. "I'd better get going. I actually have parents out here somewhere."

As he left R.J. yelled, "But don't forget, you're still Kid Riley."

He laughed, waved, and disappeared out the door.

We said final goodbyes to Chancellor Doun and exited into the locker room. We collected whatever valuables were there and scanned the room. There were two exit doors. One was labeled, "TRAMS." The other was labeled, "MAINTENANCE ONLY NO ADMITTANCE."

We all agreed to accidentally take the wrong door. It opened to a hallway. Janitorial closet on the left, server room on the right. At the end of the hall was a door marked, "FIRE EXIT ONLY." It did not appear to be alarmed but had a brass wound wire with a stamped lead seal locking it down. I snapped the lead seal and pushed the door open.

To our muted joy, the glistening wall of the dome was only a hundred feet away, very near the spot we had entered. The dome shone around and above us. We hurried to the exit spot. At the shimmering wall, R.J. went first to test it. The other three followed, then me. Outside, standing in the world of dead brown, we were able to relax a little. Our escape appeared to have been clean. Our stored packs were in still stacked under the brush. R.J. and I retrieved our weapons.

Diya was even more fearful of the environment than we were. She constantly stayed low and scanned the terrain. She never once spoke as we followed our tracks back through the dead woods toward the ranch house and barn. The five-mile hike tired all of us.

The place still looked deserted. R.J. and I went first to clear the house and barn. There were no signs anyone had been there except us. It dawned on me we should have used brush to wipe away our tracks. I cursed under my breath. Still, there did not appear to be any new tracks. Our wings were still parked in the barn waiting to go. After a quick inspection inside the house we waved the others in.

R.J. made as smokeless a fire as possible. "Back to franks and beans," he remarked. "Even though we don't know what the franks are made of."

"One hundred percent meat," I replied.

R.J. gave a guttural laugh.

We rested and grouped together to try to figure out our next move.

I asked, "So the bottom line is we are not going back to Earth without that crystal?"

Diya nodded. "That ship's systems are far too complicated to try to bypass that."

Fantasia asked, "Have you done a thorough scanning of that console? I still have my scanner."

Diya answered, "We did. You don't get much data from scans. The technology seems to be too far advanced."

Parth said, "But you did manage to come here?"

"Yes and no. We found the crystal by accident in dirt in the shaft outside the spacecraft chamber. That shaft was an elevator up to the temple centuries ago. We had seen the

286

indentation in the console which matched the shape of the crystal. We thought it might power up the display screens so that we could perhaps learn more. We were right. We did not know that with both of us seated at the console the ship would automatically jump dimensions to the preprogrammed coordinates. That is how we got here. It was by mistake."

R.J. replied, "Well, we can't fault you there."

Diya looked around inquisitively.

Fantasia explained, "We made the same mistake."

Diya asked, "So what can we do? If there is no hope of getting back, we may need to find a way back into the underworld just to survive."

I said, "We shouldn't give up on getting back as long as there is any chance, no matter how slim."

R.J. added, "I have to agree with that. On Earth Elachia has a ship out looking for us but they'll never find us here."

"But what chance do we have?" asked Diya.

I answered, "You said your associate, John was his name? You said he hid the crystal in his boot. I know it's a long shot, but we need to find his body. It may still be there. Do you remember exactly where he was killed?"

Diya winced. "Yes, but there may not be a body to find if the surface dwellers have eaten him."

That revelation caused a long pause of silence. It notched up just how much danger was lurking in the world around us.

Parth finally said, "A search would be a difficult tactical undertaking, Adrian. Would we split up leaving some of us vulnerable, or would we all be fighters?"

I asked, "Where were you and he separated, Diya?"

Diya's expression darkened. "Near the center of the city. We wanted to check a burned-out store for cans of food. I waited out back. John went in. We did not have any weapons. Someone else inside yelled at him to stop. John tried to run. He yelled for me to get away, that he would catch up, but outside the back door he was shot and fell. From far away I saw two men search his body, but John had nothing they wanted."

I said, "I'm sorry to ask this, but did you see them take his boots?"

"They did not. But as I've said, many surface dwellers consider humans to be food. I did not dare stay around there. I managed to get to my bike and ride south away from there. I was starving. When I reached the dome I had to take any chance I could. That is how I ended up in the underworld."

R.J. said, "It's a long shot, alright, but we know exactly where he was and his body wouldn't have been moved too far, if it was moved at all."

Parth said, "There are many possibilities. The man's boots could have been taken. The crystal would have been found, or it may just have fallen out into the dirt, or the man's body was taken for food and the crystal found then or lost, or the body may still be there with the crystal still in the boot. Many possibilities as I've said."

I said, "When we took off there, I counted maybe five or six men shooting and chasing us. That was the biggest gang we saw. Diya, how many people did you encounter while you were there?"

"From the rooftops we saw gangs of two or three to perhaps five."

R.J. said, "So there's our recon intel. We could run up against patrols of two to five."

Fantasia said, "Five against five."

I said, "We need more guns."

R.J. said, "Let me be the one to review just how ugly this little mission will be. We're talking about taking the plane to the next city, landing on a road somewhere deserted, and hiking into the city in search of a body. From there we can't even say what will happen. Then if we somehow get the crystal, we hike back to the plane, take off on a road, and head for the cave. Does that about sum it up?"

No one answered.

I shrugged. "The alternative is spending the rest of our lives here underground, if we're lucky."

Silence.

I tried to sound hopeful. "R.J. help me find some paper and a pencil or something to draw with."

We searched and came up with a dirty sheet of paper and a very fat carpenter's pencil.

"Diya, would you draw us an exact picture of the crystal so we know what we're searching for?"

Diya nodded and went to work.

R.J. said, "We've still got our maps at least. Maybe we can pick out some roads that aren't too far away."

R.J. and I stretched the best map out on the floor near the fire and began selecting the best possible landing sites. Fantasia handed out glasses of water.

Diya called out, "Okay, I have it. I am proud of my artwork. It is a close approximation of the crystal. I've included the gold setting the stone should have had in order to match the console indentation. You must remember our crystal did not have the gold setting. We had to adjust our crystal in place with paper to make it work."

Diya handed the paper to Fantasia.

Fantasia stared down at the image. She tilted her head forward as though she didn't understand it. Finally she asked, "Diya, what color is the crystal."

"Bright red," replied Diya.

Fantasia looked up in a daze. "Oh my God!" She hurried over to her pack, knelt and dug down in it. She pulled out the necklace she had purchased in Tirumalai and held it up. "Like this!?" she asked.

Diya stood. "That is it! Yours even has the gold setting ours did not. The setting holds the crystal in just the right place above the console. Where did you get it?"

Diya stood next to Fantasia as she held up the necklace to examine it with a new appreciation.

R.J. stood bent over with a piece of fresh firewood in his hands as though he was waiting for the joke to be declared. I looked over, still on my hands and knees above the map, trying to process what had just been said. Parth looked up at them with raised eyebrows, hoping for reconfirmation.

Fantasia draped the necklace over Diya's head. "Here, you're the one who knows how to use this."

R.J. added, "Just don't leave without us."

Without getting up I asked, "Are you sure?"

R.J. said, "Please, don't give her a chance to change her mind."

Diya, still excited, said, "No, no. I am certain. These markings on the setting. They are the same as those in the ship. It is unmistakable."

Parth added, "I believe I have finally found nirvana."

We sat together and looked at each other to consider what Fantasia's crystal meant.

290

"There's something I'm not sure I understand," said Fantasia "When we entered that ship, there was a crystal in the navigation console. I remember seeing it held in place by pieces of paper. But when we arrived here, the crystal was gone. Power in the spacecraft shut down. How is that possible?"

"Yes, it is a conundrum," replied Diya. "I believe the ship here is an exact copy of the one on Earth. It is both the same ship and not the same ship. And I would hypothesize that the ship will consider your crystal to be one and the same with mine. They are interchangeable."

"The quantum science of inter-dimensional travel is difficult to comprehend," replied Fantasia.

"I'm just thankful we don't have to go into that city," said R.J.

Parth added, "Our losses might have been unbearable."

Fantasia said, "This means we can fly direct to the cave."

R.J. said, "At least as close as we can get to it."

Parth asked, "Do we have the fuel, Adrian?"

"We were just about full when we took off. At the rate we used fuel on the way here my best guess is that it will be close. The worst that can happen is we run out and have to put down on a road early. In a way it doesn't matter. We might not have been able to take off on the length of road we have with full tanks and five people anyway."

Fantasia said, "I still have our following map in my scanner. It will lead us directly back to the cave."

Parth said, "The people here have actually done well recovering from a doomsday war, but I am looking forward with great anticipation to our return to Earth."

R.J. said, "I'll never speak badly of Earth hot dogs ever again."

I said, "We should leave early. I'll study the maps we have tonight. You all may want to make yourself some kind of ear plugs. The cabin will be loud and we'll be enroute for quite a while."

Blankets were gathered. We all made beds on the floor near the fire. We took shifts keeping it going and staying alert for intruders.

In the morning coffee and beans were passed out. R.J. had to make a joke about the aircraft cabin being too small. My preflight went well. We found a bicycle pump and took turns daring to add air to the tires. Everyone went about their business in quiet. They were secretly holding their breath, hoping we would get clear the trees.

When at last there was just nothing left to do we loaded up. R.J. all the way in the back for weight and balance. Parth and Diya in the middle seats. Fantasia and me in the front. I set the parking brake and explained the throttle and toe brakes again to Fantasia. The keys were still under the pilot's seat.

Under the intent gaze from all of them I gave a short countdown from three. I spun that prop as hard as I could while falling back away and the little airplane coughed once and kicked in alive from that first pull. She jostled around a little too much from a slightly too advanced throttle so I had to race around and get in the pilot seat to back it off. We taxied out of the barn, prayed there were not snipers waiting for us, and bounced along the driveway to the road. I pondered for a moment whether I should do a run-up, then decided if both mags died we'd know they were bad anyway and we were going one magneto or two. I slid the throttle in full and let her go.

The brown forest raced by. The silence in the noisy cabin was intense. The airspeed indicator had stopped working but I could feel her getting light. A touch of rotation and up we went, leaving the treetops below. R.J. let out a nervous sounding, "Yee-ha."

It was good to be above brown world. It was as though we'd already escaped it. There was no melancholy at leaving. The best view we had was forward. We all craned our necks periodically to look back at the big Oldtown dome, shimmering in the hazy light. It was impossible not to think of Main Street, the Colton brothers, and the saloon which would carry Candy Shrack's name until the next guest wanted to run the place. All those people who had become an integral part of our lives for those three months, lived as a lifetime.

I leveled off at three thousand. We watched the next bomb-blasted city approach below. It was Britonia-lost, where Diya had left her associate John. He was down there somewhere, or at least parts of him were. He would stay behind in brown world forever. I stole a glance at Diya. She was looking down at the city thinking of him.

R.J. called out, "I can see the jeep."

Everyone switched to the port windows.

We quickly left the city behind. Our wings carried us over brown dusted roadways, dead forests and dried out stream beds. The distant mountain range we were aiming for came into view. The reassuring drone of the aircraft engine kept steady. I continually expected it to abruptly die, but it did not. Jeffson, the small town we had first visited appeared ahead. Seeing it was a reminder of how far we had come. We passed over and it became time to find the mountain cave we needed.

Fantasia followed her scanner closely. Now and then she would point out something familiar. Another twenty minutes of studying the terrain and she began to be excited.

"There, there!" she called out, pointing at one particular cliff side.

I brought the bird around for a low pass. The trail we had taken down the mountain came into view. The small plateau at the mouth of the cave did not have any undesirables waiting for us. I kept five hundred feet and began ovals back and forth looking for the best, closest roadway.

A funny thing was bothering me. You can land small aircraft on a much shorter field than is needed for takeoff. In my search for the best stretch of road, I kept dismissing some because they would not allow a takeoff if we changed our minds for any reason. That led to an absurd mental argument of what circumstances could possibly cause us to want to take off again. But there was one valid reasoning. What if the ship didn't work? What if we couldn't get it to take us back? If such a dastardly event did happen, we would need this airplane, low fuel and all. But the best stretch of road for a landing and takeoff would leave us with a ten-mile hike through the woods. The best spot to land with no chance for takeoff would give us half that distance to walk.

Parth's leg was fully healed. All of us were in pretty good shape. R.J. and I had our weapons. I have always believed in leaving myself an out if things went bad. I set up for a landing on the ten-mile walk road.

"Is this the closest?" asked Fantasia.

"Closest if we want to be able to take off again."

Fantasia thought about it. "I agree with your decision. I sensed you were having concerns."

I set up on a downwind leg for a close look at the landing strip. We turned base and then final. Fantasia began aiming and adjusting her scanner to get a good bead on the cave location. The brown trees came up around us. We blew brown dust off of them. Touchdown was smooth. Again the tires held. We coasted to a stop. No one waited. The doors popped open. We all climbed out.

With the airplane shut down, the dead world became dead silent. There was no place off road to park so I hid the keys underneath the carpet and we left our wings parked right there in the road.

Of the five of us, Diya was the most nervous. She spotted the handgun stuck into my waistline behind me and came over to ask if she could carry it. Impressed, I drew it out and handed it over. Diya resumed her continuous looking around and tucked the gun in the front waistline of her pants.

The woods were dense enough that we had to walk single file. It reminded me of an old black and white jungle movie. I led the way just so I could stay in front of Fantasia who was concentrating more on the scanner than watching where she was going. She kept nudging me on the shoulder saying, "Bear left, bear left."

An hour into it, we stopped and passed a canteen around.

"How far?" asked Diya.

"I think we've only gone about two miles," replied Fantasia.

We buckled down and continued walking.

Two more hours of dodging brush and trees with Fantasia poking directions at me brought us to a narrow trail. There were sounds coming from up ahead. We stopped to drink and listen. It was a faint creaking noise.

We pushed on more carefully and came to a larger clearing beyond a line of brush. There was a single-story wooden building with a water wheel turning. A large stream coming from the mountains was tuning the wheel. We crouched behind the brush and watched. After a few minutes a man with a long-barreled shotgun appeared and walked a short way along the stream, inspecting it.

R.J. crept over next to me. "I don't think we want to stop in for a visit."

"There was no stream we had to cross on our way out. How can there be a stream up ahead?"

R.J. gave a concerned look. "Uh-oh. You think Fantasia's scanner is leading us astray?"

"Why wouldn't I have seen this place from the air?"

I scooted over to Fantasia. "Fan, there was no stream before, and I didn't see this place from the air. Are we lost?"

"Certainly not. The sun has been off my left shoulder all the way. See those mountains up ahead. That's where we're going, Adrian dear."

I gave her my dumb look and duck-walked back to R.J. "She says we're not lost."

"Duh."

"Yeah, duh."

Very skillfully I motioned to the others using hand signals only that we should go wide around the water wheel place to the left. Diya wasn't paying attention. She looked at Parth for an explanation.

"He indicated we are going around the place to the left," said Parth.

I threw up my hands in exasperation and led the way.

Twenty minutes later we found an explanation for the missing stream. The water flow ended at a jagged rock opening in the ground into which the rushing water disappeared. The nearby mountain was now rising high above us. Fantasia was the first to spot the ledge and cave opening in the distance. She pointed it out and gave me a wrinkled brow look.

We climbed the trail to the cave entrance, a tired and motley looking crew. The day's light was fading. The temperature was dropping. The cave was forebodingly dark. None of us had a flashlight. R.J. had matches.

A formidable torch was fabricated. We used alcohol from Fantasia's medical kit to get the thing going. Within the main chamber, to our great relief, the dimension ship still waited. As soon as the doors to the central column opened there was light. We tossed our torch, squeezed into the elevator, and took the ride up.

It was warmer in the control cabin. No one dared sit. With our packs on the floor we watched Diya remove the red crystal from its chain and hold it next to the navigation console imprint to check the shape and size. Both were perfect.

Three seats by the nav console, three others on the other side of the center column. Fantasia, R.J., and I went to the far side and left the navigation to Diya and Parth.

We all sat. Nothing happened.

Diya called out, "On the count of three I will drop the crystal in place. Ready, three, two, one, now!"

There was a blinding flash and a moment in which it felt like my soul was trying to catch up with my body. The feeling lingered for a few moments then slowly dissipated.

R.J. called out, "Well something definitely happened."

Diya fished the crystal out of the indentation and all of the console lights immediately went dark. Only the room lighting remained.

Fantasia asked, "Is everyone alright?"

"I'm still a little dizzy," said Diya.

"Me also," added Parth.

R.J. said, "There's nothing left to do but go outside and see where we are."

We slowly stood, grabbed up our packs and gathered at the elevator. We rode down in silence and waited for the magic doorway to Earth to slide open.

# Chapter 25

The door opened. Light from the elevator revealed familiar cavern walls. R.J. stepped out and went to a flashlight laying on a nearby flat rock. He clicked it on and looked around as the rest of us came out. The elevator door shut leaving only R.J.'s flashlight beams.

"This is our stuff," said R.J.

"So far so good," replied Fantasia. "All of our supplies are still here."

R.J. said, "We've got to look outside. We've got to know for sure."

No one spoke but everyone agreed. We followed R.J. through the shaft room and into the tunnel. Not far along we came to the pile of stones used to conceal the entrance. R.J., Parth, and I pulled them away to allow passage. In the main tunnel we made our way to the grated entrance and worked it open. We all stooped over and went outside.

The stars were shining brightly. There was no moon. The trees and brush surrounding the cave were green and healthy. Our previous tracks in the dirt lead away from the cave.

Diya said, "That constellation overhead is Cassiopia. You can also make out Pleiades over there. This has to be Earth."

I said, "We just took a ten-mile hike in an alternate dimension. We can't make the trip down this mountain in the middle of the night. We'll have to go back in, rest, and wait until morning."

Parth said, "That is not so bad, knowing we are here."

Most of our food supplies were well preserved in the cavern's chill. We broke open the vacuum-packed turkey and ate with the pleasure of knowing what kind of meat it actually was. We thought about bringing in firewood to build a fire but the truth was we were just too tired. We bundled up in the extra clothes and sleeping bags brought in before our accidental trip and huddled together for shallow naps. I had mini dreams of being back in Oldtown, flying an antique plane and riding in a rusty jeep. In one I was earnestly trying to talk to a man whose face was made of wires and integrated circuits. I know the others had the same sleep visions because from time to time someone would jump or moan in their sleep.

We survived the night. As soon as there was enough light we restacked the rocks against the secret passage and started down the mountain on our second ten-mile hike. Downhill made it easier and faster. It took little more than three hours to reach the edge of the village where the street market just happened to be in full swing once again. Only a few sections of crowded market needed to be navigated. Parth managed to find us a taxi back to the hotel.

To our surprise, a man was waiting inside the room Fantasia and I had rented. He was seated on the bed reading from a small cell phone device. He saw us, folded it shut, stuffed it inside his jacket and stood. He was wearing tight black slacks with black boots which came up over the calf. His dark jacket was a Nehru style. He had soldier-cut dark hair and wore dark sunglasses which I could tell were clear lenses from his perspective.

He removed the glasses and nodded. "My apologies if I alarmed you, Fantasia. Greetings,

Mr. Tarn. My name is Jules. My team was sent by Elachia to find you and bring you back to Enuro."

Before I could respond, R.J. entered the room, saw our would-be rescuer, and declared, "Uh-oh!"

Jules answered, "Ah, yes. Mr. Smith. Elachia has asked me to give you a message the moment I located you. The message is; What the hell, R.J.?"

I tried to stifle a laugh.

R.J. answered, "I will be explaining this to her for the rest of the day I think."

Somehow Jules understood.

I said, "Jules, we all had a nice ten-mile hike yesterday, a cold night in a cave last night and another ten miler this morning. We're going to need to rest up before we can go anywhere."

Jules answered, "My ship is in orbit. I'm here by shuttle. You could let us take you up to the ship and you could rest there. We'd be able to start back immediately."

I added, "I think we have some loose ends we need to tie up before heading back. Can you wait for us?"

"Certainly. My contract with Elachia is to find you and bring you back to Enuro. There is no time limit on that."

Parth had been standing in the hallway. He stepped in and asked, "I was stationed at the space center in Florida before coming here. Would you be able to shuttle us back to Florida before you go?"

"As a matter of fact, Elachia was granted a planetary diplomat visa for this trip. Flight Service will accept a transatlantic flight plan based on that. So yes; we would be glad to take you there."

I looked at Fantasia. "I was hoping he'd say something like that. It's been a very long time since I checked on my quadplex apartment. We're here on Earth. This would be a good time to do that."

"I would love to see your home here on Earth," said Fantasia.

R.J. added. "Great. I need to check on the suite Elachia and I have in Cocoa Beach."

The next morning Jules landed in our hotel's parking lot. The five of us loaded up our belongings and climbed aboard. It was smooth ride high across the ocean. The parking lot around my quadplex is not that big, but the able-bodied Jules managed to drop down into it. Fantasia and I grabbed our stuff and exited down and away from the spacecraft. It lifted off a moment later to drop R.J. on the roof of the high rise where his suite was.

My place looked the same. The key was still hidden in the buried fake rock by the door. We let ourselves in. It was stuffy as hell but everything was just as I'd left it. In the garage the Vette was still protected by the car cover and a layer of dust. The non-standard tires were still up. The power was off. Fantasia wandered around the shadowy rooms and marveled at the previous life of the man she had adopted. We sat at my 1950s yellow kitchen table and ate a candy bar from my pack. It only served to make us realize how hungry we were.

We had spotted a new diner from the shuttle windows. It was within walking distance. I found an old pair of dark sunglasses and hoped they would be enough of a disguise. We walked the sidewalk and studied Mother Earth. There had not been time for a visit the last time we were here.

Our entry to the diner was ignored by most of the customers. Occasionally another patron would stare at me for too long but none believed I was me.

"Do you remember the last time you were here?" asked Fantasia.

I nodded. "Yeah, all six seconds of it."

"I meant here, on this part of the planet."

"Wow! I'd have to think about that. It may have been with R.J. and Danica Donoro out at the space center."

"Don't you miss all this, Adrian?"

"Yes, but Enuro is as much my home now as Earth. So were I here, I'd be missing Enuro."

"What would you miss on Enuro, dear?"

"I'd miss the little blue people I've grown to love."

"What else?"

"To tell you the truth I've grown to love the lake and your castle."

"And that's all you'd miss?"

"This is a trick question, isn't it?"

"You wouldn't miss me?"

"No, I wouldn't miss you because wherever you were that's where I'd be."

"My, my, how cunning you are, darling."

"Well, how about you? Are you missing Enuro?"

"Yes. I miss the staff. They are always so jovial. And I miss the horses and the lake and manor."

"You miss your home. It's normal."

"No, I do not miss my home. My home is with you."

"I think we just agreed on something but I'm not sure what."

Fantasia gave an intoxicating smile. "Parth and Diya should come back to Enuro with us for a vacation."

"I think they want some time alone together. They've been separated and at the same time together for three months after all."

"I guess we'll have to settle just for R.J. then."

"Yes, but at least his hair has all grown back."

Fantasia laughed loudly enough to attract attention. She caught herself and lowered her voice. "I think we should go back to your place to wait for Jules. Some of the people here are staring at you too often."

I waved for the check, started to sign for it then pushed it over to Fantasia. We left under the discerning stare of quite a few patrons.

The hum of a hovercraft brought us out of my apartment in time to watch the landing. R.J. opened the rear doors and we climbed in. From the windows we watched central Florida shrink down into a continent. Jules docking with the mother ship's hanger bay was so smooth we slid in.

We sat in a luxurious lounge and felt ourselves thrown into subspace. R.J. brought drinks and we gathered at an oval white table near windows filled with stars.

R.J. said, "I had a mind-bending epiphany today."

I smirked. "Oh, this ought to be good. Let me guess: you suspect Oldtown was actually real life and we are now in a simulation."

"Close."

I mused, "I had an interesting realization myself about Oldtown."

R.J. raised an eyebrow. "Okay. You first."

"It occurred to me that Oldtown saved Jack James' life."

R.J. sat back. "Keep going. I'm intrigued."

"During the time Luke and Mae James were plotting to do away with Jack, they believed Oldtown was real life. There's no reason to think they wouldn't have done the same thing even if they hadn't visited Oldtown. It would probably have been an insurance payoff instead of a bounty, but if they were willing to murder Jack in Oldtown, why wouldn't they have done the same thing in their real-life environment? Because of Oldtown, Jack James now knows two of the people closest to him were plotting against him. He can now protect himself against them."

R.J. shook his head. "There is something profoundly ironic about that. A fake reality exposing two criminals from a true reality in time to save someone's life. I believe I'll need to digest that awhile."

"Okay, what was your epiphany?"

"Mine is a bit more transcendental. What occurred to me was that Oldtown was exactly like real life. We arrived in Oldtown. We didn't really know how we got there or who we were. There were rumors of extraterrestrials. People fell in love. Others fell out of love. There was crime and good deeds. We did the best we could to get by in there and in the end when it was over we left our guns and possessions behind. The only thing we took with us was what we had done and what we had learned. Think about it. Here in this life we don't really know how we came to be here or who we are exactly. We're doing our best to get by. There are mysteries all around us. And, when we leave here, the only thing we'll take with us is what kind of people we have been and what we've learned. Just like Oldtown."

I sipped my drink. "Wow."

R.J. went on. "Who's to say we're not prevented from knowing the big true reality until we die, just like Oldtown? Who's to say when this visit is over we don't return to our real lives from where we originally came, just like Oldtown? The effect is the same. The only things we bring back with us are the memory of what kind of person we were and what we've learned."

Fantasia smiled. "You are a true philosopher, R.J. dear. You are describing human life as a learning experience. Higher learning on a transcendental level."

R.J. said, "So that's it, Adrian. No more special missions for us, okay? No more getting involved in other people's problems. Let's just go catch that big fish in the lake and sit back and enjoy life."

I nodded. "Right."

Fantasia tried to suppress a sarcastic laugh. She stood and went to a sleeping compartment to get away.

We watched her leave.

R.J. said, "Never mind her. All I'm saying is we should lay back and not get involved in other people's problems. We'll just hang back and let people take care of their own problems. Permanent vacation."

With my most serious expression I slapped the table and nodded. "Right!"

Fantasia laughed and laughed.

www.ingramcontent.com/pod-product-compliance
Lightning Source LLC
Chambersburg PA
CBHW060533180626
46817CB00002B/557